MIDNIGHT VALENTINE

J.T. GEISSINGER

Published by J.T. Geissinger, Inc.

www.jtgeissinger.com

ISBN-13: 978-0-9969358-3-8

Cover design by Letitia Hasser, RBA Designs

Edited by Linda Ingmanson

Printed in the United States of America

To Jay, my true north

Do not stand at my grave and weep
I am not there. I do not sleep.
I am a thousand winds that blow.
I am the diamond glints on snow.
I am the sunlight on ripened grain.
I am the gentle autumn rain.
When you awaken in the morning's hush
I am the swift uplifting rush
Of quiet birds in circled flight.
I am the soft stars that shine at night.
Do not stand at my grave and cry;
I am not there. I did not die.

~ Mary Elizabeth Frye

1

——————

"Do you believe in reincarnation?"

"Megan. We've been over this before."

"And you've never given me a straight answer. It wouldn't kill you to come right out and say one way or another."

"What's important is what *you* believe, and why."

I sit up from the uncomfortable leather sofa I've been lying on every Thursday for fifty minutes for the past two years and look at Dr. Singer. He's handsome in a 1950s-engineer way, crew-cut silver hair and a pair of horn-rimmed glasses, a classic white button-down shirt. I knew within ten minutes of our first visit that I could trust him, knew also that I'd lie to him like I'd lied to every other therapist I'd visited before.

There are truths too painful to be spoken aloud. Some demons should be left to rot in the dark forever.

"It's our last session, Dr. Singer. Which means it's your last chance to help me."

Though he's trained to keep a neutral expression, he visibly winces. "Do you feel I haven't helped you, Megan?"

Of course you haven't. But it's not his fault all my shattered pieces can't be glued back together, so I smile and say something nice. "You're the best therapist I've ever had."

He studies me. Behind the horn-rimmed glasses, his eyes are the color of old denim, faded from the acid wash of too many sad stories. Too many poisonous secrets have bleached them bone pale.

"Will you call Dr. Anders when you arrive in Oregon?"

"Yes," I lie. "As soon as I'm settled."

"I hope you do. He's a good man. Highly qualified."

"You're highly qualified too. Look where that got us."

We gaze at each other while the clock ticks quietly on the wall. Somewhere outside, a dog howls. The sound is unbearably lonely.

"You're an intelligent woman, Megan. You know therapy will never work if you don't commit to it."

"I've been here without fail every week for two years. That's commitment."

"Your body's been here, but your mind has always been somewhere else. You've never been completely open and truthful. Tell me I'm wrong."

I pick up my handbag from the floor, sling it over my shoulder, and stand, ready to be done with all this. I've got a moving van waiting, a new life to start, a thousand dreams to bury in the desert sand.

"I'll make you a deal. Tell me if you believe in reincarnation, and I'll tell you something true. Anything you want to know, I'll answer honestly."

Dr. Singer stands, unfolding all those gangly limbs of his, and comes out from behind his desk. He stops in front of me and props his hands on his hips. "All right. I suppose better late than never." He's thoughtful for a moment, then says, "No, I don't believe in reincarnation. Or an afterlife, to be perfectly frank. I think this is as good as it gets, which is why it's so important to make the best of this life. To confront our problems, to work through them, so ultimately we can be free of them and enjoy the time we have."

Unsurprised by this answer, I nod. "Okay. Thanks."

In an unusual show of affection, he rests his hands on my shoulders and gazes down into my face. He says softly, "Now here's *my* question: why haven't you let me help you?"

He looks so earnest. I'm moved by his obvious sincerity, by how much he wishes he could help me, by the goodness of this person who thinks all life's problems can be solved by talking about them.

"Because no matter how much you might want to, Dr. Singer, you can't help someone who's already dead."

I pat his hand, sorry for that look of dismay I've caused, then turn and walk out the door.

∼

It's a twenty-two-hour drive from Phoenix to Seaside if you go straight through, but I stop overnight in a town with one traffic light, rent a room in a cheap motel, and lie atop the bedcovers, fully dressed, staring at the ceiling until it gets light. Then I drink three cups of terrible coffee in the small diner attached to the motel and get back on the road.

The I-5 through California is one long, boring stretch of high-way, crowded with eighteen-wheelers. I listen to a blues station as the urban sprawl gives way to fields of almond trees and cow pastures. The rolling hills of the central valleys are dotted with the rangy silhouettes of oak trees, and the long grasses are burned brown from the summer sun. I take a left turn at Port-land, then it's another hour and a half to my final destination. By the time I pull into Seaside, I'm exhausted and starving, but strangely relieved.

One more day in Phoenix might have put me over this edge I've been living on so long.

The real estate agent has already sent me the key to the house, but I decide to stop and get something to eat before going over. I pull into another diner, this one full of gray-haired old couples and one man sitting alone in a booth near the back, staring out the window into the gently falling evening rain.

Even sitting down, his size is obvious. His broad shoulders strain the seams of his black raincoat. His hands dwarf the ceramic mug they're wrapped around. He looks like he had to wedge himself between the booth and the table to sit down.

It isn't his size that really stands out, however. It's the menacing air of *stay away* that emanates from him, the way he hunches over, the way the hood of his raincoat casts dark shadows over his face. As if he doesn't want anyone to look at him.

As if he's hiding.

"What can I get you, honey?"

The waitress standing behind the counter holds a carafe of coffee. She's somewhere north of sixty, plump and red-cheeked, smiling like we're old friends. I sit on one of the stools and plop my handbag on the counter. "I'll have some of that coffee, please. And a Denver omelet with extra bacon on the side."

If she thinks it odd that I want an omelet for dinner, she doesn't mention it. She just nods and pours me a mug of coffee, then says she'll be right back.

When she heads into the kitchen, I look around, sipping my coffee. It was too dark as I drove in to get a good view of the town, but I've studied the details long enough to have them memorized.

Seaside, Oregon is a small resort city with a beach known for its surf breaks, and a 1920s promenade with an arcade and an old-fashioned carousel. The population is a hair over six thousand, a far cry from the one and a half million who crowd Phoenix. The air is different here too, fresh and bracing, filled with the scent of salt and pine instead of smog and stone baked by the unrelenting desert sun.

I hope everything will be different here. I hope I can leave all my nightmares behind.

Preoccupied with thoughts of all the work that needs to be done to the house, I drink my coffee and eavesdrop on conversations, trying not to wonder what Cass would have to say about this place. How he'd be bouncing off his stool with excitement.

It's several minutes before I realize I'm uncomfortable.

Surprised by the intensity of the feeling, I glance around. None of the patrons are looking my way. The music is cheerful, the interior of the diner is clean and bright, and everything appears normal. Boring, even.

Then why is the skin on the back of my neck crawling?

I glance over my shoulder and discover the reason. The guy in the raincoat is looking at me. No, not looking—*glaring*. Conspicuously hostile, he stares at me with total revulsion, as if I've deeply offended him in some way.

Cold, hard, and utterly black, his eyes are like obsidian.

I raise my brows and stare back at him, because I don't have time for assholes with attitude problems.

"Here you go, honey." The nice waitress deposits a plate in front of me. It's overflowing with an omelet that could feed a family of four, topped by a messy pile of hash browns.

"Wow. That's a lot of food."

She laughs, her stomach jiggling. "I should've warned you about the portion sizes. Cal—that's my husband—is the cook, and he likes folks to leave feeling like they got a lot for their money."

"Tell Cal you can raise the price of this omelet by ten dollars, and I'd still feel like I got a lot for my money." I poke at the huge, fluffy mound with my fork. "How many eggs are even in this thing?"

She chuckles. "Who knows. I gave up trying to get him to follow recipes years ago. I hope you like it, honey."

"I'm sure I will, thanks."

We share a smile, she ambles down the counter to refill someone's coffee, and I dig in. I'm not what you'd call a dainty eater, so within a few minutes, I've polished off most of the omelet and have started to make a dent in the giant pile of hash browns. Just as I'm lifting the fork to my mouth, that strange feeling overtakes me again. All the tiny hairs on my arms stand on end and my ears burn like I've stuck my finger into an electrical socket.

I set my fork down, grit my teeth, and look over my shoulder.

Moody Raincoat Guy is staring at me with an expression like he's about to jump out of the booth and open fire.

But what he doesn't know about me is that I'm not the girl who wilts when confronted with awkward or potentially dangerous situations. I'm the girl who bares her teeth and growls.

I meet his burning gaze with an unflinching one of my own. "You got a problem?"

The grip he's got on his coffee mug tightens until his knuckles turn white. He swallows, a muscle in his jaw flexing, but says nothing.

"How's that omelet, honey?"

I hold Moody Raincoat's hate-filled gaze a moment longer before turning back to the waitress. "Amazing. I won't have to eat for two days. Actually, scratch that. Do you have key lime pie?"

The unmistakable sound of a big man trying to quickly evacuate a small booth comes from behind me. There's a lot of rattling and thumping, the squeak of rubber soles on the linoleum floor, and a huff of aggravation. Then he's clomping past, dragging wind and the scent of the woods in his wake. I hear the bell over the front door jangle, then the door slams shut with a jarring noise. The force of it rattles all the windows. I'm surprised all the glass in the place doesn't break.

Looking over my shoulder, the waitress shakes her head and sighs.

"He's a real charmer," I say drily.

"He used to be." Her voice is tinged with sorrow, which piques my curiosity.

"You know him?"

Her kind green eyes turn sad. "Known him since he was a boy. Hell, everybody in this town knows him. He's lived here all his life. Captain of the football team in high school, prom king, engaged to the prettiest girl in town. Everyone loved him. There was even talk of him running for office, he was so popular in these parts. Then the accident happened, and he's never been the same since."

A cold veil of dread settles over me at the mention of the word "accident." I have to moisten my lips because my mouth has gone dry.

The waitress waves a hand in front of her face, as if to dispel a cloud of bad energy. "Sorry, Cal's always telling me not to gossip. Let me get that pie for you." She comes back with it shortly and refills my coffee. "You here on vacation?"

"Nope. I'm moving in."

"Really? That's exciting! We don't get many permanent transplants. Most everyone in Seaside this time of year is a tourist. Where you from?"

"Phoenix."

She looks impressed. "Oh, big city. I could never live in a city as big as that." She notices the wedding band on my finger and brightens. "You're here with your husband?"

That word doesn't hurt as much as it used to. I've grown callouses over all kinds of words, like husband, marriage, kids. Love.

"My husband passed away several years ago."

The waitress puts her hand over her heart. "Oh, honey. I'm so sorry to hear that."

I can tell she really is. A lot of people say the words from a reflex to be polite but don't mean them, but this friendly waitress isn't one of those people. "Thank you."

"So do you have family nearby? Portland, maybe?"

"Nope."

"Work, then?"

She's wondering why I decided to move here, Smallsville, USA. The answer isn't one of those things I've grown a callous over, so I go with a half-truth, delivered with a cheery smile.

"In a way, I suppose, though I don't have a job waiting for me. It's more like I'm going to make one." When she knits her brows in confusion, I add, "I bought the Buttercup Inn."

She lets out an excited whoop that has everyone's heads turning. Over her shoulder, she hollers toward the kitchen, "Cal! This nice little girl bought the Buttercup!"

Thirty-two is hardly a girl, and I've never been little, in stature or personality, but she's turning back to me, beaming, and who am I to rain on her parade with these pesky details?

"Well, that's fantastic news, honey! I had no idea it sold! That place has been on the market, what, eight years now?"

"Ten, according to the real estate agent."

"Suzie Martin," the waitress says, nodding. "Excuse me, *Suzanne*." She rolls her eyes. "It's hard to call someone you knew when she was peeing her pants in kindergarten by her proper name. She'd skin me if she found out."

When she gives me a pointed look, I make a zipper motion over my mouth. "My lips are sealed."

"I'm Jean, by the way. Jean McCorkle. Welcome to Seaside." She sticks out her hand.

"Megan Dunn." We shake, and it feels as if something's been decided.

Then Jean's freckled face creases with a wry smile. "I hate to be a downer, honey, but I hope you have deep pockets and a background in construction. The Buttercup's a bit of a mess."

"Mess" is an understatement. It needs a new roof, new plumbing, new windows, mold remediation, landscaping, plaster patching, painting, new floors, and electrical work. So basically everything. It's a Victorian, built in the late 1900s, full of character and quirks, zoned as a bed-and-breakfast and operated as one until there was a kitchen fire. The prior owner didn't have enough money to fix it, so he put it on the market instead. There it sat, moldering in the sea air, for a decade.

"Yeah, it needs a lot of work, but I'm looking forward to the project. Suzanne gave me the name of the best contractor in the area. I'm going to give him a call tomorrow, as soon as I can survey the place and get a feel for what I should prioritize. Hopefully, he has the time to come out soon and give me an estimate. I'm anxious to get started on the work."

Jean blinks. "Oh, I'm sure he'll have the time. Though I'm not sure you'll want him to."

"What do you mean?"

The rumble of an engine and a loud backfire make me glance over my shoulder. At the curb across the street, out in the rainy night, Moody Raincoat Guy sits on a chopper, revving it aggressively like he's waiting for a starting flag to drop. He tears off with a roar, the tires spitting water, the hood of his raincoat flipped back onto his shoulders from the force of the wind.

Jean says, "I mean you already met the best contractor in the area, honey, and by the sound of things, you didn't like him."

When I send her a quizzical look, she gestures with her chin toward the windows and the sound of a roaring engine, fading into the distance until it's swallowed by the drum of the rain.

My heart sinks. *"He's* the contractor?"

She lifts a shoulder, apologetic. "There's other guys who will come up from Portland, but they're a lot more expensive, and honestly, the work isn't near what Theo can do. I admit he's off-putting, but if you can get past the not talking, he's really the best."

Thought it's impolite to make faces, my face regularly bucks protocol and contorts to some interesting shapes, as it does now. "The 'not talking'? You mean he's mute?"

"I mean he doesn't speak."

"Is he deaf?"

"No."

"So he can speak, but he chooses not to?"

Jean sighs like she wishes there was something she could do about the situation. "To be honest, honey, I really don't know what the problem is. He talked fine before the accident, but after the accident, he didn't ever talk again. Maybe it's physical, maybe it's mental, who knows. All I know for sure is that he can hear, he understands what people are saying, he just never responds. So don't expect it if you hire him."

This keeps getting better. "How am I supposed to communicate with him if he won't talk to me?"

"You tell him what you want, and he'll do it. If he has questions, he writes on a little pad he carries with him."

She says that as if it's completely normal, a standard way of doing business. I push my plate away, wipe my mouth with my napkin, and take another swig of my coffee. "Thanks, but I think I'll try the guys in Portland. I'll get the info from Suzanne."

"All right, honey. Suit yourself. You want anything else, or should I bring you the check?"

"Just the check, Jean, please."

She walks away, leaving me staring pensively out into the rainy night, thinking about Moody Raincoat Guy, former local wonder boy turned mute, glowering diner patron with eyes like midnight at the bottom of a well.

I wonder if his heart is full of ghosts too.

2

---

he movers arrive early the next morning, and I'm occupied for the rest of the day sorting through boxes and getting things organized in the house. I barely slept, as usual, tossing and turning on the air mattress I brought with me in the car.

The sound of breaking waves isn't nearly as soothing as I'd imagined it to be.

The Buttercup Inn sits on a massive dune near the ocean's edge. Whatever color the old Victorian used to be, it's a dingy gray now. The windows are rimed with a layer of salt, and everything smells of sea and sand.

And mold. The inspection showed none of the toxic black mold that can cause illness, but various walls have been colonized by patches of the furry green version of the stuff, and when I opened the basement door, the odor was so strong, I quickly slammed it shut.

I probably should've taken Suzanne's advice and rented a house while work was being done on the Buttercup, but I've never been good at taking advice. And despite its state of disrepair, this crumbling old inn feels like home.

We're both in ruins. We can keep each other company while repairs are made to our insides.

There are six guest rooms in the inn and one larger master suite upstairs with its own wraparound balcony. Fortunately, the master is in the best shape. It only needs mopping and some scrubbing of the bathroom countertops to make it habitable. A huge, claw-foot porcelain tub dominates the bathroom. When I run water from the tap, it comes out rusty brown, but in a few minutes turns clear. This is lucky because I love baths the way I love breathing.

I decide to leave the bath for later and give Suzanne a call about the contractors. She picks up on the first ring.

"Hello?"

"Hey, Suzanne, it's Megan Dunn."

"Hi, Megan! Did you arrive safely?"

"Yep. Came in last night."

"How was the trip out?"

I think of gas stations and bad coffee, endless hours of staring at the tailgates of eighteen-wheeler trucks. "Long."

"Yeah, that's a hell of a drive. But I'm glad you made it. If it's okay, I'll come over later. I've got a little something for you."

Realtors and their housewarming gifts. She better have bought me something nice, because though I got a good deal for the Buttercup due to all the repairs it needs, two acres of beach-front property still ain't cheap.

"Sure, I'll be here. Come over any time. I was calling to get the numbers of those other contractors in Portland you mentioned, but you can bring them with you if it's more convenient."

A short pause follows. "Theo wasn't available?"

"I don't know. I didn't call him."

"Why not?"

"I stopped at Cal's Diner on the way in, and he was there, sucking up all the happiness in the place like a black hole. No matter how good a contractor he is, I'm allergic to assholes."

Suzanne's tone turns defensive. "He's not an asshole. He's just...been through a lot."

Why is it that when a woman's been through a lot, she's expected to handle it gracefully with fake smiles and a stiff backbone, but when a man's been through a lot, he's given full license to storm around like a giant baby throwing a tantrum?

"Everyone's been through a lot," I tell Suzanne, my voice flat. "If you make it to thirty, you've got enough emotional scars to keep a therapist in business for the rest of your life. That's no excuse to go around glaring at strangers like you want to chop off their heads."

Her voice rises in surprise. "He *glared* at you?"

"Let's put it this way: if the man had a chainsaw available, I'd be missing a few body parts."

"You must've misunderstood. I mean, he's not what you'd call friendly, but I've never heard him described as a glaring asshole before. He's very hands-on with all his projects, oversees everything from start to finish, and is totally trustworthy and reliable. I recommend him to all my clients and have never heard a complaint."

"Great, so it's just me. Even more reason not to call him. I'll see you later."

I hang up before she can answer, because I know more defense of this Theo, Moody Raincoat Guy is coming, and I know I'll only get more and more irritated listening to it.

I'm not the kind of woman who thinks surliness is charming. All these alpha-holes from romance novels have given women the wrong idea that bad manners are attractive. I also hate talking on the phone, which I stubbornly refuse to remember until I'm in the middle of a conversation, wondering why I didn't just send a text.

I go back to cleaning and organizing, emptying boxes, and attempting to make a dent in the mountain of work I've got ahead of me. By the time I hear Suzanne's voice calling my name, it's six o'clock, and the sun is going down over the ocean.

It's a spectacular sight. I stand in the middle of the master bedroom and stare out to sea, nearly blinded by the huge orange ball and its glittering reflection on the water. This alone might be worth the price of the place, even if I never fix a single thing. Born and raised in Phoenix, I've never seen a sunset over the ocean. I find it strangely moving.

Cass would've loved this.

"Megan? Are you in there?"

I cross to the glass doors that lead to the balcony, pull them open, and look over the edge. There stands Suzanne on the brick patio below, her neck craned and a hand shading her eyes as she stares up at me. Gusts of wind blow her dark hair all around her face. She waves.

"Oh, hi! Your doorbell isn't working!"

"I'll be right down."

I take the stairs two at a time and head out to the back patio. It's enormous, as wide as the house, with an excellent view down to the beach. Off to one side, there's a fire pit made of huge chunks of stone thrown together in a circle, ringed by half a dozen ancient Adirondack chairs, which look so weather-beaten, I can't believe they haven't collapsed into piles of rubble.

I open the French doors and wave Suzanne inside. "C'mon in."

She picks her way across the patio, careful not to twist an ankle on the uneven bricks. Why she's wearing high heels, a short skirt, and a blouse unbuttoned almost to her navel to visit me is a question I'm not sure I want an answer to.

Cass used to tease me that I'm a lesbian magnet because of the frequency I'm hit on by women. I used to tell him that's because lesbians have good taste. Then he'd wonder aloud if I could find a lesbian who might also find him cute, and I'd wonder aloud what was the best way to get rid of a dead body.

As it turned out, cremation.

The list of things I'll never joke about again is almost as long as the trail of tears I've left behind me.

"It's getting blustery out there! You can really feel the end of summer!" Suzanne sweeps into the room on a gust of cold wind, pushing her hair out of her eyes and laughing. She's about my age, attractive in a brassy way, one of those women who wears perfume that inhabits a room long after she's gone. I close the doors behind her and gesture toward the grocery bag in her arms.

"You need help with that?"

"It's not heavy. It's just a bottle of wine and a little something I made for you." She looks around the empty living room. "Did the movers not make it yet?"

"They came this morning, but as you can see, I didn't bring much with me. Mostly just my clothes and books, some bedroom stuff."

When she looks confused, I feel forced to explain. "My place in Phoenix was very Southwest, lots of cowhide and leather. None of it would fit here. I'm planning on getting an interior designer to create a modern-meets-Victorian vibe, keeping all the cool character of the Victorian era but updating it with contemporary touches."

Suzanne looks impressed. "That sounds amazing, Megan. I have several great designers I can put you in touch with if you need recommendations."

"Yeah, that would be great. Why don't we go into the kitchen? At least there's a flat surface in there."

I lead the way as Suzanne follows, her heels clicking hollowly over the wood floor.

The house is built around a central rotunda which rises up two stories and highlights an elaborate curved staircase. We walk past the empty drawing room, music room, parlor, and guest bedrooms, and arrive at the kitchen. Like the rest of the house, it's big and airy. Unlike the rest of the house, the windows are all boarded up and covered with a tarp on the outside to protect from weather damage. Evidence of the fire still remains: soot clings to the ceiling, scorch marks mar the black-and-white checkered floor.

"Oh Lord!" exclaims Megan, surveying the damage. "My cleaning crew was supposed to come out here before you arrived!"

"Someone must've come out, because the floors have been swept and the banisters have been dusted. And there are no cobwebs anywhere."

She shudders dramatically, wriggling her shoulders. "Ugh, don't talk to me about cobwebs. Spiders scare the bejeezus out of me."

I have to smile. I used to be afraid of spiders too, until I had bigger things to worry about. PTSD tends to put things like arachnophobia into perspective. "I promise I'll kill any that might jump out at you."

Looking around warily for any critters preparing to pounce, Suzanne heads over to the large marble island in the center of the kitchen. She sets down the bag, pulls out a bottle of wine, and puts it aside, then withdraws a plate covered in aluminum foil.

"I baked you a key lime pie. You said it was your favorite."

I'm touched. I can't believe she remembered that detail. We must've spoken about it months ago during one of our many phone conversations before the house went into escrow.

"That's so sweet of you. And here I was expecting a half-dead plant."

She props a hand on her hip, all sass and sarcasm. "I'll have you know I *never* do the half-dead plant thing. I'm a classy girl. Usually it's a half-dead flower arrangement."

We share a smile until I notice the label on the wine and almost have a heart attack. "Suzanne, that's a *very* good bottle of Burgundy."

She's pleased I recognized it. Her grin goes from ear to ear.

"Thank God you know your wine, because I had to go into Portland for something nice. When I told the guy at the wine store how much you paid for this place, he steered me right into the back where the good stuff was all kept behind a locked door."

I pick up the bottle, running my thumb over the label of the Château Corton Grancey, blinking hard because water has begun to pool in my eyes.

"This was the wine my husband and I used to have on our anniversary every year," I murmur, swamped with memories of Cass. "We went to France on our honeymoon and discovered this old man on the side of a country road one afternoon. He'd fallen off his bicycle and hurt his knee, so we gave him a ride back to his house. Which turned out to be this incredible wine estate—he was the patriarch of a family that had been making wine in Burgundy for more than two hundred years. He made us stay for dinner with his family and served us this."

I have to stop because my throat has closed around the lump in it.

After five years, this still happens. Something will remind me of him, and suddenly, I'll hear his laugh, I'll feel his arms around me, I'll smell that soap he liked to use, the scent still lingering on his skin after a shower, and it'll be like no time has passed at all. The knife is plunged into my chest all over again. All over again, my heart bleeds.

I've died a thousand deaths since the day I lost Cass. People say time heals all wounds, but that's a lie. Grief is a chronic disease. The pain just keeps on coming.

"What are the chances of that?" says Suzanne in a voice like she's sure she's made a terrible mistake.

"No, it's amazing." I meet her eyes. "Thank you. Really. It's a very special gift, and so is your pie. I'll have them together for dinner tonight."

It was an attempt to be lighthearted, but Suzanne looks horrified by the thought of me eating pie and drinking wine alone on my second night in town. She clutches my arm.

"Why don't you come with me tonight? My friends are having their annual cocktail party in honor of the last day of summer. I was on my way over when I stopped by."

So this is the reason for the heels and short skirt. I'm relieved I won't have another awkward *You're very attractive, but I'm not into girls* speech in my future.

"I couldn't barge in like that—"

"No, no, it's very casual, and I know they'd love to meet you. Everyone's curious about the woman who bought the Buttercup. It'll be a good way for you to meet a few people!"

When I balk at the mention of meeting new people, Suzanne renews her efforts even more energetically.

"You can just pop in for a few minutes if you're too tired to stay long, and I can introduce you around—oh! And the building inspector will be there! Not only is he a good guy to know for all the permits you're going to need on this place, he's really cute."

When I wrinkle my nose, she insists, "Like, *really* cute."

"I'll go if you promise not to try to set me up with the building inspector." When she looks like she's about to offer up a few other names, I warn, "Or anyone else!"

She pouts, but damn if she doesn't pull it off. Usually, grown women pouting like two-year-olds makes me want to punch someone in the throat.

"All right. I promise not to try to set you up with anyone. Tonight."

When she smiles smugly, I can see that Suzanne and I are going to have issues in the future about her insistence on thrusting single males at me and my insistence on being uninterested in said males. Better to deal with it now rather than later, when I want to strangle her.

I've been through this with the friends I left behind in Phoenix. People will give you a year to get over your dead husband, tops, then they start throwing men at you like confetti. Young widows make people nervous.

"Suzanne, you seem like a very nice person, and I hope we'll be friends. But if you ever try to set me up with anyone, I'll start a rumor that you only charged me two percent commission on the Buttercup Inn."

She inspects my face with narrowed eyes. When I don't flinch, she demands, "Do you have any idea how fast that would get around this town? All my past clients would be mad I charged them more, and any new clients would expect a discount!"

"Yeah, small towns are a pain that way, aren't they?"

"I don't believe you. You're bluffing."

I lift a shoulder, nonchalant. "Only one way to find out."

We engage in a stare off, which lasts until Suzanne breaks into another pout. "You're too pretty to be this mean."

I scoff. "Passive-aggressive flattery doesn't work on me, girl-friend. I practically invented the backhanded compliment."

She rolls her eyes and sighs dramatically, throwing her hands in the air. I wonder if she majored in theatre in college before she went into real estate. Then she relents.

"Fine. I won't try to set you up. But I can't vouch for anyone else. The ladies of Seaside are a pushy bunch. Once they find out you're single, they won't rest until they've married you off to one of their underachieving, mouth-breathing offspring."

I lift my brows. "Sounds like the dating pool here is swimming with winners."

I get another one of her dramatic sighs, this one accompanied by a toss of her head. "I'd move to Portland, but it's overrun with real estate agents. I like being a big fish in a little pond, even if that pond has a serious lack of hot men."

"What about the super cute building inspector?"

She turns practical, not even having the decency to look chagrined. "He's a foot shorter than me. When I said he was 'cute,' I meant in a 'look at the cute little fella' way."

"You were gonna set me up with a man who's eye level to my belly button, weren't you?"

She keeps a serious face for a split second, then breaks down laughing. "My mother keeps telling me I'm too picky and should look on the bright side: I'd get to set my drink on his head if there wasn't a cocktail table nearby."

"Wow. I think I love your mother."

"Oh, yeah, she's a character. Eighty years old and she can drink the rest of us under a table. Now go put on a dress and some lipstick. I can drive over. I'll wait for you in the car."

I look down at my jeans and David Bowie T-shirt, then back up at Suzanne. "I don't own a dress, and I don't wear lipstick unless I'm going to church. Which I haven't set foot in since I was married." I lift my arms. "This is as good as it gets."

Suzanne's pursed lips aren't quite a pout, but they're not *not* a pout either. She eyes me up and down. "I don't mean to be rude, but you've got coffee stains on your shirt, dirt stains on your jeans, a smudge of something that could be bird poop on your cheek, and your hair's a little...funky. You look like you might've recently been living under a bridge."

Inevitably when someone starts a sentence with, "I don't mean to be rude," they're about to be rude. She's lucky I'm tired, or I'd be inclined to give her a hard shove and watch her topple over on those skyscraper heels of hers.

"If you're one of those super girly-girls who refuses to go out of the house without an hour's worth of prep, full makeup, and a bra, we can't be friends."

Suzanne isn't fazed by my disdain. "I am, in fact, one of those 'super girly-girls' because I like to look my best—which isn't a crime, by the way. It's called being put together—and when you have thirty-eight double Ds, going out of the house without a bra is like getting into a car without a seat belt: careless, dangerous, and something you can get in trouble for."

All the cleavage she's baring is dangerous too, but it's none of my business how much skin she likes to show. Truth be told, if I had boobs like hers, I'd probably be showing them off too. They're pretty spectacular.

Sometimes I feel sorry for men, having to try to maintain eye contact while two of their favorite things in the world are smiling up at them from the open neckline of a woman's blouse.

"Okay. You win. I'll go change and brush my hair, just for you. Feel honored, because I wouldn't do it for anyone else. And they better have delicious fried things at this so-called party, or I'm walking out." I make my way out of the kitchen and down the hallway toward the stairs.

She calls out after me, "You can't walk out, I'm your ride!"

It occurs to me that a town this size might not have decent taxi service, but it wouldn't be much of a problem anyway. I'm accustomed to taking long walks alone in the dark. It's one of the only things that's kept me sane the past few years.

When I enter the master bedroom, I notice a handprint on the sliding glass door I hadn't seen earlier. It's backlit by the setting sun, so it glows against the glass like it was breathed there by a ghost. It strikes me as oddly compelling, so I cross the room for a closer look.

It's big and surprisingly detailed, as if the person who made it however long ago pressed his hand there with the fingers spread wide and stood unmoving for a long time, looking out at the ocean. The ridges, lines, and whorls seem strangely intimate. I feel like I'm looking at a clue someone left behind. A secret moment in time marked by skin.

The lifeline that runs down the center of the palm is broken in half right in the middle, as if part of it was erased.

I lift my hand, spread my fingers, and hover my palm over the ghostly print on the glass. When a gust of wind rattles the glass, I jump, sucking in a startled breath.

Then I scold myself for being an idiot, wipe the print off the glass with the sleeve of my shirt, and go get ready for the party.

3

*B*ecause I've perfected the Don't Give a Shit approach to my personal appearance, I'm ready in under five minutes. Suzanne attempts another pout when she sees me reappear in a clean pair of jeans and another Bowie T-shirt, but she smiles instead when I arch a warning brow.

Only Mr. Spock from Star Trek has a brow arch full of more threat, suspicion, or withering disdain than me, a fact I take great pride in.

The drive to Suzanne's friend's place is only another few minutes across town, then we pull into the driveway of a brightly lit Craftsman. It's blue with white shingles and has white lights wound around the trunks of two towering palm trees in the front yard.

"At least let me carry the wine," I say as Suzanne leans over to get a wrapped bottle from the backseat. "I can't walk in empty-handed."

"If I let you carry the wine, *I'll* be walking in empty-handed."

"Yeah, but they already know you. You can get away with it. They'll think I'm some kind of freeloader with no manners if I do it."

She scrunches her face and looks at me. "Are you always like this?"

"Disarmingly honest? Yes."

"I was thinking more along the lines of worryingly odd."

"Oh, yeah," I say, nodding. "But there's no need to worry. I'm harmless."

She taps her long acrylic fingernails on the steering wheel and shakes her head, looking me over. "Harmless as a bear trap, I'd say. I can't *wait* to see the expression on Mike's face when he sees you."

"Who's Mike?"

When she smiles, I warn, "Two percent, Suzanne. Don't forget our deal."

"Oh, keep your panties on. But you can't blame me when half the men drop dead when you walk in and the other half instantly file for divorce. Even in boyfriend jeans and no makeup, you look like a supermodel, you bitch. If I didn't make so much money off you, I'd hate your guts."

She hands me the bottle of wine and exits the car, leaving me smiling. Though we're pretty much opposites, somehow I think Suzanne and I are going to get along just fine.

The front door of the house opens to Suzanne's brisk knock, then I'm looking up—way up—at a young man with a mop of curly dark hair and a shy smile. He's in his early twenties, tanned, lanky, and adorably bashful, gazing at Suzanne from under long, curving black lashes that have no right belonging to a male.

"Hey, Suzanne," he says softly, toeing the floor.

When she says, "Mike! Hiya, handsome!" and kisses him on the cheek, he blushes so furiously, I'm worried he might pass out.

Suzanne is either oblivious or accustomed to Mike's obvious infatuation. She turns to introduce me as if the poor guy isn't about to faint from the mere sight of her. "Mike, this is Megan Dunn. She bought the Buttercup Inn, so I brought her as my date."

Mike turns his big brown eyes to me, then exhales a long breath that contains a lot of vowels. His cheeks darken to the point he looks sunburned, and now I understand that Mike is a virgin with a capital V who also has a vivid imagination, the raging hormones to fuel it, and not enough social graces to land himself a girlfriend to assist him with his predicament.

I remember being that young and desperate. Growing up is a special kind of hell.

"Hi, Mike. Nice to meet you. I love your shirt. Queen's one of my favorite bands."

He gazes at me like I've just descended from the heavens on a golden chariot. "No way."

I nod seriously. "Way. I mean, they're no Bowie, but who is?"

After a moment wherein he simply stares at me with his mouth hanging open, Suzanne takes charge. "Always great to see you, Mike." Smiling, she grabs my arm and pushes past him, dragging me along into the foyer of the house.

"God, the poor thing," I whisper as she guides me into a living room that looks like something out of a Martha Stewart book. "You should be trying to set *him* up, not me."

"That would be inconvenient, as he's decided to enter the seminary."

I almost trip over my own feet. "He wants to be a *priest*? Does he know they're not allowed to have sex?"

"It's a pity, right? He's so cute. I feel sorry for whatever population of elderly nuns he's going to traumatize." She lifts a hand in greeting. "Sunday! Hi! I brought you a present!"

A woman wearing a flowing, bohemian-type dress turns to us from where she's standing chatting with several people in the living room. She raises her hand in greeting, and her armful of gold bangles twinkle in the light.

"Hi, Suze! Who's your friend?"

We stop in front of the group, and Suzanne introduces me like I'm some kind of rock star while everyone politely smiles and tries not to be too obvious as they look me up and down and judge my outfit.

"*This* is Megan Dunn, the woman who bought the Buttercup Inn. She's incredibly smart, incredibly funny, and, as you can see, prettier than a thousand-dollar bill. I've decided not to hate her because she also happens to be cool."

I'm starting to get that Suzanne has no filter.

"Megan, this is Sunday, Mike's mom." She points at the woman with the bangles, and we nod and smile at each other. "And this is Chris—Sunday's husband—Tina, who owns the best beauty salon in town, and Colleen, who teaches at Seaside Elementary."

"Hi. It's nice to meet you all. Sorry for crashing your party, Sunday, but Suzanne didn't leave me much of a choice."

Sunday tosses her hair over her shoulder and laughs. "No worries. I know how excited Suze gets when she has the opportunity to be a matchmaker. Has she already told you about Doug?"

I look sideways at Suzanne. "If Doug is the short building inspector, then yes."

Everyone laughs. I notice Sunday and Tina looking at my wedding band. They share a glance, and it's obvious I've been a topic of conversation in this town long before I ever arrived. I wonder how long they'll wait before they try to pry the story out of me.

"Oh, you brought wine! Thank you so much, you didn't have to do that!"

Sunday takes the bottle of wine from my hands while Suzanne stares sourly at my profile, and I try not to smile. "I didn't want to walk in empty-handed."

"That was really thoughtful. Let me introduce you around."

Sunday takes one of my arms, and Suzanne takes the other. Then I'm paraded around like a prize hog and introduced to approximately fifty people whose names I promptly forget. My face starts to hurt from forcing a smile for so long.

Doug, the building inspector, turns out to be the kind of guy who tries to make up for his lack of height by being aggressively obnoxious. He talks too loud, interrupts everyone, and stares at my chest the entire time I'm standing in front of him. I can tell Suzanne thinks it's hilarious. I decide to get myself invited over to her house so I can replace all her shampoo with hair remover.

I extricate myself by asking where the restroom is. I hide in there for as long as I can without it being weird, then head into the kitchen, avoiding eye contact as I go.

The kitchen is as cheerful and bright as the rest of the house, and blissfully empty. Coolers overflow with sodas and beers on ice, and a selection of wines and liquor stands ready on the island beside rows of glasses. It's obviously a self-serve setup, which suits me since I won't have to interact with anyone for a few moments.

I find parties draining. Socializing in general is draining now, after so many years of self-imposed solitude.

I grab a Coke and lean against the counter as I drink it, watching the rain fall outside through the sliding glass doors that lead to a covered patio.

It was ninety-eight degrees the day I left Phoenix. The only time it ever rained there was during the monsoon season, and then it was thunderstorms and lightning, nothing like this gentle, melancholy mist, scented of the ocean.

Seaside was Cass's idea. It was his dream to open a B&B near the beach when we retired, and this was the town he decided it should be in. We spent hours hunting the internet for weather stats and demographics, real estate prices and tourism information, until we winnowed down the choices of cities.

We knew the moment we saw the pictures on the internet that the Buttercup was what we'd been looking for. Decrepit yet hauntingly beautiful, it spoke to us on a visceral level. We flew out one weekend to look at it and fell in love even more. Our plan was to buy it and spend every holiday and vacation coming out to work on it, a little at a time, until all the work it needed was finished, then move here and open it up as a B&B again.

He loved to plan things in advance like that. He was always looking toward the future.

We were so young. We didn't know yet that the future isn't guaranteed.

After Cass was gone, the dream seemed pointless. I figured the Buttercup would sell to someone else, but it never did. I'd check on the listing every few months, and, sure enough, it was always available.

Some part of me felt like it was waiting for me. One day, I decided I'd made it wait long enough.

I hear people approaching from the living room and know I won't be able to make conversation because of the damn rock in my throat. I leave the can of soda on the counter, cross to the sliding glass doors, and slip outside into the night.

The patio is covered, its roof supported by several large brick columns. There's a wrought iron table and chairs in the center, a built-in barbeque off to one side, and terra-cotta flower boxes overflowing with hot pink and red geraniums all around the perimeter. The backyard lawn stretches into darkness past the low lights that line the patio edge.

After the warmth of the house, the rain beckons to me. I cross the patio and step out on to the grass. It's springy beneath my feet, pleasant to walk on. I go about ten yards out, past the reach of the lights, then stop, close my eyes, and lift my face to the rain.

I open my mouth to catch a few cool, sweet drops on my tongue. I hear muffled laughter and music from inside, the sound of voices floating to me on the night air. Then I hear the words that haunt me the most, the thing Cass used to whisper into my ear every night before we fell asleep in each other's arms. The last thing he said to me before he died.

I love you, sweet pea. I'll love you till the end of time.

How long will it be until I can no longer remember the sound of his voice? How many years does it take to forget the love of your life? Will I wake up one day and the memory of his kiss will have vanished, trampled to dust by the relentless forward march of time?

"Babe," I whisper, my heart twisting. "I miss you so much. Why did you leave me?"

A tingle like a mild electric shock zings up my spine. From one heartbeat to the next, I realize I'm not alone.

My eyes fly open. I swing around and look back toward the house. I'm momentarily blinded by the lights, but when my eyes adjust, I see a figure in the shadows leaning against one side of the columns that support the patio.

It's a man. A big man with wide shoulders and long legs. His hands are shoved deep into the pockets of his black raincoat. The hood of the raincoat is pulled over his head, but even in the shadows, I can see the glint of his dark eyes.

He stares at me with an unblinking gaze, his expression grim. *Theo.*

As if he heard his name in my mind, he straightens. He pulls his hands from his pockets and stands there staring at me with his hands flexed open like some kind of psychopath about to pounce on me and wring my neck.

That doesn't scare me so much as piss me off. I call out, "Lurk much, pal?"

When he doesn't respond—because, oh yeah, talking isn't his thing—I take a few steps toward him. Simultaneously, he takes a few steps back. When I stop, he stops. Then we stare at each other while I try to decide if I should find a rock to throw at him or calm down and act like an adult.

I'm embarrassed he caught me standing alone in the rain, talking to myself, but it isn't his fault I'm strange.

When his gaze sweeps over me, snagging on my chest before flashing back up to my face, I realize several things at once.

One, I'm not wearing a bra. Unlike Suzanne's double Ds, my B cups don't require scaffolding to hold them up. Two, I've been standing in the rain in a white T-shirt, which means, three, I'm probably giving this nontalking Theo quite a show.

I hunch my shoulders, grab my shirt, and pull it away from my stomach, trying to make all that look nonchalant.

He doesn't move. He doesn't look away. He just stands there, staring, his jaw like granite and his black eyes burning holes into my head.

The tingle in my spine increases until it feels like an itch.

"There you are!" Suzanne's voice rings out over the patio as she pulls open the door and spots me on the lawn. "What're you doing standing in the rain?"

"Nothing. I'm coming."

I glanced away from Theo for a second to look at Suzanne, but when I look back to the place he was standing, he's gone. I catch a glimpse of moonlight reflected off a slick surface around the side of the house. It's Theo, striding toward an open gate, his shoulders stiff beneath the raincoat. He disappears through the gate and melts silently into the night.

Finally, I can move. I hurry back toward the patio, shaking the rain from my hair, wondering why he was standing alone in the dark, why I felt compelled to come out to the patio, and what would've happened if Suzanne hadn't appeared when she did.

I go to bed that night pondering what Suzanne said when I told her I saw Theo in the backyard.

"Oh no, honey, it must've been someone else. That man wouldn't be caught dead at a party."

Somehow, I can't scrub those words from my mind.

4

———————

The next week was a blur of activity.

Suzanne's cleaning crew, an efficient team of five young women, showed up the day after the party and got to work. They tore through the house, scrubbing walls and washing floors, exclaiming in surprise that the place wasn't as dirty as they antici-pated. I wondered who'd gotten rid of the cobwebs and swept before I moved in, but forgot about it in the press of everything else that had to be attended to.

I called three contractors from Portland to come out and give me a bid, only two of whom showed up. One of the contractors was a guy in his sixties who looked at my ass one too many times for comfort. The other one was a perfect gentleman, but the quote he gave me was so high, it made me laugh out loud before I tore it in two.

The following week, I got two more quotes from two more contractors. One was closer to my budget, but the owner said he couldn't start the work for ninety days. The other was from a guy who kept suggesting I'd be more comfortable having my husband deal with "this kind of thing," as if my vagina were a handicap to rational thinking.

Meanwhile, the lights flickered, the pipes in the walls clanged, the ceiling in the master bedroom sagged so badly in one corner, it looked like a boil ready to burst, and the shingles on the roof flew off one by one anytime there was a strong gust of wind.

Worst of all, an ominous crackling coming from one of the electrical outlets in the parlor made me fear that a fire would break out, and I'd die of smoke inhalation in my sleep.

So on a Friday evening when the fog is so dense I can't see the rose bushes that had gone wild around the path leading to the front door, I dial the number Suzanne originally gave me when I asked for a referral for a contractor.

I assumed Hillrise Construction would have an answering service which answered the phones, considering the owner's general hostility and disinclination to speak, so I'm not surprised when a machine picks up. The outgoing message is one of those toneless, electronic voices you get when you neglect to customize it.

"Please. Leave. A message. After. The tone." *Beep.*

"Hi. My name is Megan Dunn, and I was referred to you by Suzanne Martin. I bought the Buttercup Inn and need a quote for repairs."

I leave my cell phone number and am about to hang up when the distinct *click* of the line being picked up stops me. Then I'm listening to silence.

"Hello?"

I could swear I hear a low exhalation, but no one speaks.

Holy shit. It must be him. No-talking Theo with the crazy eyes. "Um...is anyone there?" More silence, but someone is definitely there. I hear rustling and a faint creak in the background, as if whoever answered has sat down.

Why the hell would he pick up the phone if he doesn't talk?

I start to get irritated, because I've got the patience of a four-year old who's missed a nap. "Okay, well, look. I need to get a quote on repairs for the Buttercup Inn. Is that something you can help me with?"

I never knew silence could be so loud. It's absolutely deafening.

I'm about to tell him to go jump off a bridge, but it occurs to me that I could have fun with this instead of letting it aggravate me. "Hey, here's an idea. I saw this on TV once, some dumb show I forget the name of where a guy had laryngitis but had to try to warn his girlfriend a killer was headed over to her house. I'll ask a question, and you can answer by using the phone buttons. One beep for yes, two beeps for no. And three beeps for maybe, if you feel like you might need that option. Okay?"

The silence lasts so long I start to worry he already hung up and I'm listening to a dead line, but then I hear it. A single, sharp electronic *beep*.

Son of a bitch.

"Good. Okay, so...is this Theo?"

A slight pause, then a *beep* that somehow sounds resigned.

"Hi, Theo, this is Megan Dunn. We've already met. Twice, actually. Once at Cal's Diner, and once in the backyard at Sunday and Chris's house party a few weeks back. Do you remember?"

Beeep.

The tone is longer. More emphatic. He remembers. For some strange reason, my pulse picks up and my armpits go damp.

"Right. So anyway, Suzanne says you're the best contractor around and I've already been through five other guys—that sounded wrong, but you know what I mean—so I was wondering if you'd have time to come out this week and take a look at the place."

Two sharp, successive *beeps*, and that's an unequivocal *No*. But I have to confirm, just in case. "No? You won't come out?"

Beep. Beep.

Jesus. How can someone sound like such a dick using only a single button on a telephone?

"Well, fine," I say curtly, heat creeping into my cheeks. "Sorry to have wasted your time. Have a nice life." I'm about to throw my cell phone across the room when over the line comes a rapid mess of electronic noises.

He's pushing all the buttons at once.

When the cacophony stops, I'm livid. Through gritted teeth, I ask, "Were you trying to tell me something there, Sunshine?"

BEEEEEP!

I decide I need a drink if I'm going to continue this bizarre conversation, so I head into the kitchen and unscrew the top of the crappy bottle of wine I bought at the store the other night. I pour some into a glass, guzzle half of it down, swallow, then blow out a breath, all the while acutely aware of the throbbing silence on the other end of the line.

Then my mouth falls open because I'm listening to a telephone rendition of "You Are My Sunshine," played by hitting the right keys to make the correct notes of the song.

Moody Theo has a sense of humor.

"That was interesting. Are you having fun?"

Beep. Beep. Beep.

Maybe.

I burst out laughing, because this is total insanity. "Can I just take a moment to say that this is the weirdest conversation I've ever had in my entire life? This even beats the time I walked in on my dad wearing my mother's underwear. I don't expect an answer to that, by the way, I'm just thinking out loud here."

We breathe at each other for what feels like a long time. "Okay. Starting over. When you say you don't have time to come out this week, does that mean you won't come out, period?"

Beep. Beep.

Why that should make me feel relieved, I have no idea. I clear my throat and try to proceed in an orderly fashion. "So would it be correct for me to infer that you might have time...the week after next?"

Beep. Beep.

"So like, what? Next month?"

Beep. Beep.

Not next week, not the week after that, and not next month. Before I give my temper free rein and decide he's screwing with me, I try a last resort. "This weekend?"

Beep.

Oh. Okay. "Tomorrow?"

Beep.

"Morning or afternoon?" When I don't hear a beep, I realize my mistake. "One beep for morning—say between nine and noon—two beeps for afternoon between twelve and fiveish."

Beep.

"Okay, then. Morning it is. Uh...thanks, I guess?"

When he exhales, hard, I wonder what he's doing. I wonder if he's looking out at the ocean, or lying on his back on his bed staring at the ceiling, or sitting in a chair with the phone held to his ear, his eyes closed and his heart thumping the way mine is.

"Theo?"

Beep.

I don't know what moves me to say it. I don't know why I feel the strange skittering over my skin that raises goose bumps on my arms, or why my stomach is in knots, or why it's become so imperative to have an understanding with this odd, mysterious man. All I know is that the words rise from my throat and leave my mouth unbidden and unrehearsed, in a voice that's undeniably raw.

"I know what it's like to have life pull the rug out from under you."

I hang up before he can respond. Then I stand in my empty kitchen, the relentless boom of waves crashing against the shore the only sound besides my labored breath.

~

I don't sleep that night, because I never do. Chronic insomnia is one of those things I've learned to live with, like soul-crushing grief and people who talk too loudly on their cell phones in public. When a knock comes on the front door in the morning, I'm ready. I've psyched myself up for another weird encounter with the Hulk Who Does Not Speak, but when I open the door, I'm surprised to find a stranger with cornflower-blue eyes, a huge grin, and a square jaw garnished by an unruly blond beard. He's carrying a manila envelope.

"Hi!" he booms, sticking out his hand. "Preston Cooper, Ms. Dunn, but everyone calls me Coop. Pleasure to meet you!"

When I stand there looking at him askance, wondering what he's selling, he adds, "I'm the foreman at Hillrise Construction."

"Oh! Sorry, I wasn't expecting you." Though I suppose his flannel shirt and work boots should've been a clue. "Please, call me Megan."

We shake hands, then his broad forehead crinkles into a frown. "Did I get my days wrong? I coulda swore Theo said today."

"No, sorry, I didn't mean I wasn't expecting Hillrise. I wasn't expecting *you*. I thought Theo would be coming out to meet me."

He smiles broadly, shaking his head. He has an overbite, which I've always found charming. "Naw, no need. He's got your quote all put together already." He hands me the manila envelope.

Puzzled, I open the flap, pull out a sheaf of papers, and look them over. After a moment, I glance up at Coop, who's beaming.

"How could he have put this together without looking at the house?"

"He's the best in the business is how. Theo knows everything about every house in town."

It's more likely he's buddies with one of the other contractors and got a copy of their quote. Maybe he's going to give them a kickback on the job. Whatever, that's his business. I flip to the last page of the papers in my hands, frowning when I see the total. "He's missing a zero here."

"Yeah, you'd think. But that's not a mistake. That's the price for the job."

The cries of the seagulls wheeling overhead punctuate the ensuing silence. I stare at Coop, feeling like I'm missing something. "Is your boss a little...?" I make a circular motion next to my ear.

Coop looks disturbed by my question. His smile is hesitant. "That's funny. He said you were a firecracker."

My eyebrows hike so far up my forehead, they might have melded with my hairline. "He told you about me?"

"*No*," he says emphatically, which is an obvious lie.

I cock my head and stare at him, which makes him squirm. "Coop."

"What?"

"Is Hillrise's office nearby?"

He looks worried. "Why do you ask?"

If I'm going to hire Hillrise Construction for this job, I need to have a real conversation with its owner. Two unsettling stare-offs and a bizarro phone call aren't going to cut it. I spot Coop's truck —an enormous red Ford—at the curb.

"Let's take a ride. I need to have a chat with your boss."

Coop's split-second pause is odd. "That's not such a good idea."

"Why not?"

"Let's just say he doesn't appreciate people showin' up unannounced."

"So text him. Tell him we're on our way."

Coop thoughtfully rubs his beard, looks up at the sky, then checks his watch. Sucking his teeth, he looks back up at the sky, and now I'm done with this ridiculous stalling.

"Spit it out, Coop."

He props his hands on his hips and stares at his boots for a while. Then he clears his throat before carefully choosing his words. "He's not exactly a people person."

"I know he doesn't talk, if that's what you're getting at."

"There are...other issues."

"I'm also well aware of his sunny disposition. The man could frighten Frankenstein. But he doesn't scare me. And if I'm going to invest a substantial amount of money with Hillrise, I need to have a face-to-face meeting with the owner, so I can look in his eyes and feel like I can trust him to do a good job. Because, honestly, our two meetings so far have left me with the impression that his elevator doesn't go all the way to the top floor, if you know what I mean."

Uncomfortable under my hard stare, Coop shifts his weight from foot to foot. "Okay, look. The way it works is that I meet with the clients to get the specs, then Theo puts together the quote and hires the subs, then I manage the job from start to finish. He'll come out to check on the work, but he doesn't have much one-on-one contact with the clients."

There's another tiny pause wherein Coop almost says something else, but he stops himself and just looks at me. The air is thick with unspoken words.

Suzanne had told me Theo was very hands-on with all his projects, overseeing everything from start to finish, but that's the *opposite* of what Coop just said...

"Wait. He doesn't want to meet with me, does he?"

Coop looks startled, then guilty.

Bingo.

He holds up a hand, shaking his big blond head. "Hold on, I didn't say that at all—"

"Why would he not want to meet a potential client?" I ignore his denial, jerking my thumb toward the house. "This is a huge job. What's the problem?"

Coop inhales a long breath, searching for words, but my patience expires before he can find them.

"You know what? It doesn't matter. You text Theo right now—or however it is you communicate with him—and tell him I'm coming over. Or he can come here, whatever's more convenient. But I'll be damned if I'm going to do business with someone who won't even give me the courtesy of a meeting."

I fold my arms over my chest and stare at Coop, my gaze unblinking.

His cheeks puff out as he slowly exhales. Then he digs his cell phone from the front pocket of his jeans, muttering, "Well, hell."

It takes a geological epoch for Coop to send a text message, because he uses one finger, squinting and pecking at the keyboard on his iPhone until I want to tear my hair out. When he finally presses Send, he glances up at me with a hesitant smile.

Apparently, Theo is much quicker on the draw, because the chime from an answering text comes through within seconds. Coop reads the message, but is silent.

"What did he say?"

He chews the inside of his cheek. "Um."

"Give me the phone."

Coop's blue eyes grow wide.

"Coop," I insist, holding out my hand. "*Give* me. The *phone*."

He hands it over with an expression like a puppy who's been scolded. I look at the screen.

DO NOT BRING THAT WOMAN HERE UNDER ANY CIRCUMSTANCES

The message is all in caps and bolded, like Theo's shouting from the other side of the screen.

I waver for a moment between feeling insulted or wanting to laugh. This is so odd and unexpected, I can't decide how to feel about it. Logic tells me there's nothing I could have possibly done to earn this stranger's dislike, but he clearly has a strong aversion to my presence. He's like a bear with a thorn in its paw—only the thorn is me.

"That woman," he wrote. Like I'm a carrier of the plague.

I look up at Coop with my brows drawn together. "Have you known Theo a long time?"

"Sure. We both grew up in Seaside. We were on the football team together in high school. He was one of the groomsmen at my wedding."

Gathering my thoughts, I hand him his phone. "Okay. I won't put you in an awkward position by trying to force you to tell me why your friend doesn't like me, but I'd appreciate it if you could tell Theo that I said...ouch."

Coop lifts his brows. "Ouch?"

"Yeah. Ouch. Just tell him that. And that if I see him again, I'll cross the street first so he doesn't have to. Thanks for coming out."

I hand him the manila envelope with the quote in it and close the door.

5

I call Craig, the contractor who gave me the astronomical quote, and spend twenty minutes with him on the phone, haggling over the price. When I tell him the other quotes I got were half the price his was, he tells me with a shrug in his voice that if budget is my main concern, I should go with someone else.

I hate to admit I like his chutzpah. A man with unflappable self-confidence is incredibly appealing.

We settle on a ten percent discount if I pay him cash. He laughs when I tell him he shouldn't charge me sales tax either. "That's not how it works," he says.

"Don't patronize me, Craig, I know exactly how it works. You're not going to put the job on the books if it's paid in cash, so you won't have to pay sales tax, so you should pass that savings along to me. Considering you padded your quote with enough pork to make a politician proud, you're still way ahead of the game."

After a short silence, Craig says, "I meant I can't take off the sales tax because there *is* no sales tax. Oregon doesn't have it."

"Oh. Right. I forgot."

"But I'll tell you what. The state just passed a construction excise tax to raise funds for affordable housing. It's based on a percentage of your building permit valuation. I'll take care of that for you."

He tells me how much it will amount to. I think for a moment before saying, "Double it, and you've got a deal."

Into his disgruntled pause, I remind him, "Cash is king, Craig. Even if you don't have to pay state sales tax, you'll be paying the Feds on anything you deposit into your bank account, am I right?"

"Have mercy on a poor guy, Megan!"

He suggests another number, then I suggest another, then we agree to split the difference. He tells me he'll send over the contract for my review on Monday, and we say goodbye and hang up.

Pleased with myself, I look around the front parlor with my hands on my hips. I'm excited for the first time in years.

It's really going to happen. I'm going to make our dream come true, babe.

The phone rings. I pick it up, expecting it to be Craig wanting to go over some forgotten detail, or perhaps Suzanne, but it's Coop, sounding bashful.

"Hi, there, Megan, this is Coop."

"Hi, Coop. What's up?"

Long, awkward pause. "Uh...I'm still standin' outside your house."

I walk to the windows, and there he is, out on the sidewalk near his truck.

"Are you having car problems?"

"No, I'm, uh, just waitin' on Theo. He's comin' out to see you. I texted him what you said, and, uh..." Coop clears his throat. "Well, anyway, he's on his way. I thought I'd give you a heads-up."

The circus never stops with this guy. "That's unfortunate, Coop, because I just got off the phone with Craig from Capstone. He's going to handle the job."

Coop scoffs. "Craig? That self-important SOB? You *like* flushin' your money down the toilet?"

"No, I don't. Which is why I negotiated a discount."

"Lemme guess. He probably quoted you..." He thinks for a moment, looking up at the house, then names a number which is only a few hundred dollars off from Craig's quote, which is very irritating.

"You seem like a nice guy, Coop, but this conversation is pointless, considering your boss has no interest in working with me."

"I never said that," he says quickly. Our gazes meet through the window. I see how serious he is suddenly, his easy grin nowhere in sight.

"I wasn't going to tell him you did," I say, sensing this is somehow a matter of great importance.

When Coop blows out a breath, looking relieved, my hunch is proven right. Before I can say anything else, however, he straightens, looking down the street.

"He's here." He flashes me a look full of warning, then hangs up, steps out into the street, and holds up a hand.

Fascinated, I watch as a classic Mustang slowly rolls up the street, engine rumbling. It's black, with windows tinted so dark, I can't see inside, and chrome wheels that gleam in the sun. The car stops in the middle of the street, then Coop walks over and bends down to the driver's-side window.

Several minutes pass and Coop is still standing there, talking to Theo. Or drawing pictures or whatever it is he does to communicate with Mr. Incommunicado.

"What the hell is it with this guy?" I mutter, growing more irritated by the moment.

Finally, Coop straightens, and the Mustang pulls up to the curb. The engine shuts off. I want to look away, but I'm rooted to the spot, staring out the front parlor window, waiting for what feels like an eternity until the driver's door opens and Theo steps out.

Black hair.

It's my first thought when his broad shoulders rise up over the roof of the car. I've only seen him in a raincoat, his head covered, but now I see he has a lot of thick, black hair, the length past the collar of his leather jacket. It's messy. Windswept and untamed, like he only ever combs it with his fingers.

When he turns and looks toward the house, it's like he knew exactly where I was standing. Our eyes meet with the sensation of a key fitting into a lock: a smooth, inevitable *click*.

A tremor runs through me, something close to fear but more primal, a pulse of restless energy that makes me want to break into a run.

I've never met anyone with more naked emotion in his eyes. His face is stony, but his eyes burn with a thousand unspoken things, all of which are dark.

I resist the urge to step back. We stare at each other until it becomes uncomfortable. I move first, turning to head to the front door, taking deep breaths to calm the sudden throbbing of my heart.

When I open the door, Coop and Theo are walking up the brick pathway toward the porch. Coop is in the lead, smiling nervously. "Hi, Megan!" he calls, as if he hasn't seen me in forever.

"Hi, Coop. Long time no see."

Coop ambles up the steps onto the porch that wraps around the front of the house, but Theo stops at the first step and looks at me, as if for permission.

"Sure, Dracula," I say drily, unamused by this strange situation. "You're welcome to come in. I'll put away the garlic and crosses."

A muscle in his jaw flexes. He doesn't look amused either. He steps slowly up, one big boot at a time, until he's on the porch and I have to look up as he walks toward me with thunderclouds churning over his head. He stops a few feet away and stares down at me as Coop looks back and forth between us, visibly worried.

But I can't pay attention to Coop anymore. Not with the boiling cauldron standing in front of me. The rumbling mountain of magma about to blow. The seething pool of silent emotions clad in a leather jacket and jeans. If I were a cop, I'd arrest this guy on the spot for disturbing the peace. All by himself, he's a riot threatening to destroy the entire town.

On the left side of his neck, a snarl of scar tissue peeks over the collar of his shirt. His nose was broken once and not fixed well. There's a ragged white scar above his left eyebrow that disappears into his hairline, and he walks with a barely perceptible limp, favoring his left side. And those dark, dark eyes. God, how they burn.

Whatever the accident was that he was involved in, it's left its mark on this man, in more ways than one.

Coop does the introductions. "Megan, this is Theo Valentine. Theo, Megan Dunn."

When he glowers at me, as he does, I sigh, because I'm really over this. "I'd say it's a pleasure to formally meet you, Theo, but my mother didn't raise a liar."

In the depths of his bottomless black eyes, there's a flicker of humor. His lips twitch as if he's about to say something, but then they still, and I realize that was his version of a smile.

"I told Coop that I've already agreed to work with Craig from Capstone, so there's really no need—"

Theo brushes past me and walks into the house.

I turn and look at him, a huff of outrage on my lips, then turn back to Coop, throwing my hands up in exasperation.

"Sorry." He shrugs. "But you did say he could come in."

Theo heads to the staircase, then takes the stairs two at a time like he owns the place, his boots echoing hollowly off the wood. As he disappears from view, I shout, "Where are you going?"

Coop says, "He wants to start work on the master bedroom first so you'll be comfortable while the rest of the house gets done."

"How thoughtful." My tone drips sarcasm. "But he's not working on anything, Craig from Capstone is."

Coop makes a face like we don't have a say in it, which is ridiculous because this is *my* house!

"Oh, for God's sake," I mutter, heading toward the stairs. Coop closes the front door, then we're both clomping up the stairs, me leading the way with steam pouring out of my ears.

I don't care what happened to make Theo Valentine such a jerk. This nonsense stops now.

I find him in my bedroom, standing at the end of my bed. He's staring down at the mattress, strewn with sheets and a blanket, all a twisted mess because I toss and turn all night every night and I haven't made my bed since I became a widow. I stop in the doorway and fold my arms across my chest. Coop is right behind me, breathing down my neck in palpable anxiety.

"Theo."

He turns his head a fraction, but otherwise doesn't move.

"I appreciate you coming out. I do *not* appreciate your manners, which are atrocious, or that chip on your shoulder, or whatever the heck it is you're doing right now. Which is all sorts of creepy, by the way."

He turns all the way around and stares at me. His eyes scorch the air.

"Oh, hi! Nice of you to join us back here on earth! Are you done with your little inspection of my bed? Because if you are, you know where the front door is. Don't let it hit ya."

Behind me, Coop smothers what could be a laugh or a groan with his hand.

Then—surprise!—Theo's black brows draw together into a scowl. From an inside pocket of his coat, he whips out a pen and a small spiral notebook, flips open the cover, then scribbles something, his hand moving like lightning over the page. He thrusts the pad out so I can read what he's written.

Sorry. Not good with people. Don't hire Capstone.

Not good with people? Hello, understatement of the century. "That ship has already sailed, Sunshine. Craig's sending over the contract Monday."

More furious scribbling. Then he walks closer and thrusts the pad right into my face.

I'm better!

I bat his hand away. "You're also a pain in my ass. And, frankly, maybe a little unhinged. The thought of having you around for the six months or so it's going to take to finish work on my house is less than appealing."

He stands there, nostrils flared, scowl darkening, vibrating annoyance and frustration, until Coop clears his throat. Theo's black gaze flashes over my shoulder.

"Maybe you should show her the plans, T."

I ask, "Plans? What plans?"

But Theo has decided this is a good idea, because he's already shoving past us and heading back downstairs at a run. The front door opens, then slams closed.

Astonished, I look at Coop. "Seriously, he's abnormal. I can't believe anyone would hire that guy."

Sounding apologetic, Coop says, "He's not usually this bad."

"How comforting. Can you give me a single good reason I'd hire someone who hates my guts?"

Coop's blue eyes soften into something that looks suspiciously like pity. "He doesn't hate you," he says gently. "Believe me, if he did, we wouldn't be here. You just...agitate him."

I laugh, because that's another whopper of an understatement. "You don't say? Wait, don't tell me—he's secretly in love with me, right?"

Coop solemnly shakes his head. "No."

I inspect his face, which is devoid of anything even approaching laughter. "Please tell me you realize that was a joke."

"Oh. Okay."

I lift my brows. "Do they not allow sarcasm in this town? Because if that's the case, I might as well scrap the whole project and move somewhere where people can appreciate my biting sense of humor and deep love of snark."

Before he can reply, the front door opens and closes again—with a resounding slam, because apparently Theo Valentine doesn't do anything gently—then three loud thuds vibrate the floorboards beneath my feet.

I look at Coop in disbelief. "Did he just stamp his foot on the floor to call us downstairs?"

Coop's sigh is resigned. "'Fraid so. We better get down there before he loses his patience."

I bark out a laugh that's half humor and half outrage. "This is him being *patient?*"

"You really don't want to know," Coop mutters, then heads out of the room.

When we get downstairs, we find Theo in the kitchen. On the marble island, he's set a large, rectangular book. It has a blue linen cover, embossed with the words "Buttercup Inn" in silver foil, in an old-fashioned typestyle with lots of swirly lines. Beside the book are several rolled-up folios that appear to be architectural drawings.

My curiosity piqued, I walk closer. "What's all this?"

Theo simply gestures to the book, as if to say, *Look.*

I open the cover, start to turn pages, and lose my breath.

The book is filled with page after page of gorgeous, full-color computer renderings of the Buttercup Inn. Only not the way it is now—the way it would look after extensive renovations.

There are lavish gardens and splashing fountains and a rolling green lawn in the front. The exterior of the house is painted a soft shade of butter yellow, trimmed in white. Inside, the rooms are decorated with beautiful furnishings that pay homage to the era the house was originally built, paired with more modern pieces that effortlessly update the ambiance.

The wraparound porch features several seating areas where guests can congregate, and the backyard has been turned into the most amazing adult playground, with fire pits surrounded by sofas, a dining table under a retractable awning, several lawn game areas including one featuring a giant Jenga, and an infinity pool overlooking the sea.

It's exactly how Cass and I envisioned it would be, down to the smallest detail.

This isn't simply a project rendering. This book is a blueprint of the inside of my head.

Stunned, I stand in frozen silence until Theo takes charge and unfurls one of the rolled folios. It's an architectural drawing of the Buttercup, white schematics on a background of pale blue illustrating the technical particulars of the building, including floor plans, site plans, and detail drawings, giving an engineering perspective of the work to be done.

If the book was a blueprint of my mind, these drawings are a map of my heart.

Unnerved, I flip back to the first page of the book, hunting for a small detail that struck me. I point at the row of purple flowers lining the front porch on both sides of the house. In a low voice, I ask, "What kind of flowers are those?"

Theo writes on his pad, then holds it out to me.

Sweet peas.

Knife to the gut. Bullet to the head. Free fall from a fifty-story building. I slam the book shut, say hoarsely, "Excuse me for a minute," and walk out of the kitchen, my stomach in knots. I head to the back patio in a half run and burst through the French doors out into the backyard. Then I stand there, gulping air, letting the sun blind me and the sea air play with my hair as I try to get a grip on myself.

Don't cry. Don't cry, you big sissy. DO. NOT. CRY.

One of the first shrinks I went to after Cass died told me that the brain has a hardwired need to find correlations, to make sense of nonsensical data by making connections between unrelated things. Humans have evolved a universal tendency to seek patterns in random information, hence the existence of fortune-tellers and dream interpreters and people who see the face of Jesus in a piece of toast.

But the cold, hard truth is that there are no connections between anything.

Life—all of existence—is totally random.

Your lucky lottery numbers aren't really lucky, because there's no such thing as luck. The black cat that crosses your path isn't a bad omen, it's just a cat out for a walk. An eclipse doesn't mean that the gods are angry, just as a bus narrowly missing you as you cross the street doesn't mean there's a guardian angel looking out for you.

There are no gods.

There are no angels.

Superstitions aren't real, and no amount of wishing, praying, or rationalizing can change the fact that life is just one long sequence of random events that ultimately have no meaning.

I really hated that shrink.

But he's with me now, reassuring me in that flat voice of his that the sweet peas planted along the front porch in Theo's vision of the Buttercup Inn have no relevance to the nickname Cass used to call me. There's no connection whatsoever between a mute stranger creating an exact replica of what my dead husband and I had envisioned for this exact house. It means nothing at all that we spent years dreaming and scrimping and planning to find *this* property, in *this* town, with *that* view of the rolling surf and *those* flowers in the front yard, and here it all is, coming together like it was fated.

It's not fated. It's a fluke. It's just life, doing what it does best: screwing with me.

If only my stupid heart would believe it.

"Megan? You okay?" Coop stands in the open doorway, one hand on the frame, his brow crinkled with worry.

"Yep. Fine." *Just super, thanks a million, I'm not at all having a breakdown on this lovely September day, nosirree.* I swipe at my eyes, angry with myself for this show of weakness. I straighten my shoulders, take a deep breath, and plaster a smile on my face. "Just needed a bit of air."

Coop doesn't look convinced. I don't blame him, because I'm a terrible liar. But I'll be damned if I'm going to admit I'm a woman on the edge of a nervous breakdown, seeing ghosts in the blueprints of my house.

I walk back inside, sending Coop another reassuring smile, and find Theo waiting in the kitchen, standing in the same spot I left him. I smile at him too, my lips stretched so tight, they hurt, but he doesn't reciprocate. He simply stares at me, a furrow carved between his black brows, a muscle jumping in his jaw.

Then he writes something on his pad and holds it up.

I'm sorry.

I don't know what he's apologizing for, but that part of my brain wired to make connections is screaming that he knows I'm upset...and why.

"No worries. I'm fine." I decide not to give him some lame excuse for why I ran out, because I suspect he'll see right through it, but I don't have the energy to power the fake smile, so I let it die out. Then we stand there, staring at each other in tense silence.

It's becoming our thing.

"I'm gonna use the bathroom," calls Coop on his way through the living room. A door closes a few rooms away. He's obviously giving us a moment alone.

Theo's Adam's apple bobs as he swallows. I've never met anyone who could stand completely still yet give the impression he's about to burst into dangerous motion. He's like a cobra, coiled to strike.

In a muted voice, I ask, "How do you have all this prepared without ever meeting with me or being inside the house?"

He glances down at the book, flattens his big hand over the cover, exhales a slow breath through his nose. Then he picks up the pen and pad.

I love this house. It deserves a second chance.

It's an answer, but a careful one that sidesteps the actual question, so I think of how best to proceed. If he grew up in Seaside, he's obviously familiar with the house. Maybe he even stayed here when it was an operating B&B. But that doesn't explain why he'd have all these schematics and renderings done in such detail if he didn't already have a client who wanted to refurbish the property.

Unless he did.

"Oh, I get it. You bid on the repair work after the fire in the kitchen, right?"

He blinks, once. I'm not sure if we're using our telephone code and that's a yes, or if he's just blinking. "For the last owner, I mean." I gesture to the book and blueprints, because he's not answering, and I can't tell if that look he's wearing is annoyance or constipation.

Finally, he tilts his head to the side, a little jerk toward his shoulder that's not a nod or a shake, it's more like a *Maybe*. Or a *Whatever*. Or possibly a *You're irritating me with these stupid questions.*

Dealing with this guy is too much work. It's only half past nine in the morning, and I already need a drink.

"Forget it. Moving on to the elephant in the room. You and I have a problem. Let's be nice and call it a personality conflict. This job is going to take a long time, and I'm not the kind of girl who's going to sit up in my bedroom knitting while the men make all the decisions and run the show. This is *my* house. If I decide to hire you for this job—and I'm only saying *if*—I won't tolerate your attitude."

Slowly, he arches one of his eyebrows.

"Yeah, you heard me." I wave a hand up and down, indicating his general impression of a volcano about to erupt. "This whole grouchy caveman thing you've got going is already on my last nerve, and you've only been here for fifteen minutes. I under-stand that you've been through some kind of trauma, but so have I, and you don't see me going around glaring daggers at total strangers. Either you rein in your nasty mood monster, or we have nothing more to discuss."

I fold my arms over my chest and wait for the volcano to blow.

But it never comes. Theo just stands there, gazing at me, his expression softening until it almost looks as if he's about to break into laughter.

He props his hands on his hips, looks at the ground, shakes his head like he can't believe what a psycho I am, then meets my eyes.

He nods—slowly, emphatically, an unmistakable *yes*—then smiles.

Beyond my shock that the man actually knows how to smile, my sense of relief is overwhelming. I feel like I've successfully negotiated with a terrorist. "Okay. Good. Well, like I said, I've already made a verbal agreement to work with Craig, so I'll have to think about this over the weekend."

Theo's default scowl snaps back into place. He snatches up his pen and pad and does his thing, then thrusts it out at me, almost hitting me in the nose.

I'm the best man for the job!

I am *this close* to smacking that pad out of his hands and cracking him over the head with the Buttercup Inn book.

"Wow, you're just determined to try my patience, aren't you? Do you remember a few seconds back when I said rein it in, Sunshine? I fucking meant *rein it in*."

His face falls, his shoulders slump, and he stares contritely at the floor like a five-year-old who's been caught with his hand in the cookie jar. It's ridiculously adorable. My heart softens toward him, this riddle of a man who's a snarling bear one moment and a sad little boy the next.

From several rooms over, Coop loudly clears his throat, closing the bathroom door firmly enough that the sound echoes down the hallway.

Lord, these two men have all the finesse of a pair of grenades. "I'll call you Monday," I tell Theo in a gentler tone. "Okay?"

He glances up at me from under his lashes, then with his pen slowly circles something on his pad that he's already written. When he holds it out to me to read, I sigh.

"You don't have to be sorry, just stop acting like I ran over your dog. Deal?"

His eyes search my face. His gaze is filled with unspeakable loneliness, and that naked antipathy that I don't understand but that raises all the tiny hairs on the back of my neck and sends a charge like electricity over my skin. It's the same feeling I had at the diner and in the backyard at the party. That sense of unwilling recognition.

Of being seen by someone who doesn't want to see.

Without responding, Theo turns abruptly and leaves. The sound of his boots heading toward the front door and disappearing through it are quickly followed by Coop's farewell shout.

"Thanks, Megan! See you soon!"

The front door slams, and I'm left alone in my ruined kitchen, wondering what the hell Theo Valentine's problem is.

And why I'm becoming so eager to find out.

6

I call Suzanne, who I figure is the best source of information in Seaside, considering she seems to know everyone.

"Hello?"

"Hey, Suzanne, it's Megan Dunn."

"Megan! How *are* you?"

She sounds overly excited to hear from me, which makes me suspicious. "I'm good, thanks. How are you?"

"Fantastic! I just closed escrow on a place up in the hills that has an incredible ocean view and an even more incredible price tag. This cute young gay couple bought it and they're going to sink a *ton* into renovations. I was just about to send Theo an email to let him know they'll be contacting him."

"Speak of the devil. That's why I'm calling."

She sounds confused. "About the gay couple?"

"No, Suzanne, about Theo. He came out this morning to give me a quote on the house. It was less than half the price of the other guys', and he brought me these really incredible renderings that blew me away."

"Oh, great!"

"No, not great. Because Theo was being Theo, and I'm not sure I can deal with that for the next few months while this project gets done. I already negotiated an agreement with Craig from Capstone, and I'm leaning toward keeping it because Theo is so strange."

"Believe me, you'll get used to his silence real quick as soon as you see the quality of work he does."

"It's not his silence that's the problem. It's his weirdness. Every time he looks at me, I get the feeling he's either going to hit something or cry."

Her matchmaker instincts kick in. "Maybe he has the hots for you!"

I snort. "Believe me, this isn't the hots. This is more like the freezing colds. The guy can barely stand to be around me."

Suzanne is thoughtful for a moment. "I mean, he's odd, definitely, but I know for a fact he's harmless, Megan. He's a big guy, but he's gentle as a lamb."

"I've never met a lamb who goes around with a hurricane brewing over its head."

After a pause, she says gingerly, "Okay, I'm going to say something now."

I know that means it's going to be something I don't like. I wait for it, exhaling in annoyance.

"Maybe—and I'm only saying maybe—you're just sensitive."

I frown. "Sensitive? About what?"

"About men."

"About *men*?" I repeat, puzzled.

"You know, because of your husband."

"Oh. You think I've lost my ability to judge a person's character because my husband died, is that it?"

"It's just that nobody else has ever had a problem with Theo, sweetie," says Suzanne in a placating tone. "Except you."

Frustrated, I blow out a hard breath. "So I'm told. But I'm not imagining it, Suzanne. Even Coop said he's never seen Theo act the way he acts around me. He said I 'agitate' him."

"Coop said that? Huh. Well, that's weird."

"That's what I've been telling you!"

"Maybe he's jealous of your tan?"

"Don't be ridiculous."

"Maybe you remind him of someone he hates?"

"It's possible, but I doubt it. His problem seems very Megan specific."

"Maybe he thinks you should put on a little lipstick and a shirt that doesn't have a band logo on it to make it seem like you give an actual fuck before you go out in public?"

That makes me smile. "Inside thought, Suzanne."

"Hmm. And you're *positive* he doesn't have the hots for you?"

"Oh yeah, I'm sure he gets an expression like he just took a dump in his pants every time he sees me because he's so attracted to me. It's definitely true love."

She laughs. "Okay, I'm fresh out of smart ideas, then. Chalk it up to one of those things and stay out of his way while he works on the Buttercup. Maybe he'll warm up to you after a while."

"Or maybe he'll leave random tools on the floor for me to trip over and break my face on."

"Don't be silly, he'll do no such thing. If you don't like Theo, just deal directly with Coop. From the sound of things, that would suit both of you. I'm telling you, he's the best there is. I've got a list a mile long of people you could call for a reference if you don't want to take my word for it. And why flush money down the toilet if you don't have to? Just my two cents, but I think it's worth it to put up with him in the short run for what you'll get out of it in the long run."

I mull it over because she makes some good points. I got a big chunk of change in the settlement from Cass's accident, but I know how these kind of large renovation projects can go way over budget. And there's no guarantee the B&B will be a success after I open. I could be filing for bankruptcy in a few years if the economy tanks. I need to be practical about this. Practical, frugal, and emotionless.

Except for my intense curiosity and my sore ego, I'd be all set.

"Maybe if you told me more about him, it would make me more comfortable."

"What do you want to know?"

"About his accident," I say without thinking. "I want to know what happened to make Mr. Popularity turn into the Grinch."

On the other end of the line, there's a long sigh. "Sweetie, that story needs to be told over drinks. What're you doing tonight?"

I look around the kitchen, at the scorched floor, the boarded-up windows, the empty takeout containers crowding the counter. "Not a thing."

"Be ready at six. I'm driving. And wear a skirt, for God's sake. I have a reputation to uphold in this town, and your homeless stoner look isn't cutting it."

She hangs up without waiting to hear the argument she already knows is coming.

At precisely six o'clock that night, Suzanne arrives looking like she has an appointment to meet Hugh Hefner. I've never seen so much cleavage in my life.

"Hi, Suzanne." I warily eye her hairdo, which is teased and sprayed to '80s hair band proportions, her stilettos, which are sky-high, and her skirt, which is so tight I suspect her circulation is being compromised. "Please tell me we're not going clubbing."

She looks at me as if I've been smoking crack. "There aren't any clubs within an eighty-mile radius. We're going to Booger's."

Booger's? This is why I never go out.

"Don't give me that look!" Suzanne scolds when she sees my expression. "It's a very nice, upscale restaurant."

"I think our definitions of 'upscale' might be different."

"Jeez, what're you, ninety, Grandma?"

"Thirty-two, actually."

Suzanne grimaces. "You're younger than me too? How did I not notice that on your escrow docs? It's a pity I already decided not to hate you. Nice dress, by the way."

"Thanks. I had to go out and buy it today because I didn't own one. I didn't want to get clobbered by my real estate agent."

She narrows her eyes at my waistline. "Are you wearing a waist trainer under that?"

Perplexed, I look down at myself. "What the hell is a waist trainer?"

She groans, throwing her hands in the air. "I changed my mind. I *do* hate you. Let's go, you're making me thirsty."

I lock the front door, she grabs me by the arm, and we're off to Booger's, which I suspect will be about as pleasant as a visit to the gynecologist.

When we arrive, I'm surprised to find I was wrong. Whoever named the place was off his rocker, but the location is spectacular. Booger's sits at the end of the beach promenade, overlooking the ocean. It has a kitschy seafaring theme that manages to be ironically sentimental instead of just plain tacky.

Fishnet is strung from the ceiling and hung with starfish and Christmas lights. Brick walls are covered in framed black-and-white pictures of old movie stars and dotted with big portholes for windows. Candles glow atop polished wood tables, and an enormous captain's wheel garnishes the hostess stand where Suzanne gives our name to a hostess who looks fifteen years old.

"It's cute," I say, looking around.

Suzanne nudges me with her elbow and grins. "Would I steer you in the wrong direction?"

"The name, though."

"It's the nickname of the owner. Someone caught him picking his nose in elementary school, and it stuck."

I grimace. "Hopefully, he's abandoned the habit and doesn't pick his nose in the kitchen."

"This way, please." The hostess, holding a pair of menus, gestures for us to follow her.

Suzanne gets a lot of stares as we walk to our table. Even some of the women seem interested in her beauty queen bounce. I admire her self-confidence and have to smile when a guy drops his spoon into his soup as we pass by.

Once we're seated, we spend a few minutes looking at the menu, then order our drinks and meals from the heavyset waitress who comes by. When she's gone, Suzanne says, "So. Theo Valentine."

"The man of the hour." I munch on nuts from a bowl the waitress left on the table. "Mystery man with a name like a porn star."

"He's not all that mysterious."

I stop munching and stare at her.

"Okay, he's a *little* mysterious."

When I don't relent with the stare, she sighs and gives up.

"Fine, he's very mysterious. *Now.* Before, he was just Theo, local pretty-boy jock set to take over the world. All the girls were in love with him, of course. You don't get that quality of man meat much in this town."

I pop another fistful of nuts into my mouth. Around them, I say, "You truly have a way with words, Suzanne."

She smiles serenely, twirling a lock of dark hair between her fingers. "He was a couple of years behind me at school, but God, did I have a crush on him. I'm a pushover for swagger, and he had it in spades. He went to college in Washington, but came back because he and Colleen were still together and she didn't want to leave Seaside. They were supposed to get married. You met her at Sunday's party, do you remember? The schoolteacher with the pretty blue eyes?"

I do remember. Her eyes weren't the only things that were

pretty. She had sleek brown hair and beautiful skin, a figure even voluptuous Suzanne might be jealous of.

"Let me guess. They never got married."

"Nope."

"So what happened?"

"Theo's accident happened. And from the way she tells it, from the moment he woke up in the hospital, he wanted nothing more to do with her. Wouldn't even look at her. Never spoke to her or anyone else again."

"Yikes. That's harsh."

Suzanne taps her manicured nails on the table. "Yeah, Colleen was devastated. I still don't think she's over it. I've tried to set her up with every single man from here to Timbuktu, but she always says no. I suspect she's hoping one day Theo will snap out of his silent funk and take her back."

"So what's with his whole not-talking thing? Were his vocal cords crushed or something?"

"Your guess is as good as mine, sweetie. His doctor won't tell anybody anything, of course, but I know a few of the nurses who were at the hospital when he was brought in the night of the accident and were there during his recovery. They both say the same thing: Theo refused to speak, he refused to answer questions about why he wouldn't speak, and he went into a rage if pressed about it. Trashed an exam room when a physical therapist got too pushy is the way I hear it. Then of course the doctor wanted to send him to a psychiatrist, but he refused that too. Just checked himself out of the hospital as soon as he could walk again, and that was that.

"Everybody in town felt bad for him, so he kept getting jobs, and after a while, nobody cared anymore that he didn't talk, because his work wasn't affected. In fact, it seemed to get even better. And he's *fast*. He can tear down a house and completely rebuild it before his competition has even gotten around to putting in bids. Whatever demon is driving him, it has a good work ethic."

The waitress arrives with our drinks, giving me a moment to think. I sip my iced tea, even more curious now about the mystery man. I'm about to ask Suzanne what kind of accident Theo was in when a deep voice interrupts.

"Well, look who it is. Fancy meeting you here."

I look up. It's Craig from Capstone, standing beside our table, smiling down at me.

"Craig! Hi, what a surprise. What are you doing here?"

Suzanne kicks me under the table. I glance sharply at her. She's gazing up at Craig with big moony eyes and a blinding smile, batting her lashes. She's pulled back her shoulders so her cleavage is displayed at its most advantageous angle for someone looking down.

He's getting the VIP treatment because he's handsome. That rugged, cowboy type of handsome where you just know he's really good at chopping wood and taming wild stallions and shooting poor game birds out of the sky and stuff like that. He's got dark blond hair, dimples you could fall into, and a smile as easy as a Sunday morning.

And he's not wearing a wedding ring, a fact that Suzanne's sharp eyes didn't miss.

He says, "I was in the area this afternoon to meet a client, thought I'd catch a bite before I went back to Portland." He notices Suzanne and her cleavage. His smile widens. "I hope I'm not interrupting."

"Not at all!" simpers Suzanne with a little wiggle of her shoulders that makes her boobs shake and Craig's eyes widen.

I pull my lips between my teeth so I don't smile. "Have you two met?"

At the same time, Craig and Suzanne say, "No."

"Suzanne, this is Craig Kennedy from Capstone Construction. Craig, this is Suzanne Martin. She's in real estate."

No sooner have the words left my lips than Suzanne is scooting over in her side of the booth. "Nice to meet you, Craig!" she says brightly, all smiles and sweetness. "Are you having dinner alone?"

"Yep."

Don't say it, Suzanne.

"Why don't you join us?"

Shit.

Craig looks at me. Of course I'm not going to be Ultra Super Mega Bitch and send him away, so I smile and pretend to be welcoming. "Yes, please join us."

Craig slides into the booth beside Suzanne, and the two of them sit there grinning at each other while I wonder at what age it becomes socially acceptable to say whatever you're really thinking and do whatever you want, regardless of what's polite. Seventy? Eighty?

God, I can't wait.

The next two hours are hell. Between Craig's and Suzanne's blistering hormones and my dinner—which was supposed to be calamari but instead tastes suspiciously like fried rubber bands—I start to feel sick.

And sweet Jesus, can Craig talk. Once he sits down, he doesn't take a breath. On and on he goes, about his work, his company, his plans for expansion, yada yada yada. It's exhausting. Not once does he ask Suzanne or me a question. It's like we were only born to sit and listen to him blather on while we smile supportively and strain our spines as we show off our boobs.

I don't even have the pleasure of getting plastered, because I never drink unless I'm at home. And I can tell by Suzanne's third glass of wine that I'm going to be the one driving there.

At quarter past eight, my patience has been worn to a nub by Craig's ceaseless drone. I catch the waitress's eye and motion for the check. When it comes, Craig takes it from her hand, waving dismissively when I protest.

"It's my pleasure." He smiles at Suzanne, who smiles dreamily back at him.

I doubt it would be his pleasure if he knew I'm seriously considering not hiring him for my ridiculously expensive renovation, but maybe Suzanne's ample assets will soften the blow.

"I can't believe we've never met before," she complains prettily, toying with the sleeve of his shirt. "I give my clients referrals for your company all the time, but I've only met your foreman."

"Well, now you've met me." Craig's smile looks dangerous. "I hope it wasn't a disappointment."

Suzanne giggles like a schoolgirl, and it's all I can do not to throw my napkin in her face. "This was wonderful," I say, "and it was so nice to see you, Craig." I slide toward the edge of the booth, hoping they'll take the hint. When they don't, I add pointedly, "But I'm feeling a bit tired, so…"

Pulling himself out of the spell of Suzanne's boobs, Craig remembers his manners and stands. "Of course. I should let you ladies go. Megan, it was a pleasure to see you again. I'll be sending that paperwork over Monday."

He shakes my hand. I try not to feel like we're making a deal. He turns to Suzanne, still sitting in the booth, looking forlorn that he's leaving. "Suzanne, I honestly can't remember the last time I had so much fun talking to someone."

She says, "You need to get my number so you can have fun again soon."

Damn. This girl is a go-getter, that's for sure.

But, shockingly, Craig doesn't take the bait. He says lightly, "Yeah, if I need a real estate agent I'll definitely give you a call. I can get your number from Megan."

Suzanne's smile freezes in place.

Craig says, "Ladies," makes a motion like he's tipping his hat, then turns around and walks away.

When he's gone, Suzanne's voice comes out flat. "What the hell was that?"

"He must have a girlfriend." When she looks at me, I shrug. "You guys obviously had mad chemistry. It's the only explanation."

"So it wasn't in my head? He was flirting with me, right?"

"Totally. At one point, I thought he was going to take his junk out and ask you to fondle it under the table."

"Which I totally would've. The man is smoking hot!"

She says that so loudly it has people's heads turning. I stand, take her hand, and help her out of the booth, staggering a little when she gives me her weight because I wasn't ready for it.

"Whoa," she says, steadying herself. "I think you might have to drive home, sweetie. The room is tilted."

"All right, hotshot, I've got you. Don't impale my feet with those heels of yours. Here we go."

We make our way through the restaurant—my arm around her shoulders, her arm around my waist—and I try to ignore the snickers I hear as we go.

I have a funny feeling this isn't the first time Suzanne hasn't been able to walk out of a restaurant unassisted.

hough it's less than a ten-minute drive from Booger's to where Suzanne lives, she promptly falls asleep in the car after giving me her home address. I don't mind, because I'm used to being alone with my thoughts, but I'm a little worried about her.

In a small town, everyone knows everyone, and their dirty laundry too. Maybe all those stares she got on the way in weren't about her outfit.

I use the map app in my phone to navigate to her house. She lives in a lovely little bungalow with pink azaleas lining a white picket fence that encloses a tidy yard. I park the car in the driveway, then go around to her side to help her out. When I open the door and unbuckle her seat belt, she's snoring.

"Suzanne." I gently poke her arm. "We're home. Wake up."

She rolls her head toward me, mumbling something about cats. I write it off to the booze, then drag her out of the car as gently as I can, wondering if she was drinking before she came to pick me up, because she's really out of it.

We stagger to the front door. I have to rummage around in her purse for the keys because she's literally sleeping standing up, leaning against me. When I get the front door open, I'm assaulted by the smell of cat piss.

Then the little beasts descend in full force, caterwauling to raise the dead.

"De Niro!" Suzanne slurs, cracking open an eye. "Pacino! Stallone! Shut the hell up, Mommy's head hurts!"

I help Suzanne over the threshold and into the house. She collapses onto the living room sofa, and all three cats—a calico, an orange tabby, and one big, fuzzy black bastard—jump up on her like they're about to eat off her face.

"Shoo!" I wave my arms around, hoping to dislodge them from poor Suzanne, but they just sit there and look at me like I'm stupid. They don't, however, make any move to devour her, so I watch them warily for a moment, waiting to see what they'll do.

They settle in around her, curling up their tails as they nestle on her chest, her stomach, and between her legs, and watch me back.

"Okay, beasties, I'm leaving you in charge of Mommy. We good?"

The big black one—I think that's Stallone—yawns. I'm being dismissed.

I head into the kitchen in search of water for Suzanne and find an open bottle of wine on the counter, a third full, and an empty wineglass beside it with hot-pink lipstick prints that match the color Suzanne wore tonight.

Now I'm not so much feeling sorry for her as feeling furious that she drove over to pick me up after having that much wine. When she's sober tomorrow, we're going to have a nice long talk about how driving under the influence of even one glass of alcohol can be deadly.

If anyone knows how true that is, it's me.

Grinding my teeth, I get a bottle of water from the fridge, then set it on the coffee table next to the sofa. I turn the lamp off on the side table, slip off Suzanne's heels, and settle a blanket over the lower part of her legs, leave her handbag and keys on the dining room table, and lock the front door before pulling it shut behind me.

It takes about fifteen minutes of walking before I've calmed down enough that my hands no longer shake.

It's a beautiful night, but it's chilly. The moon is full, the air is thick with the scent of the ocean, and the stars are out in full force. They never blazed this brilliantly in smog-choked Phoenix. Wishing I'd brought a coat to dinner, I walk through Suzanne's quiet neighborhood until I reach the main boulevard leading into town, then I head south toward home.

Seaside is one of those towns whose sidewalks curl up when the sun goes down, and tonight is no exception. The boulevard is deserted. The only thing keeping me company are the moths dancing silently around the streetlamps overhead. I walk, unhurried, absorbed in thought as I listen to the distant boom of the surf and the crickets' serenade, the music of the night.

You'd love it here, Cass. You'd love it so much.

Out of nowhere, a classic black Mustang blasts past at top speed, engine rumbling like a wolf's growl, the draft in its wake blowing my hair and skirt sideways. About fifty yards past me, the driver slams on the brakes. The car screeches to a stop in the middle of the street. Then it sits there, engine idling, brake lights glowing red in the darkness, steam billowing from the tailpipe like smoke from the nostrils of a dragon.

"You've gotta be kidding me," I mutter, knowing exactly who it is.

The car shifts gear and slowly begins to reverse.

When the Mustang has backed up far enough so it's beside me in the street, it stops. The passenger door pops open and swings wide. Theo's eyes glint in the dim interior—he's leaning over the seat, looking out at me.

Waiting.

After a moment's hesitation, I get in, pull the door shut, and pretend this is all no big deal by checking things out.

Like the outside, the inside of the car is pristine. I could eat right off the dashboard, and I'd be shocked if the ashtray has ever been used, even to hold coins. There's not a speck of dust or a stray hair in sight. He must keep a vacuum in the trunk.

But even in such a sterile environment, his mark is unmistakable. A blues station plays softly on the radio—some siren with a whiskey-soaked voice croons about lost love—and the air is warm and smells like him, soap and leather and brooding masculinity, a hint of forest at night.

Maybe he's a shape-shifter, a lone wolf who hunts in the woods when the moon is full.

I need to stop watching the Syfy channel.

I blurt, "I'm sorry I cursed at you this morning. That wasn't nice."

Theo exhales in a big gust, like he's been holding his breath. Then he puts the car into Drive and we start moving, at a much slower pace than he was driving before. A small silver medallion swings from a chain on the rearview mirror, winking in the light. It's a patron saint medal, but I can't tell which one.

My curiosity about him intensifies.

Is he religious? Did he have a spiritual conversion after his accident? Or is he like me, a former believer who keeps the medal as a reminder of his lost delusion that somewhere out in the universe, someone actually listens to our prayers?

I glance over at him. In the shadows, his profile is all hard angles, from the slash of his nose to the hard edge of his jaw. He appears tense and uncomfortable, and I wonder why he bothered to stop when he's so clearly aggravated by my presence.

"I wish I knew why you don't like me."

Startled, he blinks. He looks over at me with an expression of anguish that's so raw and vulnerable, I know what I've said has hurt him, and also that my assumption he doesn't like me is true.

Those two things together don't make any sense, but nothing about this man makes sense. Every interaction I've had with him so far has confused and frustrated me. He's like a puzzle missing so many pieces, it can never be solved.

I continue with my confession, because the dark has a way of coercing them.

"I'm a very likeable person. At least I *think* I am. I've never had an enemy in my life. I'm actually a bit boring—my idea of excitement is binge-watching a new series on Netflix. So imagine my surprise when a complete stranger takes an obvious and intense dislike to me before I've even spoken a word to him. Imagine how small and hurt that would make me feel. Not to mention really fucking pissed."

He looks at me like I'm stabbing him in the gut with every word.

"I know. It's not fair. We're in a confined space, I'm doing my famous verbal diarrhea thing, and you can't respond. And I cursed again. Which is an unusual thing for me because I was trained from birth by a mother too concerned with other people's opinions that only classless women with inferior vocabularies ever use foul language, but honestly, the word 'fuck' is so useful for so many different situations I can't resist the occasional slipup."

I pause to take a breath and sort my thoughts. "Where was I? Oh, right. You not liking me and me not liking that."

Poor Theo looks like he'd rather be sitting in an electric chair than the driver's seat, but too bad. This is my opportunity to vent, and I'm taking it.

"You know how in romantic comedies there's usually some stupid situation that arises that could be resolved without all the drama if the couple just had a conversation? Like, just sat down and hashed the problem out? I feel like that's the deal with us. Like if you would just...I don't know, write down what I did that irritated you to the point of looking at me like you want to slam a dog poo pie into my face, then maybe I could apologize, or not do whatever that thing is again, and we could go on and have a decent working relationship while the house is under construction and not have to tiptoe around each other because there's this huge black cloud of animosity following us around. You know?"

He doesn't know. I can tell because he looks as if he's about to puke, and his hands are curled so tightly around the steering wheel, it's in danger of snapping in half.

"Never mind. Forget I mentioned it. Honestly, it's your prerogative to dislike whomever you want. I'm just being sensitive. No, scratch that, I'm not being sensitive! Any other rational person would feel the same way! Nobody *likes* to be disliked!"

Theo's swallow is audible, and now I feel like an idiot.

I sigh and drag my hands through my hair. "I'm going to be quiet now."

We drive for a while in silence until we come to a stop sign. I shiver in my seat, rubbing my hands over my arms for warmth. Seeing that I'm cold, Theo shrugs out of his jacket and hands it over to me.

"Oh. Thank you." I drape it over my front like a blanket, enjoying its warmth and trying not to start laughing because this is so weird and I'm so uncomfortable and I only have two knee-jerk reactions when I'm feeling awkward: laughter or sarcasm.

We start driving again, then it's only a few more turns until we're at my house. He pulls into the driveway, shuts off the car, and gets out. Before I can open my door, he's opened it for me. He holds out his hand.

So he's a gentleman psychopath who hates my guts. Noted.

I allow him to help me out of the car. When I hand him his coat, he takes it, but instead of putting it on, he settles it over my shoulders. Then, like an old-fashioned suitor, he takes my arm and leads me up the path to the front porch, holding aside a thorny branch from one of the wild rosebushes so I don't get whacked by it as I pass by.

This is so confusing.

He pauses at the bottom of the porch steps, but this time, I'm not inviting him inside. I slide his jacket off and hand it back to him with a murmured "Thank you," then turn to go into the house.

Theo stops me with a touch on my elbow. Surprised, I turn back to him. He reaches into his coat. I think he's going to remove his writing pad, but instead, he takes out a business card. He hands it to me, his eyes shining like gems in the low light.

"Um. Thanks." I stand there for a moment, unsure of what to do next, until he points at the card. "Yes, I have your number. I'll call you Monday, no matter what I decide."

He shakes his head like I don't understand what he's trying to say. Which, naturally, I don't. "You don't want me to call you Monday?"

I swear his eye roll is sarcastic.

He pulls his jacket on, takes the card in one hand, and with the other points to his email address on the bottom. He taps it three times.

"You want me to email you instead?"

This time his head shake is a hard jerk. I can tell he's getting frustrated. He makes a rolling motion of his hand, but I have no idea what he means.

"Oh, for God's sake, Theo, cut me a break, will you? I suck at charades."

He gives me back the card, then whips out his little notepad. He scratches something on it and holds it out for me to see.

You can email me before Monday if you want to talk.

When I look up at him, he drops the pad to his side and stares at me. That muscle is jumping in his jaw again. His eyes are unnaturally bright, as if he's running a fever.

"Do *you* want to talk?"

He looks away, draws a breath, closes his eyes. Then he looks back at me. He nods—then shakes his head.

"Yes and no."

He nods again, because I've interpreted him correctly.

"Well, hell, Theo," I say, irritated. "Make up your damn mind."

His lips curve upward. He covers his mouth with his hand to hide his smile, then clears his throat.

It's a startling sound, because it's a *sound*. I stare at him, breathless, my pulse picking up pace until it's zooming.

He doesn't notice my sudden stillness. He just nods—three times, so I can't mistake his meaning—then turns around and walks back to his car. He gets in and drives away without a backward glance.

I stand on my porch for a long time, Theo's business card clutched in my hand, the pounding of the surf ringing in my ears. Then I go inside and fire up the computer.

Into Google's search box I type: *Can mute people make sounds?*

8

*A*ccording to Wikipedia, mute people can make all kinds of sounds, destroying my rapidly ballooning conspiracy theory that Theo Valentine *can* talk but just doesn't want to.

I read aloud from the webpage. "Inability to speak is not the same as inability to make noise. Grunts, groans, yells, etc. don't require vocal cords as they can be made by forcing air in or out of the lungs. Depending on the severity of damage to the vocal cords, short words such as 'me' or 'you' may be possible. If vocal cord damage is total, only primal sounds such as screams are possible."

Then I glimpse the section titled "Selective Mutism." It includes a list of symptoms that are familiar: social isolation and withdrawal; difficulty maintaining eye contact; reluctance to smile; difficulty expressing feelings; sensitivity to noise and crowds. There are a bunch of other things that should have Theo's picture next to them, but that condition usually appears in childhood.

Hmm.

There's also a condition called reactive mutism, in which a

person decides not to speak, usually after suffering some kind of severe trauma.

So it *is* a thing, but I have no way of knowing if Theo's problem is with his vocal cords or his mental state.

Or both.

I go upstairs, run myself a bath, get undressed and soak, my thoughts in a jumble, until the water grows cold. Then I climb out, towel off, change into my usual lie-atop-the-covers-and-stare-at-the-ceiling T-shirt-and-boy-shorts outfit, and get into bed.

At 3:00 a.m., I drag myself up, go back downstairs to get my laptop, and return with it to bed. *Okay, Mr. Valentine. Let's see what you've got to say for yourself.*

To: Theo@hillrise.com
From: Bowie4Evah@yahoo.com
Subject: New Homeowner in Need of Advice

Dear Dr. Valentine,

So I met this man a few weeks ago, and I need your advice. Everyone keeps telling me what a wonderful guy he is, how great his work is, how I should absolutely hire him to do this huge renovation on my house—my dream house, mind you—but there's a problem.

I cause this individual severe gastrointestinal distress.

If I were a sadist, I would simply hire him and let him stew in his own sour juices while the job was completed, but I have a heart. I want to give this poor man a jumbo bottle of Tums to make him feel better. But the guy doesn't want my antacid offerings, he just wants to peel the skin off my face with the blistering heat of his dislike.

What do you suggest?

Sincerely,

Confused

After I hit Send, I re-read the email several times. Satisfied the tone is sufficiently tongue-in-cheek, I'm about to close the laptop when the chime announcing the arrival of a new email sounds. Lo and behold, I've got a response. *That* fast.
Is he an insomniac too?

To: Bowie4Evah@yahoo.com
From: Theo@hillrise.com
Subject: Re: New Homeowner in Need of Advice

Dear Confused,

I suggest being up front with him to clear the air. For instance, you could initiate a conversation on the topic during a late evening drive in his car. I'm sure that wouldn't be awkward *at all*.

Sincerely,

Dr. Valentine

Ha! The snarky bastard! I break into a huge grin and immediately compose my response.

To: Theo@hillrise.com
From: Bowie4Evah@yahoo.com
Subject: Sadly...

I already did that. Sir Grumpsalot didn't appear to appreciate my attempts to clear the air of the thick fog of his disgust. I was thinking I could write him a haiku to demonstrate my intellectual charms and win his admiration?

> *Haikus are poems*
> *That often do not make sense*
> *Hippopotamus*

To: Bowie4Evah@yahoo.com
From: Theo@hillrise.com
Subject: Re: Sadly...

- #1 – Sir Grumpsalot?! I prefer Captain Crankypants, thank you. Unless addressing me formally, in which case you'd use my proper title of King Crabby Poo.

- #2 – That is probably the best haiku ever written. Not only does it perfectly describe the art form, you worked in the word hippopotamus, which, in my opinion, is vastly underrepresented in poetry. Well done.

To: Theo@hillrise.com
From: Bowie4Evah@yahoo.com
Subject: Re: Re: Sadly...

Your powers of observation are astute. I am shocked, sir, *shocked* that you guessed my original email was about you.

Would it be rude at this juncture to observe that I like you much more in email than in person? Though I must admit, you give good phone too.

To: Bowie4Evah@yahoo.com
From: Theo@hillrise.com
Subject: YES IT WOULD BE VERY RUDE

But your poem and your devotion to the late, great David Bowie have scored you a few sympathy points. (Yes, I noticed your T-shirt, your email address, and the print of the *Heroes* album cover tacked to your bedroom wall. Side note: what do you think he was doing with his hands? Signaling the mother ship?)

Now if only I could be assured that you have equally good taste in guitarists as you do in singer-songwriters.

To: Theo@hillrise.com
From: Bowie4Evah@yahoo.com
Subject: No need to shout, King Crabby Poo

I scoff at your challenge. It's too easy. Top 5:
  1 – BB King
  2 – Les Paul
  3 – Eddie Van Halen
  4 – Jimmy Page
  5 – Jimi Hendrix

To: Bowie4Evah@yahoo.com
From: Theo@hillrise.com
Subject: Wow

How can you expect me to like someone who puts Jimi Hendrix *last*? I think we're done here.

To: Theo@hillrise.com
From: Bowie4Evah@yahoo.com
Subject: Re: Wow

I never said the list was ranked in order. Check your assumptions, KCP.

And while we're on the topic of assumptions, would it be safe for me to assume if I hired you to renovate my house, THIS version of Theo Valentine would appear? Because this guy I can handle. This guy I like.

I wait for the blinding-fast response he's been giving me, but it doesn't come. After five minutes, I decide he must've taken a bathroom break or something, but at fifteen minutes, I'm afraid I won't hear from him again until the morning—if at all. Maybe his sense of good humor only lasts for a twenty-minute window starting at 3:00 a.m.

But then an answer comes through and stuns me with its honesty.

To: Bowie4Evah@yahoo.com
From: Theo@hillrise.com
Subject: This guy

I want you to like me, but you shouldn't. I'm not stable. I'm not even sure if I'm sane. You said something in the car about that moment in a romantic comedy where everything could be solved if the people having problems just talked, but what I'd have to say if we talked about the problem wouldn't be romantic, or funny.

It would be scary as hell.

Let me be clear: that isn't a threat. I'm not a danger to you, or anyone. I'm just...fucked up. The kind of fucked up that doesn't have a cure. The kind of fucked up that hears voices and sees ghosts and sometimes can't tell what's real and what isn't. Especially at night, when all the monsters I can usually keep locked up during the day refuse to be contained.

Which is why I don't sleep. Which is why I've tried every available medication from antipsychotics to pot. Which is why I stay away from people, except when I'm working, the only thing that keeps me grounded in reality.

Which is why we can never be friends, Megan. We can never be anything.

I want to work on the Buttercup because I love it. I love it in a way that couldn't make sense to you, and still doesn't make complete sense to me, but that house feels like an anchor to me. Like an island in the middle of a huge, black ocean.

Like the needle on a compass pointing true north.

If you decide to hire me, even after this ridiculous confession which I shouldn't have sent but had to, I'll kill myself making that house perfect. (Not being literal, but you know what I mean.) If you decide not to hire me, I understand. Craig is a solid guy. He'll do a good job.

Theo

I sit in bed with my mouth hanging open, reading the email again and again. Finally, I close my laptop and lie back down, my head buzzing and my nerves jumping like I've had ten cups of coffee.

We can never be friends, Megan. We can never be anything.

I stare at the ceiling until the sun slips over the horizon and floods the room with light.

Then I compose an email to Craig at Capstone telling him I'm

looking forward to getting his contract on Monday and asking
how soon he'd need the first payment of cash.

For the rest of the day, I'm unsettled. I can't stop thinking about
Theo's email. I read it about a dozen times, trying to understand
what he could have meant by the problem is "scary as hell."

Logic tells me to keep away from him. I'm too old for this kind
of drama. But the mystery of Theo Valentine is one my curiosity
finds irresistible.

I decide not to call Suzanne. I'm still angry at her, and I know
I'll pester her for more details about Theo, which is the last thing
I should do. I've got my own problems to deal with. I don't need
to add his to the pile.

I order takeout again and eat it standing up in the kitchen
over the sink, then take a bath and go to bed.

During the night, a storm blows in. The rain pounding the
roof sounds like gunfire. Thunder booms in the distance, and
flashes of lightning illuminate the room in sudden, bright white
light.

I fall into a fitful sleep and dream of endless fields of purple
sweet peas swaying under the summer sun.

When I get out of bed at 8:00 a.m., the sky is a dull, heavy
gray, which perfectly matches my mood. I stumble downstairs in
my robe, my head thick and my eyes bleary from hours of tossing.
I get the coffeemaker started and stand there yawning as a cup
brews. When the phone rings, I answer it absentmindedly.

"Hello?"

"You're *not* going to believe this!"

I yank the phone away from my ear, because Suzanne's
excited shout just pierced my eardrum. "A little warning would be
nice before you break the sound barrier, Suzanne," I grumble,
reaching for the mug.

"I just saw on the local news that Capstone Construction's headquarters was destroyed last night!"

I freeze. "Destroyed? What're you talking about?"

"It was hit by friggin' lightning! Can you believe that?"

My brain is having trouble processing her words. I squint at the coffeemaker, not entirely sure I'm not still upstairs in bed, dreaming. "Lightning," I repeat slowly.

"Yes, lightning! You heard the storm, right?" She doesn't wait for me to answer before plowing ahead. "Apparently a big-ass bolt of lightning hit the building and started a fire, which destroyed pretty much everything before the fire department arrived and put it out. Turn on the news and check out the pictures—the building is a smoking pile of rubble!"

By now, I'm wide awake, adrenaline acting much faster than coffee could. "That's awful! Was anyone hurt?"

"Not according to the news. But that building is toast. I hope Craig had good insurance." Her tone is gleeful. Obviously, she hasn't forgiven Craig for his diss at the restaurant. "Way for the universe to help with your decision on who to hire to rebuild your house, right? It's like it was fated! What a fluke!"

A strange sensation comes over me, a dark kind of déjà vu. I recall something I thought when Theo came out and showed me his Buttercup Inn book, and I was so overcome with emotion.

It's not fated. It's a fluke. It's just life, doing what it does best.

An army of goose bumps marches up and down my arms. Distracted, I murmur, "Fated and a fluke are two different things." Then my attention snaps into focus, and I get practical. "I'm sure the fire won't have that much of an effect on Craig's ability to do business. Maybe temporarily, sure, but he's probably got all his files and everything backed up remotely, and the actual work is handled by subs—"

"Capstone hardly uses any subs. Craig handles most every-thing in-house, with dozens of specialists certified for everything from electrical to A/C. All those guys are employees, and he owns all his own equipment. Owned, I mean."

That takes a little wind out of my sails. "Oh. Well, he'll just have to find a location for a new headquarters. How long could that take? A few weeks?"

"Are you kidding? The market for commercial real estate in Portland is tighter than the Pope's asshole. I did an extensive search only last week for a client and something the size of what Craig had is practically nonexistent."

I'm starting to get irritated because Suzanne is taking way too much pleasure in the demise of poor Craig's business. "Then he can buy or rent something smaller until a bigger place becomes available. He seems like a very capable guy. I'm sure he'll land on his feet."

"His size-sixteen feet," she says in a new, throaty tone. "Did you see those puppies? They were like skis—"

"Were you drinking before you came to pick me up Saturday night?"

A brief silence follows my question. "Hello, awkward segue."

"Hello, awkward beatdown of my real estate agent if the answer is yes."

More silence. "I only had one glass."

"Bullshit. You were way too wasted by the time dinner was finished to have had only one glass before you left. Correct me if I'm wrong."

Suzanne's sigh is a long, pained exhalation that doesn't sound nearly as contrite as it should. "It was only a few miles to the restaurant, Megan, and I was totally under control. You would've noticed if I wasn't in shape to dri—"

"My husband was killed by a cop who only had one drink in his system before he got behind the wheel of his squad car, Suzanne," I interrupt, my voice hard. "Don't you dare talk to me about control."

Now her silence sounds shocked, and I'm damn glad. I let it

stretch out way past the point of uncomfortable, because it's her turn to say something—and that something better include an apology, or I'm never speaking to her again.

She begins haltingly, her voice shaky. "I'm...I'm so sorry, Megan. I didn't...I had no idea." She draws a breath. "I don't really know what else to say except I apologize. Truly. It won't happen again."

I'm still angry, but at least she sounds sincere. I scrub a hand over my face. *What a way to start a day.*

Then Suzanne says something that stops my heart dead in my chest.

"That's what happened to Theo too."

All the hair on the back of my neck bristles. "What?"

"I don't think I ever got around to telling you on Saturday. Theo was on his way home from his girlfriend's house when his car was hit by a drunk driver who blew through a red light. T-boned in an intersection. Theo's car was totaled. My nurse friend said that when he arrived at the hospital, he didn't have a heartbeat." She makes a small, uncomfortable laugh. "Obviously, they got it restarted."

Thump. Thump. Thump. My heart throbs to life with a sharp, painful beat that reverberates through every nerve in my body. My head swims with memories, terrible, black memories. I'm so dizzy, I have to clutch the counter for support.

"Are you still there?" Suzanne asks when I'm silent too long.

T-boned in an intersection. Car was totaled. Didn't have a heartbeat.

What are the odds?

"I'm here," I rasp. But I'm not really. I've traveled back in time, back to an intersection in the middle of the night in Phoenix, where I'm on my knees on the asphalt, sobbing and screaming for help, holding my dying husband in my arms, listening to the last thing he'd ever say to me.

I love you, sweet pea. I'll love you till the end of time.

I breathe shallowly, my palms sweating, my hands trembling, the room closing in until I can barely draw a breath.

I recognize the signs. I'm about to have a panic attack.

I drop the phone and run through the house until I reach the French doors leading to the back patio. I burst through them, gulping air, my eyes tearing, the cold morning air a slap on my hot face. I run across the patio and down to the beach, stumbling over my feet, and head straight for the water.

It's freezing cold as it hits my shins, but it's the shock of reality I need. I stand knee-deep in the ocean, shivering violently, my arms wrapped around my body as waves rock me, the gentle morning surf murmuring soothing things to cool my boiling mind.

I close my eyes and breathe deeply, sucking air into my heaving lungs.

Air scented of blood on asphalt, and the haunting, honey-like perfume of sweet peas.

9

*W*hen I finally get myself together and trudge back inside, a half hour has gone by, and I've missed four calls from Suzanne on my cell.

I text her back that I can't talk and we'll touch base later. Then I change into dry clothes, turn on the TV in my bedroom, and watch the local news with a feeling of cold disbelief.

According to the newscast, the lightning strike on Capstone's building was massive. The resulting fire engulfed the building within minutes. The whole thing was captured on video by a security camera at a building across the street. The images are insane, like something out of a movie.

The newscaster mentions several times how unusual it is that the lightning didn't hit the telecommunications spire on the high-rise building one block over—the spire that's twenty times the height of the tallest point on Capstone's roof.

There's a brief discussion about the weather system that caused the lightning, then the station breaks for a commercial. I want to call Craig, but I'm sure he's got much more important things to deal with this morning. I'll give him a few days to get his bearings before trying to determine what this means for our project. In the meantime, I send him a quick email just to say I saw the news and am sorry, but grateful no one was hurt, and to take his time getting back to me with the contract.

Within five minutes, my phone rings.

"Hello?"

"Megan, it's Craig Kennedy."

He sounds understandably tense. "Oh, Craig, I'm so sorry to hear about what happened! I just sent you an email."

"I know. It came through on my phone. Thank you, that was thoughtful."

"I know this is a stupid question, but are you okay?"

"As good as can be expected. I'm out at the building now. It looks like a bomb went off. We're lucky it didn't happen during work hours, or there would've been a body count."

A grisly image of barbequed bodies pops into my mind. I force it back, along with a brief wave of nausea. "Yes, that's true. Equipment can always be replaced."

There's an awkward silence, then a rough throat clearing. "Yeah. If my insurance hadn't lapsed a month ago."

"Lapsed?" I repeat, my voice high.

His voice comes over the line in a frustrated growl. "My fucking incompetent bookkeeper just informed me that I never signed the check to renew the policy. It was cut, but for some reason never made it to my desk for my signature, and she forgot all about it. Until now, because the goddamn fire reminded her!" He groans. "Sorry. I'm sorry, I shouldn't be using that language, I'm just so frustrated."

"Of course you are. Totally understandable," I say faintly, focused on a large, meandering crack on my bedroom wall that's been growing since the day I moved in. It bears an uncanny resemblance to a bolt of lightning.

"That's not the worst of it," says Craig grimly.

"You're kidding."

"I wish I were." He sighs heavily. "I found out this morning that my general contractor's license is being suspended."

My jaw drops.

When I don't say anything, Craig continues. "There was a labor code issue with a disgruntled office employee a few years back. Total bullshit, but she filed a complaint with the state license board. Long story short, we were investigated, and I found out a few minutes ago the investigation didn't go our way. My attorneys are going to appeal—"

"Appeal! Yes, that's great!" I know I'm clinging to that possibility like a drowning swimmer clings to a life vest because then I wouldn't have to deal with this disturbing idea my brain wants to run away with that somehow the lightning, the lapsed insurance policy, and the suspended license have destiny's fingerprints all over them.

Because I don't believe in destiny. I don't. I *won't*. I know better. I've spent too much money on therapy to start believing in providence now. This situation is just one of those random things that happen in life, a misfortune, an accident. A fluke.

This *isn't* the universe trying to tell me I should hire Theo Valentine to renovate my house.

Craig sighs heavily. "Yeah, but in the meantime, I can't work on a suspended license. And the appeal process could take months. So, unfortunately, I'm not going to be able to take your job, Megan."

I close my eyes and pinch the bridge of my nose between my fingers. "I'm really sorry to hear that, Craig. I was looking forward to working with you."

His voice comes out gruff. "Well, that's good to know, because now that we won't be working together in a professional capacity, I was wondering if you'd let me take you on a date."

Shocked, I stare at the lightning-bolt crack on the wall until my vision blurs.

"Hello?"

"Yes, I'm here, I'm just...surprised."

"I know my timing's weird, but it occurred to me after I got off the phone with my attorney a few minutes ago that life is short. Things can change at any minute, in ways you can't predict."

"You don't say," I murmur, feeling like I'm having an out-of-body experience.

"So I thought, shoot—why not just go for it? I think you're a beautiful girl. Ballsy too. There aren't many guys who negotiate as hard as you do. I like that."

He likes how I negotiate? What the fuck is happening right now? I have to take a moment to compose myself before I answer.

"That's...very flattering, Craig. But I have to be honest and tell you I thought you and Suzanne really hit it off at dinner. Why don't you ask her for a date?"

In the pause as he chooses his words, I hear street noise in the background. "She's not really my type."

"Smart, sexy career girls aren't your type? I find that hard to believe."

"Listen, I don't want to say anything negative about your friend, okay? She's just a little too obvious for my taste."

A flash of irritation hardens my tone. "Obvious. That's guy code for desperate, slutty, cheap, or all of the above, right?"

He pauses again, longer this time. "I'm sorry if that was offensive. Maybe it wasn't the right choice of word. I just don't find her as attractive as I find you."

"You could've fooled me. You two were all over each other at dinner."

"No, she was all over me. I kept trying to get your attention, but you seemed distracted."

I was distracted by all the hormones in the air, but from what he's telling me, *his* hormones were aimed in my direction. God, are my instincts that off? Maybe being celibate for five years has dried up my intuition along with my poor uterus.

I stand from the bed, walk to the windows, and stare out at

the restless sea. It's the same leaden gray as the sky, and my heart. I muse aloud, "I haven't been on a date since I was a teenager. I wouldn't have a clue what to do."

"I'm gonna take that as a yes," he says, his voice warm.

"It wasn't."

"It wasn't a no either."

I have to smile at his cocky tone. "I hate to be a downer, Craig, but I'm pretty sure you just told me you're unemployed. Dating might not be in your budget right now."

He chuckles. "Oh, you think I only want you for your money, is that it? I can honestly say that's the last thing on my mind when I look at you."

Now he's outright flirting. I've always been the absolute worst at flirting and am generally suspicious of people who are skilled at it. But his resiliency in the face of disaster is something I admire. If I were in his shoes, I'd be a sobbing mess right now, not calling up some dude I like to ask for a date.

"I tell you what. I'll think about it, how's that?"

"Deal," he says instantly. "How long will this thinking process last? Just so I know when to make reservations at this awesome restaurant I'm gonna take you to."

I shake my head, smiling. *This guy is unbelievable.* "Call me on Wednesday. And be prepared to be disappointed, because I'll probably turn you down."

Craig's chuckle is full of self-confidence. "Nah, you're gonna say yes. I'll talk to you Wednesday."

He hangs up before I can contradict him.

I disconnect and stand watching as four huge pelicans swoop down from the sky and skim the surface of the waves, wings outstretched, hunting for food. I follow their path as they fly north toward the curve on the shoreline, until my attention is caught by something else.

Someone stands alone and unmoving on the deserted beach. Even from this distance, I can see that the person is large, with wide shoulders and long legs. He's wearing a black windbreaker with the hood pulled up over his head, gazing south down the shore like he's searching for something.

He's too far away for me to see his face, but I have the strangest sensation he's looking right at me.

He stands there a long time, motionless, hands shoved deep in his pockets, until he turns and walks away, head lowered into the cold morning wind.

Though the weather isn't good, I'm too restless to stay indoors, so I decide to get some exercise. I put on my walking shoes and head toward the historic seaside promenade that borders the ocean for a mile and a half, ending in a large turnaround that boasts a huge statue of Lewis and Clark in the middle. The turnaround is made to redirect tourists to get back down Broadway, but also signifies how Lewis and Clark turned again for home after reaching the Pacific Ocean.

Surprisingly, a lot of people had the same idea I did. Once I get near downtown, I encounter a lot of walkers, runners, couples with strollers, and dogs of various sizes happily enjoying the windswept day. Out on the beach, kids dig for clams in the wet sand left by the low tide. Someone flies a red kite. The view of Tillamook Head, a rocky, wooded promontory jutting into the Pacific, is gorgeous.

The east side of the prom is lined with condos, shops, restaurants, and the Seaside Aquarium, where I admire a skeleton of a gray whale displayed in the front window. I eat a corn dog from a street vendor, then, still feeling hungry, head over to Booger's to get something more substantial.

The entire time, I think about Theo Valentine. He's on simmer in the back of my mind, a restless disturbance just beneath the surface.

We can never be friends, Megan. We can never be anything.

It's the second part of that statement that bothers me most, though I can't say exactly why. If we're going to do business together, we don't have to be friends, but we have to be *something*. More than acquaintances, certainly. Partners, at least in a business sense.

But I don't think he was talking about business. It felt personal. It's almost as if he was refusing an offer for intimacy that hadn't been made.

Or warning me not to make it.

Which is ridiculous, considering I find him about as attractive as a rabid gorilla. I mean, he does bear a striking resemblance to Keanu Reeves: exotic dark eyes, a razor-blade jaw covered in scruff, an appealing look of befuddlement, like he's lost his way home.

When he's not glowering like an axe murderer, that is.

He's the polar opposite of my golden, happy-go-lucky Cass, a man whose laugh came easy and often. I wonder what Cass would've made of Theo. He had an almost spooky intuition about people. I used to joke he could read people's auras, but he'd reply that a man's true heart was always in his eyes. You just had to look close enough to see.

Shaking myself out of the dark spiral my thoughts are about to dive into, I pull open the heavy wooden door of Booger's and step inside. In my haste and distraction, I don't look up, and bump hard into the back of someone standing at the hostess stand, waiting to be seated.

"Oh! God, I'm so sorry! I wasn't looking where I was..."

The person turns to stare down at me. Black hair. Black eyes. A razor-blade jaw covered in scruff.

Theo Valentine.

"Right this way," says the hostess to Theo, gesturing for him to follow her. But he isn't paying attention to her. He's gazing at me with a look of intense concentration, those dark eyes unblinking.

A flash of anguish surfaces in them, there then instantly gone.

We stare at each other. I experience a sensation of weightlessness, like cresting the peak of a high hill on a roller coaster, that split-second lack of gravity before you plummet over the edge.

"Sir?"

When Theo turns his attention back to the hostess, it's a snap of disconnection, as if a little flame inside my chest has been snuffed out.

He holds up two fingers.

"Oh, sure." The hostess smiles at me, pulling another menu from the basket on the side of the wooden stand, then turns and walks away.

Theo follows her without looking back. I stand frozen for a moment, unsure, then blow out a breath and decide to see where this interesting little detour takes me.

I follow behind Theo as we make our way to a table in the back. This time it's me getting all the curious stares. I wonder if King Crabby Poo has been seen in public with a woman since his accident, because judging by all the shocked looks I'm getting, this is a momentous event.

Either that or a pigeon crowned my head with a big, hairy turd.

The hostess stops beside a table in the farthest corner of the restaurant. "Here you go!" she says brightly, in a tone that makes me think this is Theo's regular spot. He pulls out a chair, then looks at me.

I sink into the chair he's holding and send the hostess a nervous smile. Instead of sitting in the chair across from me as I expected, Theo lowers himself to the chair *beside* me. Now I'm in a corner against the wall, with no way to exit unless he lets me out.

I try not to be freaked out that this is always the way Cass and I sat at restaurants. Next to each other at a table against a wall, me on his right, looking out at everyone so we could watch all the people and speculate on their conversations and their lives.

The hostess hands me a menu. "I'll be back in a few minutes to take your order." Then she leaves, abandoning me to my fate.

Being the well-mannered extrovert that he is, Theo ignores me. He pulls out his cell phone from the inside pocket of his leather coat and begins to compose a text.

"Hey."

He glances at me, a lock of hair falling into his eyes.

I look pointedly at his phone. "That's rude."

He hits Send, sets his phone down on the table, folds his hands on the tabletop, and stares at me. Then my cell phone chimes with an incoming text.

I fish my phone out of the back pocket of my jeans and look at the screen, already knowing who it is.

You have to stop stalking me like this.

I flash him an exasperated look, only to find him doing something with his mouth that looks like it could turn into a smile if it only knew how.

"I've seen you smile before, Theo. Go ahead. It won't kill you."

He covers his mouth with his hand to hide the fact that he's smiling so big, he's actually showing teeth. That feels like a victory, like I've just scored the winning touchdown in the Super Bowl.

I type him a response.

Excuse me, King Crabby Poo,
but YOU are stalking ME.

His phone chimes, he reads the text from me, then composes his response, his thumbs moving so fast, they're a blur.

You're not excused. Why is your nose so red?
Snort coke much?

"Okay, Sunshine, it's on," I mutter, then type.

Charming. That's called walking-in-cold-wind nose. However, if I
knew I'd be bumping into you,
I'd definitely have turned to drugs
to help me through the trauma.

He snorts.

Please. Being in my presence is like soaking up
golden rays of sunshine. Just look how jealous
everyone is of you right now.

I hazard a glance around, and sure enough, almost everyone is looking at us. Some more obviously than others, but the general level of interest could be compared to that of an audience awaiting the opening act at a circus to begin.

So of course I have to smile widely and wave.

Eyeballs scatter like marbles. Beside me, Theo makes a low noise deep in his throat that sounds like something close to a chuckle.

I want him to make that sound again.

"I suppose the good citizens of Seaside are all shocked to see you out of your coffin during the daytime, Dracula. Oh, wait, there's one guy over there who isn't staring at us. Must be a tourist."

I turn to find Theo gazing at me, his eyes bright with laughter. This close, I can see that they're not black like they appear from even only a few feet farther away, they're a deep, rich brown, velvet dark as espresso, just as warm and inviting. But also filled with that indecipherable longing like a secret message waiting to be decoded. Waiting for someone to look close enough to see.

My heart skips a beat. I haven't looked this deeply into a man's eyes since my husband died.

I look away, toying with the fork at my place setting, fumbling it between my fingers because they're trembling. *Breathe, Megan. Just breathe.*

After a moment, my phone chimes.

You okay?

I stare at my fingernails, which are in dire need of a manicure. "Stop being so observant. It's irritating."

Irritating is my middle name.
Tell me what's wrong.

Uncomfortable, I laugh. "I just remembered this place has really awful food. I had some calamari the other night I still haven't completely digested."

He's about to type something into his phone when the waitress reappears at our table side. She holds a pad and pen in hand, ready to take our order. Looking at me, she asks, "Have you decided?"

I haven't even looked at the menu yet, so I go with my default food choice. "Could I get a Denver omelet with extra bacon on the side?"

She blinks, glances at Theo, then looks back at me. Her smile is uncertain. "Sure. And, uh, will you be having the key lime pie for dessert?"

I lift my brows. "Is it on special or something?"

She blinks again, looking nervous, then laughs.

I have no idea what's going on, but the poor girl seems to be completely freaked out by Theo—who's now sitting stiffly in his chair, staring at her in a weirdly challenging way—so I make an effort to move the conversation along so she can flee. "Yes, I'll take the key lime pie. Thanks."

She nods, notes it on her pad, then turns around and sprints off toward the kitchen before I can shout after her that she forgot to take Theo's order. She never even gave him a menu, come to think of it.

Bemused, I watch her go. "Well, that was strange."

Slowly, Theo turns his head and looks at me. All the warmth has leached from his eyes, his shoulders are stiff, his nostrils are flared, and his lips are flattened. His jaw is so hard, it could cut glass. He looks like he's about to jump up and start screaming.

I lower my brows and level him with a look. "Sunshine. Do you recall our little chat about the mood monster? Because he's making a reappearance."

He stares at me, breathing erratically.

"The waitress will come back," I reassure him. "We'll get your order in. Don't throw a tantrum, it's a minor deal. Damn, you're even crabbier than normal when you're hungry."

He swallows, then props his elbows on the table and drops his head into his hands.

People are beginning to stare again. I decide a change of subject is in order. "So did you hear the news about Capstone?"

Theo's sigh is a giant gust of air that sends the paper napkin on his placemat flying.

"I'll take that as a no. Let me fill you in." I take my own paper napkin and spread it over my lap in case any more dramatic sighs might be forthcoming. "So there was that storm last night, right? All that thunder, lightning, stormy stuff? Apparently, a lightning bolt struck Capstone Construction's headquarters in Portland, which caused a fire, which burned the *entire* building to the ground. No one was hurt, but the place is toast. The video on the news was pretty trippy. Some other business's security camera caught the whole thing. It was like Zeus throwing a thunderbolt from the sky—bam!"

I slap my hand on the table. Theo doesn't move. Now people are *really* looking.

I should've moved to New York. You can act like a complete lunatic there, and no one even blinks an eye.

"C'mon, Sunshine, you're gonna give me a bad reputation in this town, and I only just moved here. The way you're acting, people will start a rumor that I made you cry over breakfast."

He turns his head a fraction, peeking out at me from between his fingers.

I send him a big smile. "I usually don't make men cry until lunch."

Radiating annoyance, he leans back into his chair, slouching like a surly teenager. He grabs his phone and starts to stab his thumbs over the keyboard.

This was a bad idea. I don't know what I was thinking. We shouldn't be doing this.

I slowly set my phone back on the table after reading his text. I'm abruptly so mad, I could spit, and deeply insulted, though this turn of mood shouldn't be a surprise. Though he can be charming when he wants to be, his default mode is Hate Megan.

"Tough. I'm here, you're here, I've got food coming, and I'm hungry. You can go back to hating me after I eat."

He exhales. Even that sounds aggravated. He starts to type something into his phone, but I cut him off before he gets two words in.

"Don't bother, Theo. If you want to leave, go right ahead, but my butt is parked in this chair for the foreseeable future."

He looks at me. I refuse to look back at him, so then he's staring at my profile. After a moment, almost imperceptibly, he leans toward me. Then I could swear I hear him quietly inhale.

Is he smelling me?

The waitress arrives with two plates. She sets one in front of me, the other in front of Theo. Both plates hold Denver omelets with extra bacon on the side.

"Wait, this is a mistake," I tell her, gesturing at the food. "We only ordered one omelet. You actually forgot to take his order."

The waitress looks panicked. Wringing her hands, she looks at Theo. "You didn't want your usual order, sir? I'm so sorry, I just assumed. That's what you always get. That and the key lime pie. Every time you're here, at least as long as I've worked here. But I can certainly take it back and bring you a menu..."

She continues to blather on nervously, but I'm not listening anymore. I'm looking at Theo. I'm looking at his face. At his eyes.

His beautiful, haunted, secretive eyes, which stare back at me with all that horrible anguish and longing.

10

*T*heo grabs his fork, tears a gash into the side of the omelet with it, and stuffs a huge chunk into his mouth. He chews exactly twice, swallows the whole mouthful in one go, then stabs into the omelet again, as violently as if it's the belly of his worst enemy, his fork clattering against the plate. He wolfs down that bite too.

The waitress decides Theo seems satisfied with his food, sends me a relieved smile, then clears out as fast as she can.

"I know the Heimlich maneuver if all that angry chewing makes a hunk of ham lodge in your throat."

Theo stops chewing long enough to glare at me, but he should know by now that I don't back down when he's making his trademark serial killer face.

"So this is interesting," I say calmly. "I think I've discovered the root cause of your mysterious problem with me."

He falls so still, it appears he's not even breathing.

I point at his plate. "Denver omelet with extra bacon on the side, and key lime pie. It's what I ordered the first night I got to town, when you were sitting in the booth behind me at the diner. You remember?"

His face drains of color.

I cannot for the life of me understand what is wrong with this man.

"You were mad because I copied your order, right?"

Looking startled, Theo blinks. I can't tell if I've caught him off guard because I'm right, or my statement is so far out of left field, he's still trying to process what the hell I'm talking about. So of course I commence Verbal Diarrhea Mode, which never in the history of ever has solved anything, but we're all stuck with our stupid personality traits.

"I mean, if this is what you always get here, it's probably what you always get every time you go out to eat. It makes sense. I do the same thing. Hell, I love Denver omelets and key lime pie! Strangely enough, they're my two favorite foods! So you overheard me ordering what you'd ordered, and you...I don't know, maybe you thought I was mocking you?"

His expression is a study in confusion.

"You're right, that can't be it. You didn't have a plate in front of you when I arrived, so I couldn't have known what you had. Hmm. So maybe you just can't stand it that someone else in the world likes the same two foods you like? Considering your general aversion for the human race, that is. Or maybe strange coincidences make you as nutty as they make me because you know there's no such thing as causal connections between anything, but the dumb part of you refuses to believe it?"

I run out of breath, and theories.

Theo stares at me for a long time, his gaze searching my face, his body still as a statue's. Then he carefully sets his fork down, picks up his phone, and starts typing. He doesn't even bother to send it, he just holds up his phone so I can see what he's written.

You don't have a future as a detective.

I send him my sweetest smile, which could cause cavities, it's so saccharine. "And you, Sunshine, don't have a future as a clown. So here we are, two people not doing jobs they'd suck at, eating omelets together on a Monday morning and irritating the shit out of each other, though only one of them knows why. Ain't life grand?"

I pick up my fork and proceed to dig into my breakfast.

After a moment, Theo types into his phone and holds it out for me to see.

> *For someone who doesn't curse,*
> *you sure curse a lot.*

I look at him. He lifts a shoulder, like, *Just sayin'*. Then I start to laugh, because it's either that or start crying.

"You're seriously killing me here, you know that? I've encountered hyperbolic geometry problems less incomprehensible than you."

> *Hyperbolic geometry? Is that your way of*
> *letting me know you've got a big brain?*

With a roll of my eyes, I push his phone away from my face. "Sunshine, my brain is so big, it's almost the size of your bad attitude."

Then a miracle occurs: we smile at each other.

"Everything okay with the food?"

The waitress has appeared at our table side once again. From the kitchen door on the other side of the restaurant, three kitchen staff in white stare at us, whispering behind their hands.

When I cock an eyebrow at them, they disappear back into the kitchen in a flash of starched aprons.

Theo makes the OK sign at the waitress. Coming from anyone else, that gesture would be friendly, but he manages to make it look hostile. Terrified, the waitress leaves without a peep.

Watching her go, I sigh. "God. You could make a nun want to commit murder. You ever think about, I don't know, being *pleasant* every once in a while? Or would that clash with the whole Mr. Tall, Dark, and Broody thing you've got going on?"

He turns and looks at me, his eyes shining, the corners of his lips curved up. Batting his long lashes, he makes an innocent face and points at his chest.

"Yes, you." I turn back to my omelet with a shake of my head, surprised to find myself smiling again. Am I beginning to enjoy his whiplash-causing mood changes? Now that would be a plot twist.

We eat. I wonder if he's as aware of me as I am of him. Every little movement he makes registers in my brain, like a Richter scale tracking the magnitude of an earthquake. I've never met someone so contradictory. In my experience, men are generally much simpler creatures than women, but this particular man is more complex than a Rubik's cube.

Or maybe he's just nuts.

"I want to talk to you about something you emailed me," I say casually to my plate.

Theo takes that as his cue to pull his statue impersonation again, but I was anticipating that reaction and don't let it rattle me.

"You said you weren't stable. Which, honestly, is obvious. I won't pry into your personal life, but on one hand, you're telling me to hire you, and on the other hand, you're telling me you hear voices and see ghosts and have a history with drugs, legal and otherwise. Can you see how that would be problematic from a prospective client's point of view?"

I wasn't expecting an answer, so when I don't get one, I keep right on talking.

"I like Coop, a lot. I hear great things about your company, your work ethic, and your talent. That book you brought with the computer images was incredible. And your competition is quickly eliminating itself. But you, Mr. Valentine, are worrisome. To be completely honest, I don't know what to make of you. I don't think I can trust you. And if we were to work together, trust is a nonnegotiable. You said we can never be friends, and I can accept that...but I won't accept uncertainty about your ability to do your job. I have to *know* you're going to be there, be professional, and be absolutely rock solid, regardless of whatever your personal issues are."

I lift my head and look at him. He gazes back at me with a pained expression, his face pale.

"That house is more than just a house to me," I tell him, my voice low but strong. "It's a lifeline. It's a kept promise. It's probably the only thing I'll ever love again. Do you understand?"

He stares deep into my eyes, long past the point of politeness. Then he sends me a text.

Yes. More than you'll ever know.

I blow out a hard breath, because hello, enigmatic statement, sit right down and join the conversation. I get another text right on the heels of the first.

*I'm sorry if I hurt your feelings with the
friend comment. The last thing I want to do
is hurt you. It's just that being around you is hard.*

I look up from my phone and into his eyes. My heart thumping, I demand, "Tell me why."

He sits there beside me, breathing unevenly, wild-eyed and tense.

"Theo. You're not getting the job unless you explain yourself. I'm done with this cloak-and-dagger routine."

He looks down at the demolished remains of his omelet, as if for help. Then he briefly closes his eyes, thinks for a moment, and picks up his phone.

Because you're so hideous.
Honestly, I've seen prettier faces at the zoo.

"Okay," I say, irritated because I thought I was close to getting to the bottom of this incomprehensible situation. I toss my phone onto the table, where it lands with a clatter. "Good to know you think this is such a joke. It's been interesting knowing you. Have a nice life."

I push my chair back, ready to barge past him or climb over him if he won't move, but he reaches out and touches the back of my hand with his fingertip.

Static electricity crackles over my skin, hot and sharp as a knife. I yank my hand away, suck in a startled breath, and stare at him, blinking in surprise.

His lips part, and I swear, I *swear* he's about to speak. But then he exhales a sharp breath, angrily shakes his head, and reaches into his wallet. He throws money down on the table, leaps from his chair, and leaves me sitting alone, gaping after his retreating back as he strides off through the restaurant.

Several minutes later, another text comes through on my phone.

Because you make all my broken parts bleed.

When the waitress arrives with two plates of key lime pie, I'm sitting right where Theo left me, reading his text for the hundredth time.

~

The long walk home in the cold doesn't clear my head or settle my nerves, and I'm still rattled when I open the front door of the house. I spend a few hours on the internet researching more contractors until I have a small list of new prospects. Feeling dejected when I can't get through to the first two I try to call, I decide I'll leave it until tomorrow.

I pass the rest of the afternoon in a funk, paying bills, doing laundry and other distracting busywork chores, until it's time for bed. I get undressed and climb under the covers to the sound of my stomach growling. After the Strangest Breakfast Ever, I wasn't in the mood to eat.

I make his broken parts bleed? What on earth am I supposed to do with that?

Nothing, answers my pragmatic side. *Forget it. The man is a lost cause.*

The problem with lost causes is that they're so seductive to those who know what it is to be lost.

Around midnight, I'm staring at the ceiling in the dark, thinking about Mr. Mysterious, when I smell something burning.

My heart slams into my throat. I jolt upright, throw off the covers, and turn on the lights. Everything in the bedroom looks normal, but that acrid scent is unmistakable. I run downstairs, fighting panic, and follow my nose through the house, hitting every light switch I pass until the house is lit up like a Christmas tree.

I find what I'm looking for in the parlor.

Black fingers of smoke billow from an electrical outlet near the window. It's the same outlet I've heard crackling on several occasions. A thin gray cloud hangs on the ceiling above, moving outward in slow, widening waves, like ripples on water after a stone has been tossed in.

Cursing, I run over to the window and throw it open in an effort to clear the smoke from the room. Cold night air rushes in, and smoke starts to rush out. I run back upstairs to get my cell phone, dialing 9-1-1 on my way back downstairs. A woman's brisk voice answers.

"Nine-one-one, what's your emergency?"

"My house is on fire!"

"Tell me your address and call-back number, ma'am."

I do, she repeats it back to me, I confirm, then she asks me to tell her exactly what's happening.

"There's an electrical fire inside the wall on the first floor, west side of the building, facing the beach. I don't know how large it is yet, but there's a lot of smoke." I manage to sound rational, though my hands are shaking and I can't catch my breath.

"Where are you now, ma'am?"

"Looking at the outlet."

"I need you to leave the house immediately, ma'am! Get to a safe spot and wait for the fire department to arrive. Do you understand?"

The dispatcher is aggravated with me. I can't say I blame her, but I'm reluctant to leave.

"Ma'am!" she barks when I don't respond.

"I'm going." I spin on my heel and run toward the front door, but skid to a stop at the stairway. Inhaling a breath that feels as cold as snow, I look up toward the second floor.

The wedding album.

I sprint up the stairs to the master bedroom. The dispatcher must be able to hear my heavy breathing and the sound of my feet hitting the floor, because she asks, "Are you outside now?"

"Almost!" I answer breathlessly. "I have to get something. I can't leave the house without it—"

She hollers, "Ma'am, I need you to *exit the premises imme-diately!*"

Now I've really pissed her off. She wants to reach through the phone and strangle me. I hurl myself into the closet, grab the white leather photo album from the shelf above the rack of clothes, tuck it under my arm, and head back downstairs, taking the stairs three at a time, panting and cursing under my breath, hysteria rising like a wave of freezing water in my blood. The dispatcher says something else I can't hear over the roar of *Please no, please no, please God no* in my ears.

If the Buttercup burns to the ground and I lose the last thing tying me to Cass, if our dream literally goes up in flames, I'm not sure I'll survive it.

I'm at the bottom step of the staircase when Theo kicks open the front door.

It slams against the wall with a tremendous *boom*. Splinters of wood fly everywhere. I rear back in shock, lose my balance, and drop the album and my phone, falling on my ass in the process. Moving with incredible speed, Theo runs down the hallway toward the kitchen. He throws open the basement door. I hear heavy boots pounding down stairs. A heartbeat passes, then the entire house is plunged into darkness.

Panicked and disoriented, I scream his name.

Off in the distance, the wail of a siren breaks the night.

Within seconds, the thud of Theo's footsteps echoes hollowly on the wooden basement stairs. Then a blinding white beam of light slashes through the darkness. It moves toward me, bobbing in time to the heavy thump of footsteps growing closer. He sweeps past me on his way into the parlor, so focused, he doesn't even acknowledge my presence.

Along with the flashlight, he carries a sledgehammer and a fire extinguisher.

"Hello? Are you there?"

The tinny squawk of the dispatcher's voice comes through my cell phone, lying on the step beside me. Ignoring it, I gather the photo album in my arms and stumble after Theo into the parlor.

As I enter the room, he's setting the flashlight on the floor. It's pointed at the wall, illuminating the outlet the smoke rises from in a wedge of white light. Then he takes the sledgehammer in hand and swings it high overhead.

The sound of plaster smashing into pieces is so loud, I jump.

With long, smooth strokes, Theo swings the sledgehammer over and over until he's broken a large hole into the wall above the socket. Smoke pours out. Exposed to a new surge of oxygen, small licks of orange flame jump and flare.

Theo drops the sledgehammer, grabs the fire extinguisher, and sprays white foam over the wall, the fire, and the smoking socket, until there's nothing left in the canister and it sputters out.

The wail of the fire engine's sirens grows closer.

Theo sees me standing in the doorway, clutching my wedding album in my arms, shaking so badly, my teeth are chattering. He's breathing hard. All the cords are standing out in his neck. In the play of light and shadow over the bones in his face, he looks beautiful, otherworldly, and terrifying, like an avenging angel coming to settle a score.

I say hoarsely, "W-what...how..." My stammering is interrupted by a hacking cough, brought on by all the smoke in the room.

Theo points to me, then he jabs his finger toward the front door.

I know he's telling me to get out, but I can't move. I can only stare at him. Shock has frozen me in place.

He drops the fire extinguisher and crosses the room in a few long strides. Then, with a swift bend of his knees, he sweeps me off my feet and into his arms. He walks to the front door while I cling to him with one arm and my wedding album with the other, my heart jackhammering inside my chest.

I stare at his profile as he carries me out into the night and across the street. He sets me gently on my feet on the sidewalk, makes sure I'm steady, then turns back toward the house.

"Theo."

He stops and looks at me.

In a shaking voice, I say, "How are you here?"

Engines roaring, the fire truck turns the corner and starts to barrel up the street. Theo whips out the small pad he carries in his pocket and begins to write. When he's finished, he tears off the sheet of paper and hands it to me. I take it with trembling fingers, and he turns and strides back into the house.

When the fire engine slows to a stop in the middle of the street in front of me, I read his words by the red flashing lights, the smell of smoke stinging my nose, the sea breeze a cooling balm against my flushed skin.

I'll always be here.

11

"You got really lucky, Miss Dunn. An electrical fire that starts inside the walls is extremely dangerous. We've seen whole houses go up in minutes. These old Victorians are especially susceptible because of the outdated wiring. You're gonna need to get all the electrical replaced, like, yesterday."

A firefighter named John is speaking to me. Under his yellow-and-black fireman's helmet, John has sparkling brown eyes and a toothy grin, and seems to be thoroughly enjoying himself. I think he's disappointed there wasn't more action when he arrived, because he immediately started barking orders at his men, deploying all the hoses and every piece of equipment from the truck, and marching around the property like a big game hunter out to bag an elephant.

It was like watching a general rousing his troops for the final assault of the war, only to find one scrawny guy with a slingshot waiting for them when they got there.

"Uh-huh," I respond absently, my gaze glued to the front door of the house for any sign of Theo.

I'm standing across the street where Theo left me, in my sleep shorts and T-shirt, barefoot and shell-shocked, oblivious to the cold. My wedding album is smashed against my chest, and my arms are wound like a vise around it.

"Yeah," says John, grinning. "Electrical fires are a real bitch. Heat in the tens of thousands of degrees from the initial arc flare. Combine that with an enclosed space filled with combustible materials like insulation and wood framing, you're lookin' at a nightmare. We had one call last month where this guy had about ten things plugged into a really old power strip—"

"Here you go, ma'am."

Another firefighter appears, interrupting John's story. This one is younger and more serious than John. He settles a blanket around my shoulders, then shares a nod with his boss.

"Thank you."

"You're welcome. You okay, ma'am?"

"Yes. And please call me Megan, I'm not that much older than you."

His smile is bashful. He's cute in a clean-cut, all-American-boy sort of way. I wonder if Suzanne has met this guy. If I told her about him, she'd probably set her kitchen on fire.

"How's it going in there?" I ask him.

"We're making sure there are no other hot spots. For now, it looks like you're good, but we have to check everything before we leave. Theo was real smart to shut off the power when he arrived. That probably prevented things from being a whole lot worse. As long as the current is live, the arcing can continue farther along in the wiring. If that happens, you can kiss your house good-bye."

At the mention of Theo's name, my attention snaps into focus. "You know Theo?"

The cute fireman shrugs. "Sure. Everybody knows Theo."

Of course they do. Seaside is a small town, and Theo's lived in it his whole life. I'm the stranger here, not him.

"Did he happen to mention how he got here before you did? Is he on the volunteer fire team or something?"

John says, "Nah, he's just a night owl, I guess you'd say. We see him wandering all over the place at night. Likes to keep an eye on things."

Things? I look up and down the beach. The nearest structure is a three-story condo building a quarter mile up the coast.

I think of the man I saw standing on the beach just after I got off the call with Craig this morning. The man with wide shoulders and long legs, wearing a black windbreaker. The man staring down the beach with an air of melancholy, like he was looking for someone, or something he'd lost.

That was Theo. Now I'm sure of it.

I should be disturbed by that realization, but oddly, I'm not. There's no fear, only curiosity. Perhaps a case of wishful thinking, but my intuition tells me Theo Valentine isn't a danger to me.

If anything, though I don't understand why, I think I'm far more of a danger to him.

As if summoned by my thoughts, Theo appears in the open doorway. Across the distance, our gazes meet. He's lit in flashing red and amber from the fire truck lights. He's removed the windbreaker he was wearing when he came in and stands in a white long-sleeved T-shirt smudged with soot. There's a big black smear like war paint straight across his cheeks and the bridge of his nose. It highlights his eyes, darkly glittering under a lowered brow.

He makes a beeline for me.

"Oh, here he comes," says John. He holds up a hand in greeting. His cute subordinate waves.

They like him. Everyone likes him, this sphinx of a man who roams the town in the middle of the night, mute and sleepless from whatever demons haunt him.

A sharp pang of empathy chews at my stomach as I watch him walk toward me. Loneliness recognizes loneliness, like the howl of a solitary wolf rising to meet the distant cry of another on a cold winter's night.

When he reaches us, he pauses, nodding first at John, then the cute one. Then he looks at me, his eyes as sharp as laser beams.

I say, "I understand you might've saved my house with your quick thinking."

His stare doesn't waver. He doesn't smile, or move, or even blink. He just waits.

"John here tells me I need to get the electrical replaced in the Buttercup ASAP."

John says, "Oh, definitely. Tomorrow isn't soon enough. You shouldn't turn the power back on until you get an expert out here to fix it."

Okay, universe. You win.

"So, you'll start tomorrow, then," I tell Theo. A sense of inevitability weighs the words, as if my lips have known all along they'd be forming them. "Today, technically. First thing in the morning if you can."

Holding my gaze, Theo slowly nods.

"Just the electrical to start. Then we'll see where we're at." With us, I mean. With him attempting a show of normal human behavior. "Deal?"

One thudding heartbeat, then two, then Theo extends his hand. I shift my wedding album to my other arm, then slide my right hand into his. My palm is swallowed in his big, rough mitt. We don't shake, we just stand there, holding hands and staring at each other, something like electricity crackling in the cold air, until John clears his throat.

"Well, that's good. I feel better knowin' you'll be takin' care of the job, Theo. Place this size might take you a week or so, eh?"

Theo releases my hand, but not my gaze. He holds up three fingers.

"Three days?"

Theo nods, then John chuckles, turning to me. "Count your lucky stars, Megan. This here's the best contractor in the area."

Theo's smile comes on slow, but it keeps growing until it takes over his entire body, until he's practically glowing from the inside out. I can't remember the last time I saw something so beautiful.

I say faintly, "So they keep telling me."

By the time the firemen leave, I'm physically, mentally, and emotionally exhausted. I feel like a wet washcloth some angry giant wrung out and flung against a brick wall. I watch the fire truck rumble off down the street, lifting a hand in farewell when one of the firemen waves from the cab.

Then I've only got the sound of the surf to keep me company as I go inside to pour myself a glass of whiskey.

Theo melted into the night like a phantom before I could ask him any questions about exactly why he was at my house when the fire broke out, but if he thinks his disappearing act is going to stop me from asking tomorrow, he's got another thing coming.

I have so many questions, my head is practically exploding with them.

With the blanket wrapped around my shoulders and the album safely tucked under my arm, I shuffle into the house, shutting the door behind me. Destroyed by the savage kick it received, the doorknob falls off when I touch it. Sighing, I leave it where it lands.

Ignoring the splinter in the sole of my foot, I head to the kitchen, navigating through the dark house with a big flashlight John gave me before he and his crew left. Along the way, I'm treated to a depressing view of the guts of my house, spilling out from gashes in baseboards and holes punched through the plaster near the ceiling in various places where the men evidently searched for more "hot spots" in the wiring. The house is a mess, but it's standing.

Thanks to Theo Valentine.

Who, for some inexplicable reason, showed up before the fire department did. Who knew exactly where in my house a fire extinguisher, flashlight, and sledgehammer were located. Who picked me up and carried me in his arms with no more effort than it took me to carry my wedding album, and I'm no tiny, delicate flower.

Who added one more piece to the ever-growing puzzle with his mystifying note.

I'll always be here.

I tucked the note between the pages of my wedding album because I didn't want to lose it. It feels important somehow. Meaningful, like a clue.

I walk into the kitchen, set the album and the flashlight on the counter, open a cabinet, and grab a glass. Then I get the bottle of whiskey from another cabinet and pour myself a drink. I down it in one go, shuddering as the fumes sear my nose, then pour myself another.

When I turn around, I let loose a bloodcurdling scream.

Theo leans against the marble island with his arms folded over his chest, looking at me.

I thunder, "Jesus Christ, Theo! You scared me half to death! What the hell are you doing!"

With a worried expression, he points at me, then makes the OK sign.

"Yes, I'm fine! God!" I put a shaky hand to my forehead, breathing hard because of the sudden spike of adrenaline crashing through my body. "I thought you left!"

Solemnly, Theo shakes his head.

"Well, now I know, obviously!"

He watches in stillness as I sag against the counter for support, tightening the blanket around my shoulders and fighting to regain my calm. After a moment, I manage to pull myself together enough to stop shouting, though I'm anything but pulled together. I'm unraveling at the seams.

"Sorry. I didn't mean to shout at you, I'm just not good with surprises. Don't sneak up on me like that again, okay?"

He nods, looking contrite, and now I feel like a jerk for losing my cool. The man saved my house, after all. The least I can do is be polite.

"Okay. This is me apologizing again. But I'd like to also add that it's a little weird you were standing in my kitchen alone in the dark. Actually, it's more than a *little* weird." My laugh is rueful. "But I should be used to that with you by now. You give weird a whole new definition."

When Theo smiles, the room brightens by degrees. It's too bad he does it so infrequently, because a smile like that could end wars.

I take the opportunity to swallow more whiskey, grateful I didn't drop the glass in my shock, or I'd probably start drinking right from the bottle.

"Here." I set the glass on the counter and reach for the paper towel dispenser. I rip off a white square and hold it out to Theo. "You have some soot on your face."

He takes the paper towel and wipes his face with it, smearing the soot all over instead of cleaning it off. When he stops and looks at me for confirmation that it's better, I sigh and shake my head.

"Worse." I moisten a cotton dish towel under the faucet. Then, because apparently I've lost all touch with reality, I stand in front of Theo and start to clean his face.

Alarmed, he stiffens.

"Yeah, I know," I say. "But if you can be weird, so can I. And you did save my house after all. I can't let you leave looking like you just got off a double shift at the coal mine."

He breathes shallowly, watching me with hooded eyes, his body so taut, it could snap in two. His hands curl around the edge of the marble island, as if he's using it to hold himself up.

"Relax, Sunshine. The torture will be over momentarily." I meet his gaze. "Then I'll start the interrogation."

He swallows.

"Yeah, you should be afraid. I've got questions, pal. *Tons* of questions."

He looks pained, then resigned, briefly closing his eyes. When he opens his eyes again, he reaches up and grasps my wrist.

I freeze. My heart starts thumping. I'm not used to physical contact, having gone without it for years, and Theo's big hand wrapped around my wrist is all kinds of contact. It's skin on skin, and a sudden sharp heat in the air, and a rushing noise like the ocean in my ears.

When his fingers press lightly against the pulse in my wrist, as if he's timing the beat of my heart, I'm swallowed by a dark, painful déjà vu.

Cass used to touch me like this. His fingers always sought the places where my pulse showed itself—throat, wrist, the hollow between my thigh and hip—resting lightly against a throbbing vein until the blood beneath it quickened at his touch.

And it always quickened. The same as it's doing now, jumping to life under the light, seeking press of Theo's fingertips, beating, then beating faster until it's a wild, racing thing, uncontrollable, like a leaf spun high into the sky by a fierce wind.

This is the first time I've truly felt alive in years.

My intake of breath seems loud in the quiet room. Theo watches my face with extraordinary focus. Our noses are mere inches apart. Under the burn of his eyes, I feel exposed, all my defenses laid bare, all my carefully constructed boundaries flattened like a house of straw blown over by the big, bad wolf.

I feel naked.

I yank my arm away and back up several short steps. The blanket falls from my shoulders and slips to the floor.

Theo holds up a hand, fingers spread, like *Stop*. Or, *It's okay.*

God, who am I kidding? I have no idea what he means. Maybe he's telling me I'm a five on a scale of one to ten.

"It's late," I whisper, my mouth as dry as bone. Suddenly, all my questions don't seem nearly as important as getting him out of my house so I can be alone with the sea of fire boiling in my blood. Sweat has bloomed over my chest, and I'm breathing so fast, I'm almost panting.

This isn't fear, or shock, or anything nearly as simple as those. I recognize this feeling like I'd recognize the face of an old friend, glimpsed from afar after a long separation.

Desire has a particular flavor that, once tasted, can never be forgotten.

All from the press of his fingertips on my wrist.

He pushes away from the island, stares down at me for several beats in blistering silence, then exhales, running a hand through his hair. I'm glad for once that he doesn't speak, because it means I don't have to either.

I'm not entirely sure what words my mouth might form in the wake of the bomb that just detonated inside my body.

He knocks twice on the top of the marble island in farewell, then turns to go.

Before he leaves, his gaze lingers on my wedding album on the counter.

12

I awaken to what sounds like a herd of bulls stampeding through my living room.

Squinting into the morning light flooding my bedroom, I sit up in bed and listen. I'm disoriented, but not alarmed. I have neither the energy nor the presence of mind to be alarmed this morning. I spent the hours after Theo left in an intimate relationship with the bottle of whiskey, the remains of which are now perfuming my breath. It's a good thing there aren't any open flames nearby, or I'd be toast.

Flames—right. That herd downstairs must be Theo and his team.

The clock on the bedside table tells me it's precisely eight o'clock. I guess Theo took my direction of "first thing in the morning" literally.

I drag myself out of bed and shuffle into the bathroom, snorting when I glimpse myself in the mirror. I look like a prehistoric cave woman who spent a long night losing a battle with a woolly mammoth. I need a shower and about a gallon of coffee if I'm even going to resemble a human.

But first I need to check on the herd.

I go to the top of the stairs and holler down, "Theo!"

Thump, thump, thump, then he appears, wearing boots, faded jeans, and a long-sleeved T-shirt, this one black. He lifts his brows when he catches sight of me.

"Put a sock in it, Sunshine," I grumble. "Some of us had a rough night."

I must be getting better at reading his expressions, because this one distinctly says, *I can see that.* How he looks so fresh and perky is beyond me, considering he probably got as little sleep as I did.

"I see you let yourself in. Glad you feel so at home."

He cocks his head at my sarcastic tone, then makes a turning motion with his hand.

"Right," I say. "The front door is missing a doorknob. Funny thing how when someone kicks in a door, these little mishaps occur."

Then he makes a stabbing motion with his finger, cups his hand around his ear, and shakes his head.

"Yes, Theo, I realize my doorbell isn't working either. But there's this thing called knocking? Here, let me show you."

I demonstrate a proper knock, rapping my knuckles theatrically on the wood banister so it echoes nice and loudly through the room.

Theo rolls his eyes. Then he presses his hands together in a praying position, rests them against his cheek, closes his eyes, and exhales an exaggerated breath through his mouth so his lips flap unattractively, like a cartoon character's.

"I wasn't *snoring!*" I say defensively, embarrassed because I probably was. Cass used to tell me I could wake the dead with the racket I made after I'd had a few drinks in me.

Grinning, Theo lifts his hands in surrender. Through my embarrassment, I find myself grinning back. Though rare, his smiles are infectious. Hopefully, now that he's getting what he wants and is working on the house, they'll appear with greater frequency.

I'm not holding my breath, but one can hope.

"I'm going to take a shower. You guys good for half an hour or so without me?"

Theo nods, waving dismissively. Apparently finished with the conversation, he strides off without waiting for me to say anything else.

"And a good morning to you too, Sunshine." I listen to the thump of his boots recede toward the back of the house. For some reason, I find the sound comforting.

Because you haven't had a man around in a hundred years, girlfriend.

Under my breath, I tell my uterus to shut the hell up. Then I head back upstairs to the shower.

"There she is!" Straightening from his inspection of a hole the firefighters punched in the baseboard of the living room, Coop beams at me like I'm his long-lost sister. He's wearing a red-and-black flannel shirt rolled up his thick forearms along with a pair of dungarees. His resemblance to a lumberjack is uncanny. "How're you doin', Megan? Happy to see me?"

"Gee, everyone's in such a chipper mood this morning," I quip, trying to keep a straight face. I'm the boss here, after all. I can't let all these big, burly men think they can get the upper hand on me by acting like some giggly teenager. "Theo actually smiled at me earlier. Did you guys smoke some dope before coming to work?"

"Naw, it's just a beautiful mornin' is all!" He props his hands on his hips and looks me up and down. "And you look prettier'n a new set of snow tires, if I might say so."

Blushing, I run a hand over my damp hair and look down at

my jeans and blue sweater. "I've never seen snow tires, but I'll take that as a compliment. Thank you."

"Never seen snow tires?" He looks horrified, as if I've just told him my parents were siblings. "Where'd you grow up, the moon?"

"The desert, actually. Before here, I never lived anywhere but Phoenix."

Coop thoughtfully rubs his beard. "Been to Phoenix once. Hot as hell and dry as a nun's cooch."

"Thank you for that disturbing visual. Is there some paperwork I need to sign? A scope of work or whatever?"

"Yeah, Theo's got the contract all worked up. He left it on the kitchen counter for you."

"Okay, thanks."

I turn to head into the kitchen, but Coop says, "Megan?"

I turn back. "Yeah?"

He hesitates for a moment. "I just wanted to say thank you."

"For what?"

"For this." He gestures to the house. "For givin' Theo a shot. He really needed it."

"Needed what? I'm not sure what you mean."

Looking over my shoulder, Coop lowers his voice. "This house is kinda...important to him. Don't ask me why, 'cause I don't know, but he's been obsessed with this place for years. I think it's been a dream of his to get it back to its former glory." His blue eyes grow a shade darker. "Like maybe fixin' the house will fix him."

What is this tremor I'm feeling, this fluttering of butterflies in my stomach, this jangling of nerves? Empathy? Anxiety? I'm not sure, but this is the first time I can say with confidence that Theo Valentine and I have something in common.

"We only agreed he'd do the electrical, Coop. We'll see how it goes over the next few days. I don't want to get anyone's hopes up."

Coop chuckles. "Too late for that. I haven't seen Theo this happy in a long time."

I say sourly, "Great. So no pressure on me to keep him on the job, then. What if I'm not satisfied with his work?"

Coop looks insulted on Theo's behalf. "Tch. You'll be plenty satisfied. He's the best, and that's no exaggeration."

"And what if I'm not satisfied with *him*? He's not exactly the easiest person to be around, Coop."

Coop acknowledges that with a nod, then pierces me with a look. "Theo's not easy, I admit, but he's the best man I've ever known. He's honest, and honorable, and the kind of loyal that doesn't ever break. I'd trust him with my life. With my kids' lives. How many people do you know that you can say that about?"

"Do dead people count?"

Coop doesn't bat an eye at my odd question, which I spoke without forethought, Cass's name leaping to my tongue at the mention of honor, loyalty, and trust. My husband was a person who was good to the marrow of his bones, but he was also as fearless as a lion, especially when it came to protecting someone he loved.

He was that thing women crave at our most elemental core, a thing made all the more beautiful by its rarity: a real man.

Coop glances at my wedding ring, then looks back into my eyes. "Sure," he says softly. "Death doesn't end a relationship. Only a life."

I press my hand to my heart, because goddamn. That *hurt*. "Unfair, Coop," I say hoarsely. "You're hitting me with this heavy existential shit before I've even had my coffee!"

Coop's smile is as gentle as his gaze. "I can't take credit for that particular piece of existential shit. I read it in a book about some guy named Morrie, stuck with me." He watches me try to blink away the water pooling in my eyes. "Knew you were a softie under that tough-chick act. But I promise I won't tell anyone. Your secret's safe with me, marshmallow."

"Shut up. And it better be. Now get to work." I turn and stride away, listening to Coop's amused chuckle as I go.

I nod at several workers as I pass through the house on my way into the kitchen. I don't see Theo, which is fine, because without a hefty dose of caffeine, my head won't be clear enough to deal with whatever mood change he might spring on me.

The first thing my gaze lands on when I enter the kitchen is the coffeemaker—which is when I remember the power's off.

I stop, groan, and slap a hand on my forehead. Then I notice what's on the island and stop groaning.

Next to a sheaf of stapled papers sits a large to-go cup, the kind with the plastic lid and the paper sleeve. A curl of steam rises from the hole in the lid.

Drawn toward it as if magnetized, I cross to the island, pick up the cup, and sniff. The delicious, nutty scent of strong coffee greets my nostrils, making my mouth water. I crack open the lid and grin in delight when I see that black gold.

If this was meant for anyone else, they're out of luck. I'm claiming this sucker. I take a sip, closing my eyes in ecstasy when the coffee hits my tongue. It's exactly how I like it: unsweetened and scalding hot.

Sighing in pleasure, I open my eyes...and find Theo standing in the kitchen doorway.

"Oh. Hi." I feel flustered and guilty, as if he caught me masturbating.

Theo points at the cup in my hand, then gives me an inquisitive thumbs-up.

"Yes, it's perfect. Did you do this?"

He nods.

"Thank you. I can't function without coffee in the morning."

He nods again. I know it's only my imagination that thinks he's saying *I know*, but now I'm even more flustered. *Get your shit together, Megan. Focus.*

I straighten my shoulders and put on my boss-lady face. "So

this is the contract, I take it?" I point at the paperwork, and he gives me a thumbs-up. "Okay. I'll look it over right now and let you know if I have any questions."

Another incline of his head, this one looking regal. He's calmer than I've ever seen him. His entire aspect is lighter, as if the thunderclouds that permanently follow him around have opened to let rays of sunlight shine through.

He looks at home standing there in the doorway to my kitchen. At home and at peace.

Why that should make me feel so good, I don't know. But some part of me, a small, dark corner of my heart, just exhaled the breath it's been holding since I met him.

"Theo Valentine," I say quietly, holding his warm gaze. "Welcome to my home. I'm trusting you with the most important thing in my life. Don't screw it up."

His mouth bursts into a huge, glowing grin, devastating in its beauty. His entire face is transformed, as if there's another man hiding beneath that mask of scowls he normally wears, waiting to break free.

He swaggers over, pulls a pen from his back pocket, flips over the contract, and scrawls onto it.

You're crabby in the morning.

"No, I'm crabby *this* morning," I correct, reading around his shoulder. "My house almost burned down last night, remember?"

Except it didn't.

I read the words he's written, then glance up at his face. He gazes down at me with a secret little smile, lashes lowered, a lock of dark hair flopping onto his forehead. Then he winks.

The man *winks.*

I say drily, "Yes, Superman, you saved the day. And before I sign this paperwork, you're going to tell me how you came to be outside my house last night at the exact moment a fire started inside the damn walls."

His expression sours. He begins to turn away, but I grab his biceps. I'm shocked when I find a stony, bulging muscle beneath my hand. I knew he was big, but I had no idea he was made of steel.

At my touch, he freezes. Nostrils flaring, he glances down at my hand on his arm, then looks back up at me. I half expected his gaze to reflect irritation or disdain, but what I see in those expressive brown eyes of his is a depth of suffering so bottomless, it leaves me breathless.

He looks at me as if I'm torturing him with my touch. As if the mere laying of a few fingers on his clothed arm has caused him such misery, he might not be able to stand upright much longer. The rawness, the palpable *realness* of his pain is astonishing.

I snatch my hand back and stare at him in confusion, knowing I've made a terrible mistake, but not knowing how or why.

Then I'm horrified to realize I touched his *left* arm. The side that would've sustained the most damage in his accident, if, as Suzanne had said, he was broadsided by the other car.

I look at the ragged white scar over his left eyebrow, the snarl of scar tissue running down the left side of his neck, and blurt, "Oh God, I'm so sorry, I've hurt you!"

I back away a step but am prevented from going any farther when Theo grabs my wrist. I suck in a startled breath, then we stand there, staring at each other in a cavernous silence so tense, it crackles.

His gaze drops to my mouth. He swallows and moistens his lips, and a wave of heat spreads across my chest and up my neck. My heart starts to pound like mad, the drum of it drowning out everything else.

His gaze snaps back up to mine. I know he sees the effect he's having on me, because his eyes darken and a ruddy flush creeps over his cheeks.

"There you are!"

In the doorway appears one of Theo's workers, a redheaded guy with a tool belt strapped around his waist. He's smiling, eager, unaware of what he's walked in on.

I don't know exactly what he walked in on either.

Theo drops my wrist as if he's been scalded, turns, and strides out of the kitchen. The worker watches him go like it's totally normal behavior for Theo to leave with no warning, then turns to me with a shake of his head.

"Hi, there. I'm Toby. I'm part of Theo's crew."

A little breathless, I lean against the island for support. I hope my cheeks aren't as red as they feel. "Hi, Toby. I'm Megan. Nice to meet you."

He jerks his thumb over his shoulder. "There are some doughnuts out here if you want. Theo stopped on the way over and got 'em."

Before the words are completely out of his mouth, Theo returns, holding something wrapped in a white paper napkin. He walks to me and holds it out, giving it a little jiggle when I don't react quickly enough.

As soon as I remove it from his hands, he turns around and leaves again, pulling Toby along with him by the sleeve of his shirt.

"See ya later!" calls Toby over his shoulder as Theo drags him away.

Still a little shaky, I unwrap the little package Theo's given me. When I see what it is, my heart stops dead in my chest.

It's not technically a doughnut. It's a pastry. A bear claw, to be specific.

Cass's favorite breakfast food, which he ate at least a few times a week, including the day he died.

13

I'm standing on the back patio, staring blankly at the sea with the uneaten bear claw in my hand, when a voice calling my name pierces the thick snarl of my thoughts. I turn to see Suzanne hurrying toward me from inside the house. She's wearing a hot-pink sweat suit and flip-flops. With no makeup on and her hair pulled back into a ponytail, she looks ten years younger.

She also looks completely freaked out.

She bursts through the open French doors and engulfs me in a hug. "I just heard about the fire! Thank God you're okay!"

"Word travels fast," I mutter, wondering if everyone in town has a special gossip line on their phone that rings when there's juicy news.

She pulls away, holds me at arm's length, and looks me up and down, as if searching for damage. When she doesn't find any, she pulls me into another hug, this one tighter.

"Suzanne, I'm fine," I say after a moment, touched but also irritated by her concern. I've never been one who enjoys people making a fuss over me.

When she pulls away this time, she's on the verge of tears.

"I should've *made* you stay in a rental until this place was fixed up." She draws a hitching breath. "Jesus, Megan, if anything had happened to you, it would've been my fault."

"Don't be silly," I say firmly. "Accidents happen all the time. These kinds of things are nobody's fault."

She looks up at the house with her brows pulled together, as if she's afraid of it. "I don't know, sweetie, my mother always says an accident is just fate's way of making sure you know you're not the one in control."

I blow air through my lips, a derogatory sound that coordinates well with my eye roll. "There's no such thing as fate, Suzanne, or destiny, or an old man in white robes in the sky who watches over us and expects us to spend an hour each week sitting on hard wooden benches in a building with ugly stained glass windows praying to a statue of a dude nailed to a cross. We're alone in the universe. Everything that happens is simply chance."

I have to ignore the nagging voice in the back of my head that's asking about the bear claw in my hand. And the computer renderings of the Buttercup. And the lightning strike. And a man who just *happened* to be out for a midnight stroll on the beach in front of my house the moment I needed his help.

And half a dozen other things scratching restlessly at my subconscious.

Suzanne says flatly, "That was depressing. Remind me not to invite you over for Christmas dinner. You'll give the baby Jesus a migraine."

"Sorry. Is it too early in the morning for nihilism?"

She wrinkles her nose. "No time of day is good for negativity, hon."

"It's not negativity. It's...practicality. It's realism."

"It's bullshit is what it is," pronounces Suzanne with finality, giving me a small shake. "Don't let life rob you of hope just because it's kicked you in the balls a few times." She pauses.

"Metaphorically speaking, of course. I wasn't insinuating I think you have testicles."

"Oh, but I do," I say with a straight face. "Big steel testicles that clang when I walk."

"I was wondering what that noise was," Suzanne shoots back. "I thought maybe you had the Liberty Bell stuffed up your vag."

Then we're laughing. It feels good after all the tension and confusion of the past few days.

She asks, "All kidding aside, how are you? Really?"

I sigh, glancing back at the house. "I'm fine. A little weirded out about Theo, but that's nothing new."

Suzanne arches her brows. "Don't tell me he glared at you again. Coop let me in and said everything was going great."

I meet her gaze, relieved to have someone to talk to about the subject of Mr. Mysterious. "Theo showed up before the firemen did last night. He got here when I was still on the line with 9-1-1. He had to be, like, *right* outside the house."

She does a slow blink that's almost comical in its exaggeration. "In the middle of the night?"

"I know, it's weird, right?"

Her expression turns horrified. "You're not saying you think he's responsible, are you?"

"Oh, no, not at all," I reassure her, because she looks like she might pass out at the thought. "The outlet where the fire started has been making strange noises since I moved in, and all the lights in the house flicker. I knew the wiring was shot. And Theo had to break through a wall with a sledgehammer to get to where the flames were. There's no way he could've started anything."

Suzanne looks confused. "Break through a wall?"

"The fire started between the walls. Something to do with an arc failure. The firemen explained it, but the bottom line is that Theo, somehow, was outside my house when it happened. The question is why?"

Suzanne runs a hand over her head, smoothing away a few

dark tendrils that have escaped from her ponytail and are trailing into her face, teased by the ocean breeze. "Did you ask him?"

"Of course I asked him. And he did his usual impression of a slab of granite and refused to answer."

I don't mention his strange note. It feels too intimate, as if telling someone else would be breaking a confidence. Spilling a secret meant just for me.

Suzanne draws a breath, shaking her head. "Well, I don't know what to tell you. He does have a reputation for being nocturnal."

"Yeah, one of the firemen said that he wanders around at night, keeping his eye on things."

"So maybe just chalk it up to coincidence. He happened to be wandering in your neighborhood at the right time." When I give her a dubious look, she adds tartly, "Hey, you're the one who thinks everything is pure chance."

There's chance and then there's circumstance, and I know Theo's arrival wasn't a random event. He was here at that time for a reason, even if I don't understand what that reason is.

Yet.

My intuition and common sense both tell me it has to do with whatever his obsession is with the Buttercup. He's already admitted in an email that the house feels like true north to him. But no matter how obsessed I was with something, I wouldn't be hanging around it in the middle of the night.

Have you forgotten all the midnights you spent on your knees on the banks of the Salt River?

The thought sends a spike of pain straight through my heart, as if it's been lanced by a spear.

Suzanne glances at me sharply. "You okay, sweetie? You just went white."

It's times like these I wish I had a face that didn't display every emotion I feel like a neon sign. Normally when I get emotional, I try to cover it up with a laugh or a sarcastic comment, but something moves me to tell her the truth.

Looking out at the white-capped waves, I blow out a hard breath. "After my husband died, I used to go to the bend in the river where I'd scattered his ashes and sit there for hours by myself. Sometimes all night. I'd sit and listen to the crickets and watch the stars move across the sky and talk to him. I'd tell him everything I was doing, how life was going, what new movies were out that he'd want to see. It took more than a year before I realized I wasn't really mourning him."

My voice drops an octave. "I was waiting for him to come back."

I meet Suzanne's startled gaze. "Cass was gone for fourteen months, and I still didn't believe it. That's when I started going to therapy, because I knew my heart couldn't be trusted to tell the difference between reality and a beautiful, long-dead dream."

Suzanne looks traumatized by my confession. She says faintly, "Oh. Honey. That's..."

"Depressing as hell, I know," I say drily. "I'm a laugh a minute, aren't I? Sorry I blurted that out. My head's all over the place this morning."

"Don't get down on yourself." With a tender, motherly gesture, she tucks a stray lock of hair behind my ear. "I can't even imagine what you've been through." She hesitates for a moment. "Are you still seeing a therapist?"

"I was, right up until I moved here. But honestly, Suzanne, no amount of talking in the world can change the past. We're all stuck with our scars and our sad stories. I think the more I talked about my pain, the worse it got, like picking at a scab so it could never heal over. Now I'm just resigned to the fact that all my happy years are behind me.

"But I'm luckier than most. That's what I tell myself on the bad days: in a world full of temporary things, I have this love that will last forever. Even though Cass is gone, our love isn't. And that's how I live."

"Oh, crap." She blinks rapidly and waves a hand at her face, her voice tight. "I think you're gonna make me cry."

I smile at her. "Good thing you're not wearing mascara."

She pulls me into another hug, whispering into my ear, "I'm so mad at myself about the other night. Drinking before I drove over. It was so stupid and reckless, and I'm just so, so sorry—"

"You're forgiven," I say, cutting her off. "But do it again and I'll take a bat to your knees."

We pull apart and smile at each other. Then she swipes at her watering eyes and straightens her shoulders. "Threats of violence. I knew you were a badass, despite this whole No Fucks Given Barbie thing you've got going on."

"I don't know what that means, but it sounds unwholesome."

She suddenly notices what I'm holding in my hand and brightens. "Hey, is that a bear claw? I love those things!"

"Of course you do." I hold it out to her. "Mazel tov."

"What does that mean?"

"Congratulations. In Hebrew."

"Are you Jewish?"

"No, just weird. Don't worry, nobody else gets me either."

The only one who ever did is dead.

Suzanne and I talk for a few more minutes while she devours her pastry. She eats the same way I do, with gusto, not caring that it looks like it's the first food she's had in a week. We go inside, and she gives me the contact information for the interior designers she'd mentioned a while back, then she leaves with a promise to bake me another key lime pie.

Then I'm left alone with a house full of men and an over-whelming ambivalence.

I want to talk to Theo and determine exactly why he was outside my house in the middle of the night, but I also don't. Especially now that I'm feeling whatever it is I'm feeling toward him. This electrical awareness brought on by the simple touch of his fingers on my skin.

It's not exactly attraction. It feels darker than that. More dangerous. Like I'm standing barefoot in a shallow pool of water and he's the live wire sparking mere inches away.

I don't have enough experience with men to know if this is normal. Cass was the only man I was ever with. When you've loved the same person since you were six years old, you grow blinders to anyone else's charms.

So I do what any rational adult would do when faced with an uncomfortable situation they don't know how to handle: avoid it. I grab the contract and my coffee from the kitchen, then go upstairs and hide in my bedroom.

Five minutes later, my phone chimes with an incoming text.

In case you thought you were being stealthy,
I saw you sneaking off.

"Of course you did," I mutter, reading Theo's words. The man notices everything.

Just going over the contract.

After I hit Send, Theo immediately begins typing his response. When I see the three little dots on my phone indicating he's composing his answer, I start to chew my thumbnail in anxiety. Somehow, I know whatever he's going to say is going to make me feel worse.

That's the first time you've lied to me, Megan.

My stomach in knots, I flop onto my back on the bed and stare up at the ceiling. I hear Theo's guys walking around the house, their footsteps echoing hollowly, their voices muffled through the floor, and I wish I could hear *his* voice.

I wonder what it would sound like. Hard like his expression or soft like his eyes?

Aggravated with myself, I slap a hand over my eyes and sigh. *I really need to get out more. Maybe I should go on a date with Craig. Have a little dinner, have a nice conversation, listen to him talk. And talk.*

I don't have to ask myself how much of that time would be spent thinking about Theo Valentine, because I already know the answer.

My phone chimes.

I was walking on the beach.
I saw all the lights go on in the house,
saw you running around,
saw the smoke when you opened the window.

My heart thudding, I sit up and read his text again. Then I compose my own.

Walking on the beach at midnight?

I wait breathlessly for his answer, my palms starting to sweat. Outside, a screaming flock of seagulls swoops past the windows, and a cloud passes over the sun. A sudden gust of wind rattles the panes.

I don't sleep much. Bad dreams.

"Something else we have in common," I say thoughtfully, studying his words. On impulse, I decide to confess it.

Me too. Maybe I should take up walking.
Usually, I just toss and turn.

When he answers, my cheeks heat with embarrassment. That dark, dangerous attraction flickers to life in my blood.

I could tell by looking at your bed.

"Why *were* you looking at my bed like that?" I murmur, fighting my fingers for control. They itch to coax more from him, to write something provocative that would make him confess why he stared at my twisted sheets and blankets with such intensity, but my brain tells me in no uncertain terms that this particular slippery slope has a pool filled with man-eating sharks at the bottom.

Ultimately, my brain wins.

I'll bring the contract down in a few minutes.
I have to run some errands, so I'll be out for
the rest of the day. Text me if you need anything.

If I thought that would put the cap on the conversation, I was wrong. Theo dashes off a response that leaves me right back where I started, unsettled and questioning everything, burning to know more.

What I need can't be put into a text.

I close my eyes, filled with dread at the distinct possibility that the question of what exactly Theo Valentine needs will grow like a cancer in my mind until it consumes me.

14

---

*E*verything looks straightforward in Theo's contract, so I sign it and leave it on the small table in the foyer on my way out the door. It's a beautiful day, sunny but with big, puffy clouds floating in the sky like so many giant cotton balls. On a whim, I decide to head into Portland to hunt for furniture.

An hour and a half later, I'm standing on a street corner in the industrial part of the city, contemplating the pile of rubble that used to be Capstone Construction's headquarters.

Craig was right: it looks like a bomb went off. Or maybe a hurricane blew through and *then* a bomb went off. The destruction is total. Charred husks of a few brick walls are the only things that remain standing of the large structure. The blackened skeleton of the roof drapes over large piles of metal that I assume were some kind of machinery, but everything has been melted or burned to such a degree, it's impossible to identify what anything originally was.

One block over, the tall metal telecommunications spire atop a high-rise glints cheerfully in the morning sun.

What I know about lightning, I learned from the annual desert monsoons that came to Phoenix in July like clockwork, many of which featured violent lightning storms. I used to hate the deafening booms of thunder and the brilliant, jagged white bolts of light that split the black sky, but Cass loved it all, the wild majesty of it, the dangerous beauty.

Some artists are moved to depict the ugly and forgotten things in life, but Cass loved beauty in all its forms, the more unpredictable the better. He was an oil painter by trade, successful enough to support us while I finished my graduate degree, but he was also obsessed with photography. He loved to get out with a bunch of his storm-chaser buddies to hunt the perfect shot of a lightning strike, and many of those images decorated the walls of our home. Even the supercell thunderstorms of the Great Plains are no match for the drama found in the southwest desert storms.

So I'm no stranger to lightning. I know its unpredictability. I know its danger.

I also know its purpose.

Lightning wants to ground itself. It wants to terminate its powerful electrical discharge in a physical object, namely the earth. The reason lightning strikes tall objects like cell towers or a skyscraper more often than, say, a person lying down in a field, is because of what storm chasers call the degree of influence. Basically, the taller the object, the more it will attract lightning that's going to discharge in that area anyway.

For example, a metal spire atop a high-rise building has a far greater degree of influence than the flat roof of a one-story building a block away.

Yet here I am in front of that one-story building, which is utterly destroyed while the nearby high-rise stands untouched.

Kinda makes you wonder, doesn't it?

"No," I say aloud to that nagging voice in my head. "It doesn't."

Sure. That's why you're here. Because you're not wondering.

I mutter, "Shut up," and get back into my car.

Portland is a beautiful city, but the traffic sucks. I circle a trendy shopping area for twenty minutes, looking for a parking spot, until one opens up. Then I wander aimlessly through crowded streets lined with shops, hoping something of interest will jump out at me.

The only thing that jumps out at me is the growing list of odd happenings and strange coincidences that have occurred since I moved to Seaside.

I'm a list maker by long habit. My brain enjoys order, planning, and the sense of satisfaction that comes from checking things off a to-do list. But the series of events my mind stacks up one after another as evidence of a strange power at work leading me straight to Theo Valentine is anything but satisfying.

It's ridiculous. A total waste of time and energy.

And yet.

And yet you want to believe there's something more than the nothingness that swallowed you whole five years ago.

"Don't be a fool," I whisper, standing stock-still in front of a small art gallery.

In the window hangs a large, beautiful oil painting. It's a landscape, done in bold colors. Slashes of purple and indigo depict a mountain range in the background, its tips as serrated as the edge of a hunting knife. In the foreground, a dry riverbed is a stripe of dusty yellow meandering through an arroyo of shadowed green. Red flowers crown giant saguaros on a brown desert mesa that stretches far into the distance, leading the viewer's eye to the brilliant bursts of white cutting across the canvas from the thunderclouds over the mountains to the ground in a spiderweb of jagged, forked lines.

The piece is titled *Lucky Strike*, by an artist with the initials T.V.

I tell myself the title means nothing, the initials mean nothing, the painting itself means nothing, but the flesh of my arms has pimpled with goose bumps and my heart is up in my throat.

My phone chimes with an incoming text.

There's a shipment here for you. Should I sign for it?

It's Theo. I laugh, breathless, because of course it's him.

Yes, please. FedEx?

No, something called Craters and Freighters. It's big.

My laugh dies in my throat. I have to lean against the window of the gallery because my knees have suddenly gone weak.

Craters and Freighters is the company I hired to ship Cass's paintings from Phoenix. Part of the collection was in an art storage facility, but a few pieces were on display in the lobby of a local resort hotel. I'd made an agreement with the hotel that they could keep them through the end of the year, and then Craters and Freighters would pack up the whole collection and ship them to me in Seaside in January. By that time, the renovations on the Buttercup would be close to completion.

But now the paintings have arrived.

Three months early.

On the morning I've visited Capstone's headquarters, destroyed by an unusual lightning strike. At the exact moment I'm standing outside an art gallery, looking at a desert storm landscape exactly like the ones my late husband used to photograph, created by an artist with the initials T. fucking V.

At what point does a string of coincidences gather significance and add up to something more than chance?

I stuff my phone into my handbag and head back to my car. Suddenly, I can't wait to get home.

When I arrive, the guys are out on the back patio, eating their lunch. In addition to Coop and the ginger-haired Toby, Theo's brought two burly Latino guys who look like brothers, and one tall, wiry fellow with tattoos all the way up both arms. They all stop and look at me when I appear in the open doorway.

"Hi, guys."

Coop and Toby grin, the Latino guys nod respectfully, and the wiry guy waves, then immediately goes back to eating his sandwich.

Theo looks at me with slightly narrowed eyes. Like the others, he's sitting on an ancient Adirondack, but somehow, he manages to make it look like a throne.

Coop introduces the men I don't know, then asks, "You want a baloney sandwich? I've got an extra."

I haven't eaten yet, but I'm not hungry. My stomach is too twisted in ropes to handle food. "No, thanks. How's it going with the rewire?"

Coop shrugs. "Piece of cake. For us. Because we're awesome. Obviously."

That tugs a smile from my pinched lips. I glance at Theo. He's still staring at me with that assessing look, as if he knows there's something wrong. "Where's the delivery from Craters and Freighters?"

"Oh," says Coop, "we had 'em put it in the garage. We thought since it was empty in there, and the house was gonna be pretty jacked up with all the work—"

"The garage is perfect, thank you." I leave before he can say anything else, and hurry out to the garage, ignoring his startled look and Theo's relentless, studied observation of my face.

The garage is detached from the main part of the house. It's a newer structure, built within the last few decades to accommodate three cars. I enter through the side door and hit the light switch, and there it is, alone on the cement pad, a big pine crate about five feet tall and eight feet long, stamped with the words "Fragile" and "Handle with Care" on the sides.

I walk over to it and rest my shaking hands on the top edge.

Then I haul myself on top of it, lie down on my back, and close my eyes.

I'll call the company later to find out what the hell happened, but I need a moment to compose my thoughts. I need a moment to reconnect with these relics from my past.

It was a clerical error. Someone made a mistake, that's all. The schedules were switched, the hotel found other art they wanted to hang on their walls, there's a reasonable explanation for all of it. These coincidences don't mean anything, Megan. You're not thinking straight.

Nothing has anything to do with Theo.

I sense him there before I even open my eyes. He's a presence in the doorway, silent, but palpable nonetheless.

"Don't mind me. I'm just having a little nap."

Footsteps slowly approach. I turn my head and meet Theo's eyes. He's a foot above me, his expression bemused. He glances at the words on the side of the crate, then his dark eyes slash back to mine. His brows lift in inquiry.

I sigh and hide from his penetrating gaze by staring at the exposed wood beams on the ceiling. "It's stuff from my old house. I wasn't expecting it yet." My chuckle is low in my throat, full of dark humor. "The list of things I wasn't expecting is growing by leaps and bounds lately."

After a moment, Theo strokes a finger along the edge of the crate. From my peripheral vision, I can see that his expression has turned thoughtful. He wants to know what's inside.

I'm not going to tell him what's inside.

I'm being ridiculously superstitious, and I hate myself for it, but I can't handle any more weird coincidences. If I tell him the crate is full of oil paintings and he sends me a chipper text that reads, "Hey, I'm a painter too!" I'll have a heart attack and die on the spot.

"It's...um. Pottery."

Silence. Without moving my head, I slide my eyes sideways and look at Theo.

With exaggerated slowness, he mouths the word *Liar.*

I huff out a breath, sit up, cross my legs beneath me, and drag my hands through my hair. Propping my elbows on my knees, I drop my head into my hands and close my eyes again.

"Okay. Here's the truth: it's stuff I don't want to talk about. It's stuff that hurts me to think about, and it's gonna hurt even worse to look at." I swallow. My voice comes out thick. "It's my husband's things."

I hear him softly exhale. Then I hear the scratching noise of pen on paper, then a tearing sound. Then Theo gently nudges my elbow. I crack open an eye and see a small piece of notebook paper resting on my knee, with the words *I'm sorry* written on it.

"You don't have to be sorry. Not your circus. Not your monkeys. Don't worry about it."

He takes back the paper, scribbles something else on it, and sets it back on my knee. It reads, *Can I get you anything?*

When I look at him, he's visibly worried, his dark brows drawn together, his full lips turned down.

"A lobotomy? A nice case of amnesia? Some brainwashing, perhaps?"

He knows what I mean, but he shakes his head sharply in disagreement. I get a new note, this one scribbled furiously fast.

If the good memories outweigh the bad,
you shouldn't want to forget the past.

I read it, twice, then crush the piece of paper in my fist. Blinking back tears, I whisper, "I don't want to forget him. I want to forget who I am without him."

Then—impossibly, horribly—I'm crying.

Ugly crying, because I'm not one of those lucky women who

can weep into a handkerchief and make it look dainty. When I cry, it involves unattractive noises and great gasps of air like I'm drowning. It involves full-body shaking and snot.

A big, warm hand presses against the space between my shoulder blades. A steady, reassuring pressure, it stays until my tears slow and I'm glowing with embarrassment for breaking down in front of him. Then Theo takes his hand back, and I wipe my eyes with my fingertips and my nose with my sleeve.

Avoiding his eyes, I hop off the crate and look at my feet. My voice comes out sounding small and strangled. "Sorry about that. Anyway. I'm gonna go inside now."

Neither one of us moves. At his sides, Theo's hands are clenched. When I glance up at his face, it's strained. I think he's trying to hold himself back from taking me into his arms to comfort me, and I'm swamped by another wave of sadness.

My loneliness pounds so hard inside me, I'd probably have a total mental breakdown if he did.

A lone tear crests my lower lid and slides down my cheek. Watching it fall, Theo looks like he's been stabbed in the gut. I lift my hand to dash it away, but Theo reaches out and gently swipes his thumb over my cheekbone.

My entire body goes electric at his touch. I freeze, inhaling sharply. From one breath to the next, I become aware of his heat, how erratically his chest is rising and falling, the faint scent of soap on his skin. We stare at each other in crackling silence, my heart like a wild animal trying to claw its way out of my chest.

His hand trembles against my face. His eyes blaze with emotion. Lips parted, he leans toward me.

Off in the distance, one of the men calls his name, and the spell is broken as abruptly as it was cast.

Theo snatches his hand away, reddens, then spins on his heel, his jaw tight and his brows lowered. He stalks out of the garage, letting the door slam shut behind him.

15

For the rest of the day, Theo avoids me, and he makes it obvious. If I step into a room, he steps out. If I glance in his direction, he looks away. Whatever was about to happen between us in the garage, it's rattled him even more than it has me. He's gone back to scowls and thunderclouds, and once again, I'm at a loss.

Before the guys finish at five o'clock, Coop gives me an update on their progress. Then they leave, Theo first. I watch from the front window as he throws himself into his Mustang and roars off down the road at top speed as if he's competing in the Indy 500.

I've never had patience with mysteries. I loved math at school because of the concreteness of it, the absolute confidence you had that every single time, two plus two would equal four. There's beauty in that kind of unchanging, provable perfection.

So the pure inconsistency of this man and situation is driving me crazy.

Which is why I decide I've had enough of it. Things between us from now on will be strictly business. His problems aren't my concern, and my problems aren't his concern. It's not healthy for me to get caught up in whatever this is.

No matter how tempting this "whatever" is.

The next day, I ignore Theo completely. I go about my chores without glancing in his direction even once. By the time five o'clock rolls around, my shoulders are so tense from how hard I'm trying not to notice him that I've given myself a headache. When my cell phone rings, I answer distractedly, rubbing my forehead with my free hand.

"Hello?"

"Hey, there, Megan. It's Craig."

Shit. It's Wednesday. He's calling about the date. I haven't spent a moment considering what my answer would be since we talked on the phone on Monday.

"Hi, Craig. How are you?"

"I'll be better when you tell me what time I'm picking you up on Friday night."

I have to smile at that. "You sure do cut right to the chase, don't you?"

"I haven't thought about anything else since we talked. Say yes."

Now I laugh out loud, because he couldn't be more different from Theo if he tried. It's a relief not to have to break my brain wondering what a man is thinking. "Well, I don't know. I haven't made up my mind yet."

It's his turn to laugh. "Yes, you have, you're just being a woman."

"Oh, really? And here I thought I knew myself better than that. I guess my silly female brain has fooled me."

I was trying to be flirtatious, but because I'm utter crap at anything requiring feminine wiles, it comes out like an accusation. He backtracks so fast, I can almost hear tires squealing on pavement.

"Sorry, I wasn't saying you're silly. I was trying to be cute. It obviously didn't go over well."

Now I have to sigh, because at this rate, this phone call is doomed to leave both our egos in ruins. "No, don't apologize, *I* was trying to be cute and it didn't go over well. I need to stop pretending I'm good at witty repartee. Inevitably, it ends with me crawling under a table to hide because I've made a fool of myself."

The relief in Craig's voice is obvious. "So I haven't botched it."

"Not yet," I say warmly, which makes him laugh again.

"Oh, good. That makes me feel so much better."

Smiling, I walk from the kitchen to the front parlor, where I look out into the yard. The sound of hammering, footsteps, and the murmur of male voices drifts down from upstairs, where Coop and the guys are working on installing a new circuit box in a utility closet. I have no idea where Theo is, but I'm not paying attention to him anyway, so it doesn't matter.

"I visited your building the other day." The instant it leaves my mouth, I know how it sounds. Judging by the pleasure in Craig's response, he's thinking the same thing.

"You drove all the way to Portland to see my burned-out building?"

I close my eyes and shake my head, mentally kicking myself. "I, um, had some shopping to do, and...I found myself in that neighborhood."

Now Craig's laugh is delighted. He says teasingly, "You 'found' yourself in an industrial park? Hmm. You must need a new battery in your GPS."

I groan. "God, I sound like some kind of stalker. I promise it wasn't as creepy as it sounds."

"It doesn't sound creepy at all to me. I think it's sweet. In fact, I think you should just admit that you think I'm devastatingly handsome and charming so we can go on our first date."

I was wrong. There's no way his ego is going to be affected no matter how lame my repartee might be. You could drive a tank over this guy's ego and it would pop right back up without a scratch.

"Our *first* date?" I shoot back. "You're assuming we'll have more than one?"

"Oh yeah," he says, all confidence. "You're gonna fall in love with me over dinner and insist I take you out again. By this time next year, we'll be picking out our wedding invitations."

My mouth falls open. Then, struck by the sheer size of his nerve, I break into laughter.

Craig pounces on my amusement like a lion on his dinner. "Or maybe you're in love with me already!"

"You're nuts," I say between gasps. "Seriously nuts!"

"And you're completely infatuated with me. It's the hair, isn't it? It's my thick, glorious head of hair. Go on, admit it. I'll wait."

I'm laughing so hard, my sides hurt. I can't remember the last time I laughed this hard, but Craig and his supersized ego are reminding me how.

"Yes, Craig. *Obviously* I'm infatuated with you because of your magnificent hair. No woman alive could resist."

"Aha!" he crows, victorious. "You said magnificent!"

"I was just repeating what you said."

"No, *I* said glorious. *You* came up with a completely different adjective that had an entire additional syllable. Case closed. You're madly in love with me. What time should I pick you up Friday?"

"Wow. Are you always like this?"

"Funny, charming, and dazzlingly sexy? Yes. Yes, I am."

My eye roll is so extravagant, I might've popped something in my brain. Still chuckling, I relent. "Okay, Craig, you're on. Dinner on Friday. Pick me up at six. And don't make me regret this, I haven't been on a date in a hundred years."

His voice drops a notch. "I promise I won't ever make you regret anything where I'm concerned, Megan. See you at six."

He disconnects before I can say anything else.

I shake my head in disbelief, muttering, "Well, this should be interesting."

When I turn around, Theo is standing still in the hallway, staring at the floor.

"Oh," I say, startled to see him standing there. "Um...did you need me for something?"

Without looking at me, he pulls his cell phone from his pocket and types something into the keyboard. It comes through on my phone with a chime.

We're done for the day.

"Oh, great. Okay. Anything I need to know?"

Theo lifts his head and looks at me. Really looks at me, his eyes searching my face. Slowly, he shakes his head *no*.

Something in his gaze elicits a powerful urge in me to run to him and throw my arms around his shoulders. The feeling is so strong, I have to physically restrain myself from moving my feet.

I know he overheard my call with Craig. How much he heard, I'm not sure, but judging by the expression on his face, he's feeling some kind of way about it. Some *major* kind of way.

I whisper, "I guess I'll see you tomorrow, then."

He doesn't acknowledge I've spoken. He simply stares at me for a beat, then turns abruptly and disappears down the hallway, his boots thumping loudly against the wood floor.

I blow out a breath and press my hand over my heart. That does nothing to stop its frantic fluttering.

My insomnia that night is worse than usual. Despite my decision to keep things pure business between Theo and me, my mind runs on a hamster wheel, going over and over every look, text, and email that has passed between us, furiously trying to read between the lines of all that he doesn't say.

Considering he's mute, that's a lot.

At midnight, I give up and rise from bed. I go stand at the patio windows and stare out at the ocean, which is as black as the sky. Neither has any answers for the questions swirling in my head. I close my eyes and rest my forehead against the cold glass.

Cass. I wish you were here. I miss you. I love you. I still love you so goddamn much.

When I open my eyes, a figure has appeared out on the beach, standing in the darkness.

My heart hammering, I jerk back a step from the window. I can barely see the person because it's so dark, but moonlight sifts between the clouds overhead, casting a ghostly glow on him, crowning his dark head in a halo of white. Whoever it is stands unmoving, hands by his sides, legs spread apart, staring up at the house. I move back to the window and flatten my hand against the glass.

I whisper, "Theo?"

The figure takes a single step forward.

All the tiny hairs on my body stand on end. My hands tremble, and I start to panic.

There's no way on earth he could've heard me speak, yet, irrationally, I'm convinced he somehow knew his name left my lips, the way you sometimes feel a tug of recognition when you pass someone you've never met on the street. You know you've never seen them before, yet something tells you they're not a total stranger. Something in their eyes sparks a sense of déjà vu.

Like maybe you met in another life.

"You don't believe in kismet, Megan. You don't believe in ghosts or fate or the tarot or any of that other nonsense. You're a rational, intelligent person. You know he didn't *feel* you call his name."

Really? Try it again and see what happens.

I mutter, "Keep pestering me, you idiotic little voice, and I'll take a drill to my skull to shut you up."

Sounds like something a crazy person would do. Might as well test my theory if you're already nuts anyway.

I curse and turn away from the window. Groaning in exasperation, I start to pace the length of the room, my hands clasped together on top of my head so they don't pick up the nearest object and throw it at the wall.

"I won't say his name again. I *won't*."

Chicken.

"Fuck you, voice. Just fuck you. I've had enough of your bullshit. This is real life, not fantasyland."

So prove it and say his name again. Prove he took a step at the exact moment you said his name due purely to chance. Let's see how that theory tests out for you.

"I'm talking to myself!" I shout at nothing in particular. "It's finally happened! I've lost my mind! Might as well go adopt a few dozen cats and start wearing my underwear over my clothes!"

Or you could just go to the window, say his name, and deal with whatever happens next.

"No."

Maybe he was being literal when he wrote "I'll always be here?" Maybe he's done with wandering all through the town at night and has decided to camp out on the beach in front of the Buttercup? And by the way, wasn't it interesting how when you called Craters and Freighters to find out why Cass's paintings were delivered so early, they claimed their paperwork had yesterday's delivery date on it all along? That YOU gave them that date when you signed the contract?

Are you seriously telling me you think THAT was another random coinkydink?

I grab fistfuls of my hair and make a noise like I've been punched in the stomach. "Coincidences don't mean anything! They're just coincidental!"

Go to the window and prove it.

I let loose a string of expletives that would have my mother's hair curling. Then I stalk over to the window and glare out the glass.

He's still standing right where he was.

"Theo," I say flatly.

He takes another step forward.

I scream like I've seen a ghost and stumble back, almost falling in my haste.

Rationalize that, Megan. No amount of logic in the world can explain your connection with Theo Valentine.

"We don't have a connection," I whisper, hyperventilating and starting to sweat. "We're complete strangers. He's just a guy I hired to work on my house."

Who's standing outside at midnight, taking one step toward you every time you say his name. Denial isn't a good color on you. Stop being such a coward and deal with it.

Racked with tremors, I walk slowly back to the glass. He waits, motionless, staring up at the window, his features obscured in the shadows. I open the glass door, step out onto the patio, and grip the wood railing. The night wind catches my hair and swirls it all around my face. With my heart throbbing and my legs shaking, I stare right at him, focusing all my attention on the word I form in my mind.

Theo.

He bows his head. He starts to shake it back and forth, covering his ears with his hands. Then he turns and runs off down the beach. In a few moments, he's swallowed by darkness.

My legs like rubber, I sink to my knees on the balcony and stare down the beach at the place he disappeared until my vision is so blurred, I can no longer see.

16

When I can stand again, I go inside, my limbs numb with shock. I can't sleep, so I pace the floors of the Buttercup, spending long hours in a dark place inside my head.

By the time the sun rises, my brain is spaghetti.

I shower and dress, eat a muffin for breakfast, make myself a cup of coffee, and read the paper. I do all that on autopilot, with minimal awareness. All the other parts of my operating system are tied up in thoughts of a man who makes no sense to me, and the improbability of the situation I've found myself in.

It. Does. Not. Compute.

When Coop and the guys arrive at 8:00 a.m., Theo isn't with them.

"Said he wasn't feelin' well," explains Coop with an apologetic shrug.

That makes two of us. I feel spooked, relieved, and disappointed, all at once.

"We should've finished up this afternoon, but without Theo, it might take another day."

"Take your time," I answer, already turning away.

I grab my laptop and phone and head upstairs to the master

bedroom. I shut the door, sit on the floor with my back against the bed so I can see the ocean, and fire up the computer. Then I send Theo an email, because I only have two options to deal with this situation: avoidance and denial, or tackling it head-on.

Though I'm scared to death, tackling it head-on seems like the better choice.

So here goes nothing.

To: Theo@hillrise.com
From: Bowie4Evah@yahoo.com
Subject: I'm confused

Here's a bit of radical honesty for you: I'm confused as fuck.

I know that was you on the beach. Another strange midnight visit from my silent friend. Enemy? Frenemy? What is this? What's happening?

Am I making things up in my head?

Tell me something true or tell me to go to hell, but communicate with me, Theo. I feel like I might be going crazy.

Please tell me I'm not.

After I hit Send, I wait with a sick feeling in the pit of my stomach. I feel hungover and strung out, as if I've spent the last week drinking wine for every meal. When he doesn't answer right away, I stand and begin to pace.

After thirty minutes, a chime tells me I have an incoming email. I'm so nervous, the muffin I ate for breakfast almost makes a reappearance, but I manage to swallow it down and click open the email with trembling hands.

To: Bowie4Evah@yahoo.com
From: Theo@hillrise.com
Subject: Re: I'm confused

I apologize for not being able to come to the job today. I'm not feeling well. I'll be back tomorrow to finish things up.

Best,

Theo

The job?

"Oh, it's like that, is it?" I mutter, angered by his impersonal response.

This bastard thinks he can prance around outside my house in the middle of the night, kick down my front door, walk out on me in a restaurant, glare bloody murder at me every other time our eyes meet, act like a psychopath one minute and a lost puppy the next, tell me I make all his broken parts bleed, and generally make me feel like I'm starring in a bad soap opera, then brush me off like nothing ever happened?

So not gonna happen.

To: Theo@hillrise.com
From: Bowie4Evah@yahoo.com
Subject: Give me a break

I'm calling bullshit on your lame excuse for not showing up today. You feel fine, and we both know it.

For future reference, I hate being patronized. Have the balls to tell me what's up or don't bother coming back. Coop is perfectly capable of finishing the job without you.

To: Bowie4Evah@yahoo.com
From: Theo@hillrise.com
Subject: Re: Give me a break

I'll let Coop know you prefer that he handle things from here on out.

Not even thirty seconds passed before his response came through. Now I'm not just mad. I'm steaming.

I send a single word back to him:

COWARD.

Then I close my laptop and go about my day, telling myself that the next time Theo Valentine shows up outside my house in the middle of the night, I'll call the cops.

I almost believe it.

∼

"This here's the smart home central controller that you can program all your devices and home electronics into," Coop says, pointing to the small digital tablet installed on the wall inside the kitchen door. There are four more of these controllers in various rooms in the house, I'm told, that can do everything from turn on the heat and lights to send an alarm to my cell phone if the security system—not yet installed—is breached.

"Once you buy your new appliances, we'll come out and take care of the programming for you." Coop grins. "At no additional charge, of course. In the meantime, your cell phone is now hooked up to the system, so you can turn on the lights and open the garage door from the car on your way home, among other things."

Impressed, I scan the interface screen. There are boxes for the garage door, lighting, A/C, appliances, and audio and security systems. "What if I get a voice-command device like Alexa?"

"No problem. It'll integrate with the system seamlessly. All you have to do is say your command, like 'Alexa, turn on the master bedroom lights,' and you're good to go."

"Wow. This is fantastic, Coop, but I didn't see this in the quote. How much extra is all this?"

Coop slow-blinks. "Nothing. It's included. Theo wanted you to have the best, so...you do."

Theo—who faked an illness to avoid seeing me—wanted me to have the best. And didn't charge me for it. I suppose that makes about as much sense as anything else.

The smile I give Coop is brittle. "All righty, then. Pleasure doing business with you, Coop. Hang on a second, I'll write you a check." I head upstairs to get my checkbook from my bag.

It's Friday afternoon, the guys are done with the rewiring project, and I've got an hour until Superego Craig picks me up for dinner. I've been ruthless with myself and haven't allowed my mind to linger in Theoland even for one minute, keeping busy with interviewing interior designers and researching their websites for inspiration. Because I felt awkward going out with Craig without telling Suzanne, I called her this morning to let her know.

"Oh, for God's sake," she'd said, sighing. "I should've known. The only guys who are ever interested in me are either married, mama's boys, or in prison."

I didn't ask for details.

We hung up after she failed to finagle a promise from me that I'd call her with every dirty detail in the morning. Vicarious sex was better than no sex, she'd said, to which I'd responded that no sex would be had tonight. Period.

To which she'd responded that I'm dumber than I look.

I pay Coop, the guys leave, then I hit the shower. My wardrobe is lacking in date-night ensembles, so I wear the same dress I wore to dinner at Booger's with Suzanne. Craig's already seen me in it, but it's the only one I own. I dress it up with heels and a pretty scarf, swipe on a few coats of mascara, dab a drop of organic vanilla oil behind each of my ears, and call it a day.

Frankly, if the night doesn't end in tears, I'll consider it a success.

When Craig pulls up at the curb in an expensive-looking silver sports car, I pretend like I wasn't watching from the front window and hustle into the kitchen so he can't see me as he walks up the path to the front door. After a minute, the doorbell rings. Though I know no one's listening, I say a little prayer, asking for strength to get me through the evening.

I open the door to find Craig standing there, grinning like the Cheshire Cat. I'm surprised to see him in black dress slacks and a stylish wool blazer. He looks like he's going on a job interview. In a way, I suppose he is.

He looks me up and down and whistles low. "You sure know how to wear that dress, Megan."

"You're not half-bad yourself."

"I'm glad you think so. I spent two hours fussing in front of the mirror before driving over here."

I have a sneaking suspicion he spends hours in front of the mirror whether he has a date or not, but I smile at him pleasantly, admiring the sheen of his freshly shaven jaw and his golden hair, which probably took a lot of coaxing to achieve that artfully tousled effect.

The man could teach me a thing or two about personal grooming. If I'm not mistaken, he even gets his eyebrows waxed. Those arches of his are suspiciously perfect.

"Are you ready to go?"

I nod, happy he didn't ask to come inside, and turn the bolt on the new door lock Theo installed. He did it without me asking, a small kindness I'm grateful for.

And am not thinking about because he's banned from my mind.

Great. Not even two minutes with Craig and already your thoughts are wandering back toward He Who Shall Not Be Named.

I turn back to Craig with a big, fake smile, already knowing the night is going to be a disaster.

Craig takes me to what is probably the best restaurant in the area. It's one town south of Seaside and obviously expensive, with waiters in tuxedos gliding around silently and a pianist discreetly playing a baby grand on one side of the dining room. We're seated at a candlelit table by a window with a view of the ocean, while I try not to be overly disturbed by Craig's taste in music, which I was introduced to on the drive over.

He likes polka. *Polka*, for the love of all that's holy.

Other than that extreme failing—and a tendency to dominate the conversation, which I already knew—he has lovely manners and is easy to be around. He's smart, polite, engaging, and funny. Not to mention well dressed and sophisticated. He's the kind of man every woman's mother would love to have as a son-in-law.

"Why are you smiling like that?" he asks after a hostess brings us menus.

"Like what?"

He tilts his head, examining me. "Like you've got a secret."

I laugh. "I was just wondering how you're still single."

He leans back in his chair, smiling, obviously pleased. "So you think I'm a catch."

I don't want his ego getting any larger than it already is, so I shrug, because I'm nice like that. My nonchalance makes him throw his head back and laugh.

"You're a tough nut to crack, you know that, Megan?"

"I've never had a man call me a nut before, so no. I didn't know that. But...thank you?"

"Just an observation, not a compliment, but if you want a compliment, I've got about a dozen of them ready to go."

I lift my brows. "You prefabricate compliments to pay to women? I feel so special."

Craig's eyes grow warm. He murmurs, "Not for women in general. For you. I won't admit exactly how much time I've spent thinking about you, but it's a lot."

My cheeks heat. I glance down at the white linen napkin on my lap, flustered by the look in his eyes, which is frankly sexual. "You're very good at this."

"What?"

I glance back up at him. He's leaning over the table now, eagerly listening.

"Flirting."

His lips cant up. He blinks like a debutante, coy as sin. "Am I?"

"Yes. You are. But you already knew that."

"And you're very good at being alluringly mysterious and hard to read."

That makes me laugh out loud. "Mysterious? Hardly. I'm an open book compared to some." *Like Theo Valentine, for instance.*

I tuck a stray lock of hair behind my left ear, silently cursing myself for thinking about Theo. It's like he's taken up residence in my head and is just lounging around in there, waiting for random opportunities to shout, *Hey, think about me!*

Craig watches the motion of my hand with a contemplative look, then meets my eyes. "Okay, since you're an open book, may I ask a personal question?"

I have a bad feeling about this, but nod anyway.

"You told me during our first conversation when you called for a quote that you moved here because your husband had passed away. How long ago was that?"

A pit forms in my stomach. I swallow, moistening my lips. "Five years."

Craig asks gently, "Why are you still wearing your wedding ring after five years?"

I hide my hand in my lap and curl my thumb into my palm, twisting the plain gold circle around my finger. I feel exposed and vulnerable. My heart is caught in my throat. "The answer to that probably isn't something a man on a first date would like to hear."

Now he's really interested. His eyes glow with intensity. "I do want to hear it. Please."

I take a breath, hoping my voice comes out steady. "I don't take it off because I still feel married. I *am* still married. My husband just happens to be dead."

After a beat, Craig leans back in his chair, crosses one long leg over the other, folds his hands in his lap, and looks at me until I'm squirming with embarrassment.

"I told you you wouldn't want to hear it."

"I'm glad you told me, though. But it begs another question."

I have to swallow a groan. "Which is?"

"If you really feel that way, why are you having dinner with me?"

I think about that long and hard. I can't find an answer that won't sound either pathetic or like I'm using him for a free meal, so I tell him the truth. "Because you make it impossible to say no."

He winces. "God, you make me sound like a sexual predator."

I blow out a breath that turns into a laugh. "That came out wrong. What I meant was that you're charming."

He cocks a brow, waiting for more. Obviously, he's not satisfied by my half-hearted attempt to salvage the conversation, but I'm rusty as hell at this, and not in the mood to massage his ego.

I level him with a look. "Craig, you know you're handsome. Half the women in this restaurant gave themselves whiplash watching you as we walked to our table."

He smiles serenely. "Go on."

Unbelievable. "And you're funny. And smart. And a lot of other nice things I'm not going to list because you're already too big for your britches."

His chuckle is one of a man oozing self-confidence, who loves to hear other people tell him how great he is so they can be in agreement. I find it incredibly grating.

Self-confidence is one thing. Arrogance is another. Time to take him down a notch.

"So what's happening with your company? Any news about the lawsuit?"

If I thought that would put a dent in his ego, I was wrong. He waves my question off like you'd wave off an irritating fly and gets right back down to business.

"My attorneys are handling everything. It'll work itself out. Let's get back to you and why you really came on this date with me."

I briefly close my eyes, wishing for a stray asteroid to smash through the ceiling and kill me. "I just told you why."

He leans across the table and grabs my hand. It's so sudden, I yelp. And why are his hands so cold? The man has the flesh temperature of a corpse!

"Megan, I like you. I haven't been this attracted to a woman in years. Maybe ever."

My mouth drops open. All I come up with is a startled "Uh..."

He squeezes my hand so hard, I can already feel the bruises forming. "And I just want you to know that I get it."

He stares at me intently. I realize I'm required to respond, but I have no idea what he's talking about. "Get, um, what?"

He lowers his voice and leans closer. "That no one can replace your late husband. Obviously, he has a special place in your heart. But I really hope you'll give me a chance. I want to get to know you better." His gaze drifts down to the neckline of my dress, and his voice goes gravelly. "I booked a hotel in town so I wouldn't have to drive back to Portland tonight. After dinner, we should go have a drink in my room."

Ah. So here it is.

He wants to play hide the sausage with me.

The sooner the better, judging by the way he's licking his lips as he stares at my boobs. We haven't even ordered our entrées yet!

Smiling tightly, I withdraw my hand from his icy clutches. "If you'll please excuse me, I have to visit the ladies' room."

I don't wait for an answer. I simply rise from the table, taking my handbag with me, and turn my back and walk away.

I maintain my cool until I get inside the restroom. It's decorated in soothing shades of beige and white and has fresh flowers on the counter. It's also empty, so I'm free to toss my handbag onto the velvet divan against the wall and curse out loud.

I try not to think the worst of Craig. He's a man, after all. They have needs. And we're both single. He's not doing anything wrong by making his intentions clear. It just felt so...calculated. So *shallow*.

So unlike everything I see in Theo Valentine's eyes.

"Oh, for God's sake, Megan," I mutter, disgusted with myself. "Cut it out."

I wash my hands in the sink, then slowly dry them, buying time because I don't have to use the toilet but I'm not quite mentally prepared yet to face Craig's no-nonsense approach to dating. I don't understand why he didn't ask Suzanne out. He could've bypassed dinner altogether and driven straight to his hotel!

Then I remember he called her "obvious," and me "mysterious," and get it.

Craig likes a challenge.

And for a man who likes a challenge, first-date sex in a hotel room with a tough-negotiating, flirting-handicapped smartass who's still wearing her wedding ring after five years of widowhood is probably some kind of Olympic-level game.

I'm Mt. Everest, and he's a climber with an eye to ascending the summit.

Enough stupid metaphors, Megan. What are you going to do?

"Just turn the conversation to something else. Get him talking about himself. That shouldn't be hard."

Dammit. I'm answering the voice in my head again.

Good thing I'm a great listener.

It's official: I'm driving myself insane.

With a huff of aggravation, I snatch my handbag from the velvet divan, spin on my heel, and storm out the door of the ladies' room.

Where I crash straight into Theo Valentine, on his way out of the men's.

17

I collide with Theo, and my breath leaves my chest in an audible grunt. I drop my handbag and stumble back, teetering in my heels. He grabs me by the arms before I can fall and pulls me against his body.

His big, hard, warm body.

Breathless, I stare up at him, overwhelmed by the sheer physical pleasure of being so close. Every detail of him leaps out at me, burning a sensation into my brain: his face, his scent, the pulse pounding hard in his neck. His strong hands gripped around my biceps. The throbbing of his heart against my breasts.

A shaky exhalation passes my lips, but otherwise, I'm incapable of speech.

Every slumbering cell in my body has woken up and started screaming.

He drags in a breath, nostrils flaring. I can't tell if he's furious, shocked, or aroused, because no man has ever looked at me with this particular expression.

Then he carefully sets me away from him and steps back.

He's wearing his usual faded jeans, boots, and leather jacket. His black hair is its normal windblown mess. He's got a three-day growth of beard on his jaw, a glower darker than midnight on his face, and the wild intensity of a thousand suns blazing in his eyes.

He's so beautiful, I have to put my hand against the wall for balance.

He rakes his gaze over me, head to foot. It might as well be his hands for the effect it has. I start to shake. My mouth goes dry. My skin comes alive with electricity. I wouldn't be surprised if my hair stood on end in a corona around my head.

I finally gather enough of my wits to speak. "What're you doing here?"

Without looking away from me, he jerks his head toward the bar.

He can't have known I was coming here with Craig. *I* didn't even know where Craig was taking me. So unless he followed us here, running into him like this is another damn coincidence.

Theo jerks his chin at me, like *What about you?*

"I'm having dinner with Craig Kennedy."

The curl of his upper lip is subtle but unmistakable. It has the unexpected effect of pissing me off.

I shove away from the wall and grab my purse from the floor. When I straighten, I blast Theo with a glare. "Oh, the guy who faked being sick to avoid me doesn't like that I'm on a date? That's classic. You were right, Theo. You *are* fucked up."

I try to brush past him and go back to the table, but before I can take three steps, he grabs me by the arms and spins me around. He pushes me against the wall in the small corridor where the restrooms are set apart from the restaurant, so we're blocked from view by a duo of large potted palms.

The length of his torso presses against mine, crotch to chest. He holds me there against the wall and stares down at me. When he drops his gaze to my mouth, a tremor runs through his chest. He exhales a low noise, like a groan, only softer.

My heart thuds so fast, I feel faint. If a person could spontaneously combust, I would.

I whisper his name. He winces, as if hearing the word leave my lips is painful. With an expression like he would stop himself if only he could, he drops his head to my neck and inhales deeply against my throat.

On instinct—like a cat when it's stroked down its back—I arch into him, purring.

He exhales in a soft gust. His warm breath fans down my neck. A delicate shudder runs through his entire body. The faintest brush of his lips against my skin leaves me gasping.

I.

Am.

On.

Fire.

He raises his head and stares down into my eyes. I see yearning and anguish and that bottomless darkness in his eyes, and something in my chest feels like it's melting.

"Why do I hurt you?" I whisper urgently, searching his eyes. "Why do I feel like I know you? Why are you everywhere, even though all you want to do is avoid me?"

He puts his fingers over my lips to silence me. It's a reflex, because he blinks when he realizes he's done it, his brows drawing together in surprise. Then it's as if he can't look away from his fingers touching my mouth. He stares, fascinated, as he slowly traces the bow of my upper lip with his trembling forefinger.

I couldn't move even if I wanted to. I close my eyes and stand there, feeling every beat of my heart on a cellular level, unsure if I'm going to faint or laugh or cry.

I want him to kiss me so much, it's a firestorm in my blood.

My voice comes out low and raw. "If you won't answer me, I need you to stay away from me. Do you understand? I can't...this is...it's too much."

I open my eyes and gaze up at him. He's frozen, staring back at me with tortured eyes.

"I'm strong because I've had to be, but you make me feel like I might be losing my mind. You make me...*feel*. Things. All these goddamn *things* that I don't know what to do with, okay? I can't deal with this, Theo, all this..."

Getting choked up, I struggle for a word. "*Emotion*. Being around you is like being lit on fire and thrown out of a plane and surviving the hard fall to earth, only to realize I've landed in a village of cannibals. And it's dinnertime!"

I break away from him and stumble around the potted palms, angrily swatting their spidery fronds from my face. I hurry back to the table, arriving just as the waiter does. Craig takes one look at my expression and knows something's wrong.

"Megan?"

"I'm fine." I drop into my chair, grab the menu, and pretend to look it over, but all I can see is a certain person's face staring back at me. That face with its slightly crooked nose and scars, even more appealing because of its flaws.

"Good evening." The waiter bows. "I'm Michael, and I'll be serving you tonight. Have you had a chance to review the menu?"

Craig takes charge, earning my gratitude. I doubt if I could hold up my end of a conversation at the moment. My body is still set to Theo Thermonuclear mode.

"Good evening. We're still deciding on our entrées, but may we please have a bottle of the Sea Smoke pinot noir to start, along with the crab cake appetizer?"

"Very good, sir. I'll bring the wine out straight away."

He walks off, leaving me alone with Craig, who is looking at me intently over the top of my menu.

"I'm sorry," he says.

Startled, I glance up at him. "For what?"

"For upsetting you."

I retort, "For propositioning me, you mean."

"No," he says, holding my gaze. "I'm not sorry for that. Only that it made you uncomfortable."

Blood floods my face. I look to the menu for help, but Craig isn't letting me off the hook so easily.

"I haven't been on a real date in a long time."

I snort like a farm animal.

"I'm being serious, Megan. For the past ten years, all my attention has been on building my business."

I ask tartly, "Are you trying to tell me you've been celibate for a decade?"

"I'm trying to tell you that the women I've been with are like your friend Suzanne. Easily available. No strings attached. That worked great for me because I wasn't interested in anything long-term. Lately, I've been rethinking that."

His gaze is serious but sincere. Now I'm even more flustered. Uncertain how to respond, I fiddle with my fork.

"Here's my point, then we'll drop it because, judging by the color of your cheeks, you're not enjoying the conversation." He pauses briefly. "I'm shit at taking things slow. I'm shit at being patient. I don't like to waste time. I'm not into playing games. I'm blunt, but I'm also real. You'll always know where you stand with me, I can promise you that. And right now, I can tell you with all honesty that you're the most interesting woman I've met in years. I'm extremely attracted to you, and I think you're attracted to me too, but you're not ready to act on it.

"So we'll take it slow. We'll get to know each other. You'll tell me when I'm being overbearing, and I'll respect your boundaries. But while we're doing all that, I might occasionally slip up and do or say something you'll find offensive, and you're going to have to call me out on it because it's been a long time since I've wanted anything serious with a woman. I don't want to fuck it up."

I stare at him openmouthed. After a few moments, I gather myself enough to speak. "I'm flattered. Honestly. And I appreciate you being so blunt." I laugh a small, uncomfortable laugh. "Though I have to admit, it takes some getting used to."

Craig lifts a shoulder. "I like to put all the cards on the table up front."

Unlike some other men I know. "I can see that," I murmur, wondering what kind of cosmic joke is being played on me.

On one hand, I've got an über-assertive alpha male with a solid-steel ego handing me his feelings on a silver platter. On the other, I've got a mute recluse with an attitude as unstable as his mental health who'd rather have all his teeth pulled out than tell me anything.

This shouldn't be such a surprise. My life stopped making sense years ago.

When a mild tingle runs down my spine, I glance over at the bar. Theo, hands flattened over the bar top and elbows locked, stares back at me. His gaze shifts to Craig. And stays there.

And hardens.

"You're not saying anything," observes Craig.

"Oh, sorry, I'm just..." I take a steadying breath, then meet Craig's eyes. "Since we're being so honest, I need to tell you a few things too."

Craig leans toward me, his eyes intent. "Okay. Shoot."

"Do you see that man at the bar?"

Craig frowns and looks to his right. "Which one?"

"Black hair. Black jacket. Black clouds churning overhead."

"Oh. Valentine."

I blink, surprised he recognizes Theo. "You know him?"

Craig shrugs. "I know *of* him. We've bid on some of the same jobs. I've seen him lurking around a few builders' conferences. He has a reputation for being an odd bird. What about him?"

"He bid on the restoration of my house too."

"Are you hiring him?"

"I had his team do the electrical wiring after the fire—"

"Fire?" repeats Craig loudly. "What fire?"

I wave my hand in the air. "Long story. No one was hurt. My

point is..." I take another deep breath. "I think there might be something going on between us."

Craig lifts his brows. "You *think*? Are you saying you're dating him?"

"No. I'm not dating him. In fact, I'm convinced he doesn't like me at all."

He squints at me as if to see me better. "I don't understand. How could there be something going on between you if he doesn't like you and you're not dating him?"

I sigh, because out loud, it sounds as ridiculous as it is. "Believe me, I don't understand it either. But...just look at him. Look at the way he's looking at you. How would you describe it?"

Craig slices his gaze back toward the bar. After a few beats, he says mildly, "I'd say he wants to rip off my fucking head."

"Exactly."

After a moment, Craig quirks his lips. Then he glances back at me, his eyes sparkling. "Good."

"Good? Did you just say *good*?"

"I did."

"Okay, now *I'm* confused."

"It's a guy thing. Never mind. The more important issue is how serious this 'thing' is that you feel is going on between you. In other words, if he and I are in a race for your attention, who's ahead?"

I lean back into my chair and stare at him. "My God. You're unflappable."

Craig breaks into a grin. "Thank you. It's one of my better qualities. Answer the question."

My expression sours. "You're also bossy."

"Not one of my better qualities. *Please* answer the question."

"There's no race." I try not to look toward the bar to see what Theo's doing, though I can tell by the pinpricks of electricity running up and down my arms that he's shifted his gaze from Craig back to me. "Like I said, I don't think he likes me."

"But?" Craig prompts when I'm silent too long.

"But...I think..." I stare at the tablecloth, struggling for an explanation that makes any kind of sense. "He's drawn to me. And to the Buttercup. And he doesn't want to be."

When I glance back at Craig, he's gazing at me with a contemplative look, his head tilted to one side.

"I heard he was in an accident."

I nod, chewing my lip.

"Do you think he's dangerous? Mentally unstable?"

"No," I reply firmly, but I'm only answering the first question. He's *definitely* unstable, but that's not something I'd tell Craig. Don't ask me why, but some secrets of Theo's I'll always keep.

More softly, Craig asks, "Do you think it's possible that he's targeting you?"

The question startles me. "Targeting me for what?"

Still in that quiet voice, his gaze steady on mine, Craig says, "You're a young, beautiful widow. Alone, in a new town, apparently with some financial means if you were able to afford the Buttercup Inn. The list of what someone like him might target you for is long."

I don't like the way Craig says *someone like him*, but I'm the one who started this line of conversation. I can't back out now. "No, I don't believe he's targeting me for anything. Frankly, I think he'd be happier if I moved away and never came back."

Craig looks doubtful. "Right. He hates you so much, he's going insane with jealousy over there by the ice sculpture. C'mon, Megan. If someone gave him a baseball bat, he'd already be swinging it at my head."

"How can you be so calm about that?" His smile is smug, and I have my answer. "Of course. Because you're used to other men being jealous of you."

He chuckles. "You say that like it's a character defect."

I prop my elbows on the table and drop my face into my

hands. "I'm sorry, my brain is going on vacation now. You'll have to talk to my napkin instead."

"I have an idea."

I groan. "I can hardly wait."

"Let's go talk to him and find out what the problem is."

Horrified, I snap my head up and stare at Craig. "*No.*"

He grips the arms of his chair and rises a few inches from his seat. "Are you *sure*?"

I hiss, "Sit *down*, Craig, before I take my dinner knife to your testicles!"

At the bar, Theo straightens, livid at Craig for upsetting me, though he doesn't even know why I'm upset. I wonder where I went wrong in life to wind up here, now, dealing with this.

"Easy, tiger," says Craig, laughing. "I'd like to keep my balls, if you don't mind. If things go the way I hope they will, we're gonna need them."

Then he leans across the table, takes my face in his hands, and kisses me.

Gasping in shock, I pull away just in time to catch sight of Theo striding out from behind the bar, brows lowered, lips flattened, a five-alarm fire burning hell blazes in his eyes.

He heads straight for our table with Craig in the crosshairs of his murderous sights.

18

*P*anicked, I leap from my chair and watch Theo approach. Craig realizes where my attention has gone and straightens to his full, formidable height as he turns to face Theo. The waiter arrives with our wine just as Theo arrives at our table, then the world's most uncomfortable pissing contest begins.

Eye to eye, chest to chest, Theo and Craig face each other. By chance, they stand exactly the same height, but that's where any resemblance ends. In every other way possible, the two men are opposites. They're night and day: one dark, one light; one rough, one polished; one a deep ocean of secrets, the other matter-of-factly wearing his heart on his sleeve.

One who never speaks. One who never shuts up, even when he should.

The waiter looks at me, looks at the two bristling males, then turns around and leaves without a word. Whispers rise from tables all around us.

In a tight voice, Craig says, "Whatever your problem is, friend, it's about to get a lot worse."

At his sides, Theo's hands curl to fists. He slashes his gaze to me, and in his eyes, I see entire universes burning.

Moving slowly, holding Theo's fierce gaze, I move closer to him and flatten my hand on his broad chest. His heart is like a drum under my palm. I say softly, "Theo, I'm okay."

A low growl rumbles through his chest. He glares accusingly at Craig.

"Yes, he made me mad and he kissed me without my permission. I appreciate that you're being protective, but I'm a big girl. I can handle it."

Theo's left eyelid twitches. I swear if it weren't for my hand on Theo's chest, Craig would already be a pile of broken bones on the polished wood floor.

Craig says snidely, "What's the matter, Valentine? Cat got your tongue?"

Before Theo can explode, I snap, "Shut up, Craig."

It surprises them both. They look at me, distracted for a moment from commencing hand-to-hand combat.

"Here's what's going to happen." I give Theo a gentle shove with my hand. It doesn't budge him, but I'm sure he gets the point. "*You* are going to walk away and get your temper under control." I look at Craig. "And *you* are going to sit down and stop being an ass."

When no one moves, I harden my voice. "*Now*, gentlemen."

There's a long, terrible pause wherein Theo and Craig simply stare at each other. Testosterone crackles dangerously in the air. Then Craig smiles like a game show host and takes his seat. He folds his hands in his lap, the picture of composure, and looks at Theo with a cocked eyebrow as if to say, *Your move, pal.*

Vibrating fury, Theo inhales a long breath. His hands flex as if they're itching to curl around Craig's throat.

I'm beginning to think Craig isn't quite as smart as he thinks he is.

But finally, Theo relents. He turns on his heel and stalks away.

I release the breath I didn't know I was holding and rest a hand against my stomach in a futile effort to slow its queasy roll.

Watching him go, Craig muses, "You don't have much experience with men, do you?"

I huff, vaguely insulted, though his tone isn't accusatory, only inquisitive. "What's that supposed to mean?"

"It means that of all the things your friend Theo Valentine feels for you, dislike definitely isn't one of them."

Craig turns his head and meets my eyes. The warning in them gives me chills. "Be careful, Megan. The most dangerous creature on earth is a man with an obsession. There's no limit to what he'll destroy in his pursuit of it."

You'd assume dinner would be ruined—potentially violent confrontations are good for that sort of thing—but Craig manages to keep the conversation afloat by steering it to less inflammatory topics than how much he'd like to get into my panties, my dead husband, or the awkward kerfuffle with the muscular mute who wanted to murder him.

One blip comes when he tries to pour me a glass of wine, but I quickly decline, telling him I only ever drink at home. I can tell he wants to ask why, but he doesn't. What he does instead is instruct the waiter to recork the bottle, saying he'd changed his mind and would be taking it home with him to drink later.

He never takes a single sip of that wine. It's a classy move, one I wish I was worthy of.

But by then, Craig had ceased to exist. For every moment that passes, my desire to see Theo again spreads throughout my body like wildfire until I'm sitting at the table, utterly consumed. By the time the check comes, I'm almost scratching my skin off in impatience.

When we leave, I look for Theo at the bar, but he's gone.

Craig drives me home, keeping up a steady stream of chatter above the hideous beat of the polka braying from his stereo. He leaves me at the front door with a peck on the cheek and a promise to call me.

The first thing I do is kick off the heels and change out of the dress and into sweats. Then I go into the kitchen, barefoot, and open a bottle of wine. Fortified with a glass of liquid courage, I send Theo a text.

> *Earth to the Twilight Zone.*
> *Come in, Stranger Things.*

Not even thirty seconds pass before I get a response.

> *He didn't bring you flowers, did he.*

There's no question mark at the end. It's a statement, not a question, like he already knows the answer.

> *That has nothing to do with anything.*
> *Can we talk about what's going on?*

> *He didn't bring you flowers. He looks at you*
> *like you're a piece of meat. He kissed you*
> *because he knew I was watching.*
> *He'll never care about your heart.*

Is that his way of saying he does? I gulp some wine, my hands shaking, and read what he's written several times, trying to decide how to respond.

But I've already said my piece. He knows I'm confused and upset but refuses to give me an inch in the way of explanation. "I can't do it, Theo," I whisper, reading his text one last time. "Here's where I get off this merry-go-round."

I gave my heart away a long time ago.
Since then, I've realized that some doors,
once opened, can never be shut. And the doors
that won't open aren't meant for me to walk through.

Like I knew he would, he remains silent. In his silence is my answer.

Theo Valentine is a door that's going to stay forever closed.

I spend the evening in the kind of mean funk that can only be cured by pints of ice cream and old movies watched in bed. Several times during the night, I feel a pull calling me toward the windows, but I drag the pillow over my face and breathe until the urge to see if he's out on the beach passes.

The same thing happens on Saturday. I sleep very little both nights, but what sleep I do get is filled with strange, unsettling dreams.

I dream of my wedding day. Of walking down the aisle toward Cass, the bouquet of purple sweet peas trembling in my hands. Of meeting his gaze when he lifts the veil from my face, but his eyes aren't their normal, open sky blue. They're dark as midnight at the bottom of a well, swimming with secrets and pain.

I dream of running through a maze of tall green shrubs in the moonlight, following someone ahead who I hear but never see. His steps on the dewy grass are sure and swift, and I lag farther behind with every corner I turn. My breath steams white in the cold night air; my heart pounds painfully hard. I try to call out his name, but it's a plaintive howl that leaves my throat instead, the melancholy cry of a wolf seeking her lost mate.

I dream of babies. A hospital nursery full of newborns wrapped in pink and blue blankets. I stare at them through the nursery window, pounding my fists on the glass, screaming so loudly, it could rouse all the ghosts within miles from their graves.

I dream of Denver omelets and key lime pie, of lightning strikes in an empty desert, of black muscle cars roaring past me at top speed.

And, as I often do, I dream of blood.

Leaching into spiderweb cracks on asphalt, slick on the palms of my hands, sliding silently down my naked thighs as I sob, knowing what I've lost even before the gynecologist murmurs her apologies.

I wake panting and drenched in sweat, feeling as if something vitally important hovers just out of my reach. When the phone rings, I'm still disoriented. I answer without looking to see who's calling. "Hello?"

"Hey, Megan, it's Suzanne!"

"Oh. Hi." I scrub a hand over my face and squint into the bright morning sun pouring through the bedroom windows.

"Geez, don't get too excited to hear from me, you'll give me a big head," she says drily.

"Sorry. I just woke up. What time is it?"

"Seven thirty."

"Why are you calling me at the crack of dawn on a Sunday morning, Suzanne?" I yawn, flipping off the covers to shuffle toward the bathroom.

"I wanted to see if you'd like to go to church with me."

"No."

She laughs. "You want to think about that for half a millisecond?"

"God and I have our differences." *It's impossible to stay friends with someone after he kills the love of your life.* "My mother once said if the shadow of the cross fell on me, I'd turn to ashes. I don't think she was joking."

"C'mon, it'll be fun."

"*Fun?* Church and fun have never gone together in the entire history of religion. I think it's actually against the law for church to be anything but total misery."

She laughs again. For some reason, my foul mood seems to delight her. "Whoa, there's some major baggage behind that statement! But this church is different, I promise."

"Pfft. Do they hand out joints on your way in the door?"

"Ha. We should be so lucky. No, they're just cool."

I make a noise that indicates how much I believe her church is anywhere near the vicinity of cool.

Suzanne giggles. "Are you living with some kind of large, disgruntled animal? Because that sounded a lot like a warthog."

"How would a sophisticated urbanite like you know what a warthog sounds like?"

"You'd be surprised by the things I know," she says, sounding mysterious.

I can tell that's a loaded statement. "Okay, I'll play. Like what?"

"Like Theo Valentine put Coop in charge of Hillrise Construction..." She pauses dramatically. "And left town."

My surprise is so total, I almost drop the phone. "*Left?* When?"

"Friday night, according to what I heard."

"Where did he go?" My voice is so loud, it echoes off the walls.

"Like Coop would tell anyone." She chuffs in annoyance. "He's almost as tight-lipped as Theo. Those two are like brothers. But from what I hear, Coop held an emergency meeting with Hillrise's crew yesterday and told them not to expect Theo back anytime soon."

Too shocked to continue standing, I plop down onto the lid of the toilet and stare at the floor. I'm blinded by images of Theo's tortured expression when he looked at me on Friday night, at his expression of fury when he looked at Craig.

"What else did you hear?"

Her voice turns businesslike. "Nope, you've gotta pay to play, babes. Otherwise mum's the word."

My sigh is aggravated but also resigned. "Fine. What time are you picking me up?"

"In an hour. And don't wear jeans and a T-shirt."

"Why not? Since when does God give a shit about fashion?"

"It's a house of worship, sweetie, not a dorm party. Show the Lord some respect."

I mutter darkly, "Tell him to earn it," and hang up.

19

*B*y the time Suzanne rings the bell, I've paced the floor so much, I've almost worn a groove into the wood. When I open the door, she gives me a quick once-over, nodding in approval at my conservative black slacks and ivory cashmere sweater.

"You look great."

"I look like someone's secretary."

"No one's secretary looks like you, bombshell. Stop complaining and get your ass in the car. We're going to be late."

I lock the front door, and then we're off. I make it all of two minutes into the drive before I start pestering her for more information. "So? What else did you hear about Theo?"

She looks sideways at me. I can tell she's trying not to smile. "Why're you suddenly so interested in Theo Valentine anyway?"

"I wouldn't call it sudden." When she purses her lips, I add, "Let's just say he's been growing on me."

"Huh. Like a mold."

"Suzanne, please!"

"No, seriously, I find this interesting. You went from thinking he was an asshole to begging me with big Bambi eyes for more deets about why he left. Obviously, there's something going on."

Her pause is filled with expectation. I realize I'm not getting any more out of her until she gets what she wants from me. I slump down in the seat and stare out the window. "Fine. Yes, there's something going on."

She hollers, "*What?*" so loudly, I jump.

"Jesus, Suzanne, shout a little, why don't you!"

Cackling, she pounds her fist on the steering wheel. "I *knew* it! I knew someone would eventually get to him! I want *all* the details. Are you sleeping with him? Are you in love with him? Wait, no, answer me this first—is he hung?"

She turns to me with an eager expression, her eyes alight. I want to punch her in the face.

"Number one, you're demented. Number two, we aren't sleeping together. Number three, no one's in love with anyone. We're just...kind of...circling each other warily."

She crinkles her face into an expression that would be hilarious if I weren't so irritated.

"Oh, how romantic. 'Circling each other warily.' You make it sound like you're a pair of feral cats!"

"I don't know what we are. We're nothing." I close my eyes, remembering Theo out on the beach in the darkness, moving one step closer to me each time I called his name. "But there's something there. A connection. I can't explain it, Suzanne. All I know is that we're drawn to each other, and that drives him crazy. Every time I'm near him, it's like he's going to jump out of his skin."

She says smugly, "I told you he had the hots for you."

"I wish it were that simple." Then I tell her the whole story, start to finish, beginning with the first time I saw Theo at Cal's Diner all the way up to the encounter at the restaurant with Craig.

When I'm finished, she's silent for a while, her brows drawn together in thought. "So what I'm hearing you say is that there's incredible chemistry between you, which makes you both uncomfortable."

I think about that. It's a vast oversimplification of the situation, but it's not wrong. "I guess so. Yes."

"And you came right out and told Theo to stay away from you because you were so uncomfortable with it."

"No, I told him to stay away from me if he wouldn't tell me why *he* was so uncomfortable with it."

She looks at me with her brows raised. "Did it ever occur to you that he's uncomfortable because he can't speak, and he hasn't been in a relationship in years?"

When I don't say anything, she continues.

"He was in a bad accident, Megan. The man went through a severe trauma. And from what I understand, he was pretty badly burned—"

"Burned?" I repeat, horrified.

"Yes, burned. He was trapped in the car for a while before they got him out. You can see some of the scarring on his neck, but who knows what kind of scars he has under his clothes? The simplest explanation for all his strange behavior is that he's insecure. He's got all these physical and mental scars, he knows he's not the same man he once was, and here comes this girl who rocks his world..."

Her voice gentles. "A girl who's had some trauma of her own. Maybe he's thinking of *your* best interests by trying to stay away from you."

Could that be it? He's being protective of me? I think of how he acted at the restaurant when he saw Craig upset me and feel ashamed. "I told him he made me feel like I was losing my mind."

"What would you do if he told you the same thing?"

I have to swallow around the sudden lump in my throat. "Leave him alone."

Suzanne says briskly, "The operative word being 'leave.' Which he did. Apparently, now we know why."

I turn to her with wide eyes. "I can't be the reason he left! We've never even kissed! We've had a few strange conversations, some random weird emails and texts, an awkward encounter or two! No one in his right mind would walk out on his business, his home, his friends—"

"You're right. No one *in his right mind* would do that. But we're talking about Theo Valentine, sweetie. The man hasn't been in his right mind for years."

I groan and drop my face into my hands.

"Moving on—how was the date with Craig?"

"He listens to polka music. He takes manscaping too seriously. He has iceberg hands, an ego the size of the continental United States, and, I suspect, thinks when a woman says *no*, it really means *yes*."

Suzanne mutters, "Geez, you're tough."

"Can we get back to Theo for a minute? What else did you have to tell me about what you heard?"

We pull into a parking lot, and Suzanne parks the car. She turns to me with a bright smile. "Nothing. I just wanted you to come to church with me."

She opens her door, ignoring my growl of anger. "C'mon, heartbreaker, let's get you under the shadow of the cross and see if your mother was on to something."

She slams the door and sashays away, leaving me no choice but to follow.

I was expecting a church with a steeple like the one I attended every Sunday as a kid, but what I get instead is a building that resembles a big box store. Squat and unattractive, it's painted a sickly beige and doesn't have any windows. It sits alone in the middle of a large grassy lot, surrounded by a chain-link fence.

"It looks like some kind of detention center for the criminal justice system."

Walking beside me through the parking lot, Suzanne laughs. "I admit it doesn't have much in the way of visual appeal, but I promise what it lacks in beauty, it more than makes up for in awesomeness."

I wrinkle my nose. "Blech. You drank the Kool-Aid."

Suzanne pulls me along by the sleeve of my sweater. "Oh ye of little faith."

I plaster a pleasant smile on my face as we approach a group of people standing outside the open front doors. One of them is Coop, looking handsome in a dark gray suit.

He sees me coming and does a double take. "Megan. What a surprise."

"Hi, Coop. I'm here under duress." I shoot a look at Suzanne, who's stopped beside me. "This one seems overly concerned about the state of my soul, so here I am."

Coop looks at Suzanne. In one swift glance, he takes in her tight black dress, her skyscraper heels, and her brilliant smile. His cheeks go ruddy. Though she's not showing any cleavage— for her, the dress is actually demure—the woman oozes sex appeal.

That evidently isn't lost on Coop.

He clears his throat and squints up at the cloudless sky. "Well, that's great," he says, voice rough. "We're always glad to welcome new folks."

I wonder if I can take Coop aside for a moment to ask him about Theo, but my thoughts are derailed when Suzanne puts her hand on Coop's arm.

"I'm so sorry to hear about you and Christine," she says softly.

Coop shifts his weight from one foot to the other, scrunching up his face as he turns his gaze from the sky to his shoes. "Yep. Thanks."

Oh, boy. This doesn't sound good. And Coop is squirming, which isn't like him. I assume Christine is his wife, and I'm proven right when the conversation continues.

"How are the kids handling it?"

"They're good kids," he says gruffly, running a hand over his unruly blond beard. "They'll be fine. They're living with their mother until we can figure out a custody agreement."

"Please let me know if I can help in any way. You know I'm here for you, Coop."

She's not trying to be provocative, but his face flushes a deeper shade of red at those words, like a teenage boy with a crush.

"Should we go inside?" I say into the awkward pause.

"Yes, service is about to start."

Suzanne turns away, but Coop stops me from following her.

"Megan, can I talk to you? It'll only take a sec."

My heart flutters. I know what he wants to talk to me about. "Sure. Suzanne, I'm right behind you."

She shrugs. "Okay. I always sit in the first row, left side. Come find me when you're done."

The front row. I'm cursed.

Suzanne smiles a farewell smile to Coop, who nods back. Then Coop takes my elbow and steers me to the side of the entrance, a few steps away from the people streaming in the front doors. He starts the conversation with no preamble.

"Theo left."

"I know. Suzanne told me. What's going on?"

Coop searches my face for a moment. His normally bright blue eyes are clouded. "I was hopin' you could tell me."

"Me?"

His gaze steady on mine, Coop says, "Theo was stable before you moved here. Fucked up, but stable. Then one rainy night last month, he pounds on my door, out of his mind. I've never seen him so agitated. He needed to get drunk, he said. He didn't trust himself to be alone, but he had to get drunk. He had to forget. When I asked him what he had to forget, he said not what. Who."

Goose bumps pimple my arms. My heart leaps into my throat.

"I've never seen a man so tormented," Coop continues, his voice low. "And I was in Afghanistan with the corps. I saw a lot of guys lose their shit. People tryin' to kill you for too long can make your brain crack. But this...this was different. This scared me, Megan, and I don't scare easily."

My mouth is dry. My hands are sweaty. There are people all around us, talking and laughing as they walk into church, but all I can see is Coop's face. All I can hear are his words, underscored by the roar of my heartbeat.

"So we got drunk. Eventually, he passed out. Slept on my couch. Like a dead man, he never moved once. I sat up and watched him because I was afraid if he woke up alone, he might do somethin' stupid. Next day, he wouldn't communicate. Wouldn't eat. He sat on my sofa with his head in his hands for hours. I thought I was gonna have to call a doctor. Then he gets up all of a sudden at seven o'clock and leaves. Just takes off, no explanation. I send him a text, where you goin'? No answer. Few hours later, he's back, in worse shape than the night before. Goes into my kitchen and heads straight for the liquor cabinet. Drinks a bottle of Jack in one go.

"That can kill a man, Megan. But I let him do it because I knew if I got in his way, it would get ugly. He doesn't normally have a temper, but he was as close to snappin' as a man can get without goin' over the edge. He passed out again. Next mornin', he left without a word.

"By chance, I had breakfast at Cal's Diner that day. My friend Jean McCorkle told me she met a nice young woman two nights prior who bought the Buttercup Inn. Happened to mention Theo was in at the same time. Happened to mention he left in a state."

Coop's voice drops even lower. "Happened to mention she almost ran Theo over the night before on the road in front of Sunday Anderson's house. Came to a screeching stop just inches from his legs, she said. Appeared out of nowhere and scared her half to death. He never even looked up. Then I find out later from Sunday that you were at a party at her house...the same night Jean McCorkle almost ran Theo over on the street outside."

My heart races so fast, I can't catch my breath. I remember the look on Theo's face as he gazed out at me from the shadows of Sunday's back porch.

All that hostility in his eyes. All that strange, unsettling longing.

Coop runs a hand over his head, adjusts his tie, and exhales a long breath. "Couple weeks pass, Theo's a bull to handle the whole time. Just a bull. He's antsy, sleepin' less than usual—which isn't much to begin with—drinkin' too much. Somethin's wrong, and it's big. Haven't seen him that fucked up since right after the accident. So I sit him down and tell him I'm worried. You know what his response was?"

Afraid of what Coop's going to tell me, I shake my head.

"'How can you remember someone you've never met?'"

That startles me to the point of speechlessness. My mind forms the word *What?* but nothing comes out of my mouth. My tongue is frozen, like the ice water slicing through my veins.

Coop's still talking. He hasn't noticed my sudden stillness or the way all the blood has drained from my face.

"So I told him you can't. It's not possible. They just remind you of someone you already know. He agreed, but I got the feelin' he was only placatin' me because I looked so worried. I hoped that would be the end of it, that maybe he was just goin' through a rough patch..."

Coop focuses on me. He says quietly, "But then he told me I had to go visit a new client. Said he couldn't do it himself, though he wouldn't say why. But he made sure I knew that this wasn't any client. Told me to make sure Hillrise got the job no matter what. Even if we had to do it for free. I almost laughed, that was so dumb, but he was dead serious. So the next mornin', I find myself knockin' on the front door of the Buttercup Inn...and there you were. And now Theo's gone."

Coop pauses. His gaze is piercing. "You comin' to town and him fallin' apart and leavin' so soon after isn't a coincidence."

Coincidence.

There's that word again. The word I've been telling myself over and over again is the explanation for everything where Theo is concerned.

"I know you're loyal to him, Coop," I say, my voice tremulous. "I don't expect you to answer this. But did he say anything before he left? Anything about me?"

Coop stares at me long and hard. I get the sense he's trying to decide something. Then he reaches into his jacket pocket, pulls out a folded piece of paper, and hands it to me.

"He left this for you. I have no idea what it's supposed to mean, but he said you will."

I take the note. The paper is almost blindingly white in the bright morning sunlight. Hands shaking, I unfold it and read.

Ask and it will be given to you; seek and you will find; knock and the door will be opened.

The world tilts dangerously sideways.

Coop was right: I know what it means. It's chapter seven, verse seven from the gospel of Matthew, but that's not what makes it so extraordinary.

I have that particular verse memorized because Cass had it tattooed on his back.

I hear myself ask, "Coop, how long ago was Theo's accident?"

He looks at me strangely. "Five years. Why do you ask?"

Scalding heat flashes over my skin. I begin to hyperventilate.

"By any..." I have to stop to force breath into my lungs. "By any chance, do you remember the date?"

"Yeah. May seventeenth."

Everything starts to spin.

Theo's accident was exactly five years ago to the day that Cass died.

20

"*H*ello, Megan. It's Dr. Singer."

"Oh, thank God! Thank you for calling me back so fast!"

"I was in a meeting, or I would've called sooner. You sounded upset in your message. What's going on?"

I'm in the ladies' room at the church, where I fled without saying a word of farewell to poor Coop, who must think I'm a lunatic. I chew my thumbnail as I pace back and forth in front of the row of sinks. I avoid looking at myself in the mirror because I'm frightened of what I might find lurking behind my eyes.

"I need your honest, professional opinion about something."

"Of course. What is it?"

I stop pacing, close my eyes, and take a deep breath to calm my thundering heart. "Am I insane?"

Dr. Singer's silence is almost as loud as one of Theo's. It makes me nervous.

"Like, on a scale of one to ten, with one being a fully healthy, functional person and ten being the writer who tries to murder his family in *The Shining*, where do I fall?"

"In my professional opinion, I'd say you're at two and a quarter. Perhaps two point five."

Clammy with relief, I sag against the sink. "Really? I'm not even a three? That's good, right?"

"There's no such scale in clinical psychiatry, but I answered that way because you're an accountant. I knew you'd appreciate my being exact."

"*Was* an accountant. In my former life. Which no longer exists. Like most of the reasoning capacity of my brain."

I laugh. It sounds crazy. I know it does, because in his most gentle I'm-dealing-with-a-cuckoo voice, Dr. Singer says, "Why don't you tell me what's going on?"

I start to pace again because it feels productive. Like I might be in control of at least this one little thing. I can't control my thought processes, my fantasies, or the psychotic little voice in my head whispering impossible things in my ear about Theo Valentine, but I *can* march back and forth over this terrifically ugly brown tile.

"Um. God. Where to start?" This time, my laugh is nervous.

"Start at the beginning."

"Okay." I blow out a hard breath. "There's this man."

"Ah."

I stop pacing. "What do you mean, 'Ah?' That sounds important."

"May I ask you a few questions about this man?"

"Yes. Ask away."

"Are you attracted to him?"

Oh fuck. "I'm...I'm..."

After it becomes clear I won't add anything more, Dr. Singer says, "It's all right to admit it, Megan. You're not betraying Cass's memory if you find another man attractive."

I start pacing with renewed vigor. Back and forth I go, my heels clacking on the tile, my hands shaking, my armpits damp. "Let's just say he affects me."

"Go on."

"He...we...I keep running into him everywhere. *Everywhere.* And, uh, there are a lot of things about him...many, many things...that sort of...remind me..." I suck in a breath and blurt it out. "Of Cass."

"That's normal."

Dr. Singer sounds completely blasé. Meanwhile, I'm about to collapse onto the hideous brown tile and never get up. "Normal?" I shout. "It's *normal* that a stranger reminds me of my dead husband?"

"Do you recall our talks about what might happen when you started dating?"

"I recall I told you I'd rather be fed limb by limb to a pack of wolves than start dating."

Dr. Singer is unfazed by my snappy tone. "Indeed. And for five years, during the prime of your life, you refused to even *look* at another man. I counseled you that not allowing yourself the possibility of happiness again was unhealthy. I believe your response was 'There is no happiness for me without Cass.' So without knowing anything other than this new man 'affects' you, I can surmise from what I know of you, Megan, that you're now paralyzed by guilt."

Cold blasts over me, as if I've been doused with a bucket of ice water.

I whisper, "Guilt?"

"We've already established that you suffer from survivor's guilt. Guilt for living when someone you loved so deeply is gone. Now it seems we can add guilt for feeling a normal, natural attraction to a man who isn't Cass. Honestly, I'm surprised this didn't come up sooner."

No. No, this is too easy. Too simple. Guilt can't be the explanation for everything I'm thinking and feeling, all this madness running rampant through my veins.

"But...there are all these things that can't be explained...like the bear claw, and the sweet peas planted along the porch, and he knows how I like my coffee! And there was this painting of lightning that had his initials, and he put out a fire at my house—and the Denver omelets! The note that was Cass's tattoo! *May seventeenth!*"

I'm not making sense. I'm also starting to worry Dr. Singer, because his tone changes to the stern one he used to use when he was insisting, for the nth time, that I get on antidepressants.

"Let's talk about your panic attacks. Have you had any since you moved to Seaside?"

It feels like I've been utterly defeated when I mumble my answer. "Yes."

"I see. And the nightmares? Insomnia?"

He sounds smug, the prick. I grind my back teeth together. "Hmm."

"I'll take that as an affirmative. And from what I gather from your mention of things that can't be explained, you're still having episodes of magical thinking?"

Ah, yes. The infamous magical thinking, at which my brain is especially adept.

"This is different," I plead, sounding pathetic. "This man, he's... There are too many things that have happened. It can't *all* be coincidental. It can't *all* be meaningless. Can it?"

"Megan, I want you to listen to me carefully. You survived an incredibly violent car accident that killed your husband. He died in your arms. The day of his funeral, you miscarried your child—a child you'd been trying desperately to conceive—and almost died yourself from blood loss. Subsequently, you were told the chances of conceiving again were virtually none.

"You were diagnosed with post-traumatic stress disorder and clinical depression but refused medication that would help you cope. You dealt with your suffering like no other patient I've ever seen, with a combination of stoicism and plain old stubbornness I was unable, in two years of weekly sessions, to make even the smallest inroads toward healing. You embraced your pain because the alternative was to let it go...and in your mind, letting go of your pain meant letting go of Cass, the baby, and everything you'd lost.

"Now you've moved to a new town. You have a new home, a new life. There's a new man you're drawn to. And because you never worked through your grief, the only way your mind can cope with what it perceives as a betrayal of the bond you had with your husband is to try to convince you that this new man *is* your husband."

Dr. Singer pauses, and it lends his next words more weight. "Subconsciously, you believe that somehow, through some magical combination of events, Cass has returned to you in the body of another man."

There it is. The ugly truth, dragged out from the rock I've been hiding it under.

I'm breathless with the utter foolishness of it.

In a voice as dead as my heart, I say, "Tell me what to do."

"For starters, make an appointment with Dr. Anders as soon as we get off the phone. I spoke with him earlier in the week, and he said he hadn't heard from you."

As if from far away, I hear myself say yes.

"And please—I'd like you to start Lexapro. It's not a cure for depression, but it *will* help manage the symptoms. I can also prescribe something to help you sleep. You need help, Megan. There's no shame in getting it."

He waits patiently until I give him the name of the local pharmacy so he can call in the prescriptions. Then I listen with half an ear as he talks about possible side effects, dosage instructions, levels of serotonin, blah, blah, blah. By the time he stops talking, I'm exhausted.

"Thanks, Dr. Singer. I appreciate you calling me back."

"You're going to be all right, Megan. I promise. It's a positive sign that you're willing to start medication. Commit to your therapy with Dr. Anders, please. You're a wonderful woman. You have so much life ahead of you. So much to offer. And remember, whenever you feel the need to talk, I'll always be here."

I'll always be here.

You've got to be kidding me.

I say flatly, "Thanks again. Bye." I hang up and turn to stare at myself in the mirror. My eyes are wild, my face is pale, and I'm still shaking. I think Dr. Singer wasn't being honest when he said I was only a two point five on the nutso scale.

I'm a full-on ten. Maybe even an eleven.

"Megan?"

A gentle knock on the ladies' room door makes me spin away from the mirror, my heart lurching. "Yes?"

"You okay in there?"

It's Coop. *Pull yourself together. Go face him. Try to act normal.*

I smooth a hand over my hair, straighten my sweater, then plaster a fake smile on my face as I head to the door. I open it and find Coop standing there awkwardly, looking worried.

"Sorry. Didn't mean to disturb. Just makin' sure you're okay."

"You should tell her how you feel," I blurt, and instantly want to smack myself on the forehead.

Coop wrinkles his brow, confused. "Who? What?"

Well, the pitch has already been thrown. Might as well swing for the rafters. "Suzanne. You should tell her how you feel about her."

Coop wears all his expressions the same way I do, like laundry hung out on a line for the whole neighborhood to see. Right now, his face registers astonishment and pain.

"Shit, Coop. I'm sorry. I'm not myself today. Ignore me."

"You think she might...?" He leaves it hanging there, his eyes hopeful.

"I think she'd be a fool if she didn't."

That makes him look bashful. He shoves his hands into his pockets and contemplates his shoes. He says softly, "I've always... she's just so...she's outta my league, is what she is." His small laugh sounds embarrassed. "I never worked up the nerve to ask her out in high school. I started datin' my wife our senior year, got married pretty quick after that. The kids came."

Coop squints into the distance. He shrugs. "Y'know. Life happened."

"It keeps on happening too," I say softly. "It's never too late to start over."

Until it is.

Coop shifts his gaze to me. His eyes take on a look of worry. "Theo told me to watch out for you. Said to make sure you were okay. Somehow I don't think you're okay."

"Oh, Coop," I say softly, touched by his concern. "I'm not even in the same universe as okay, but I'm surviving."

"You gonna call him?"

Now it's my turn to look into the distance. "I'm probably the last person he wants to hear from right now."

"Trust me, you're the only person he wants to hear from."

Surprised by the vehemence in his voice, I shift my gaze back to Coop.

He says, "Look. I don't know what the hell the root of all this is, this problem he has with you. All I know is that the thing that breaks you is the only thing that can put you back together."

If that's true, all the antidepressants in the world can't help me.

I'm overwhelmed with sadness. "I told him to stay away from me, Coop. And I called him a coward."

"Did you mean it?"

My throat tightens. The hot sting of tears prickles the corners of my eyes. "No. I was just...afraid, I guess. Afraid and confused."

Coop settles his hand on my shoulder. "Call him. Leave him a message. Write him an email. Tell him what you just told me. Please, do it as a personal favor. I think it would help."

Music swells inside the sanctuary. People begin to sing, their voices carrying past the closed doors. It's a hymn, one I recognize well.

When I start to laugh—softly, brokenly—Coop asks, "What's funny?"

"This song."

"'Amazing Grace' is funny?"

"My mother sang it at my wedding."

Coop frowns. "I don't get it."

I sigh, shaking my head. "That makes two of us. C'mon, let's go inside before Suzanne sends out a search party."

I link my arm through his, and we walk through a pair of double doors into the sanctuary. It's packed with people. Everyone is standing, singing "Amazing Grace" so robustly, it's like a group audition for a reality show about church choirs. I find Suzanne in the front row and give her a quick smile as I slip in beside her.

Standing behind a wood podium on a large, carpeted dais, the pastor is a woman in her mid-fifties with beautiful silvery-white hair. When the hymn ends and everyone takes their seats, she surveys the crowd with an air of serenity. Then she speaks in a voice that carries to the last row.

"Love isn't born of the flesh. It's born of the spirit, and so can transcend the bonds of flesh, and life, and time. The poet Rumi said, 'Don't grieve. Anything you lose comes around in another form.'"

It isn't until every head in the room turns toward me and two hundred pairs of startled eyes fix on my face that I realize I've begun maniacally laughing.

$\mathcal{W}$ hen I burst through the outer church doors, the sun has vanished behind clouds, and it's begun to rain. I walk home barefoot, carrying my heels, wet and miserable, ignoring the constant buzzing of my cell phone in my handbag and the much louder buzzing inside my head.

Theo's note was referring to my text about closed doors. The bible quote has nothing to do with Cass, and neither does the hymn. Or the sermon. Or the seventeenth of May. They're all coincidences.

Sure they are. And I'm Elvis Presley.

Shut up.

You shut up!

I take it as evidence of my mental deterioration that my nagging inner voice now has split personalities that are arguing with each other. Magical thinking has dug its tentacles into my brain. No matter how many times I tell myself it's all bullshit, that Dr. Singer's explanation is valid and my grief is making connections where there are none, my heart doesn't care.

My weak, stupid heart. And my poor, broken brain. Between the two of them, it's a miracle I've lasted this long.

By the time I get home, I've got a bunch of messages on my

voicemail from Suzanne. I'm not surprised. I ran from the church as if I were being chased by lions. I text her an apology, say I'm not feeling well, and make a joke about the shadow of the cross. Then I shut off my phone, strip out of my wet clothes, and crawl into bed.

I'm still there when the cloud-shrouded sun sinks into the ocean, turning the room from gray to black.

Black as his hair. Black as his eyes. Black as the shriveled-up husk of my heart.

The thing about depression is its weight. It's so damn heavy. Every breath is a fight. Every step takes so much effort. It's like trying to move through wet sand. It's so much easier to lie down and let the sand fill your mouth and ears and eyes, to let it seep into your soul and obliterate all the nothingness.

As I lie in darkness, sinking into that sweet relief of letting go, I keep hearing Coop's words.

The thing that breaks you is the only thing that can put you back together.

When the clock reads 12:02 a.m., I rise from bed, get my laptop, and compose an email.

To: Theo@hillrise.com
From: Bowie4Evah@yahoo.com
Subject: Broken pieces

Dear Theo,

When I was six years old, I fell in love with a boy. He was smart and sweet and the best person I've ever known. He was my best friend. I married him when I was twenty-four. Three years later, he died, and so did I, in all the ways that matter.

I don't know who I am without him. He was all the best parts of me. The person you met is a ghost, a ghost walking around in the guise of a woman who has a beating heart and blood running through her veins. But my heart is a stone and there's nothing but dust in my veins. Everything inside me is ashes.

Don't let a ghost drive you away from your home. If that's even what happened. I find it hard to believe I could be the cause of such a thing, but what do I know? As it turns out, absolutely nothing.

There are people here who love you. Coop does, you know. He's a good friend. He'll help you through whatever hell you're dealing with. My husband used to say, "If you're going through hell, keep on going." I think he meant keep going until you see the light on the other side. I'd like to believe there's a light, but I'm finding that almost impossible. Hell is so damn big.

I'm sorry I make all your broken parts bleed. If it makes you feel any better...ditto.

A confession: I'm the coward, not you. If I had any courage at all, I'd put an end to the wasteland of misery that is my life, but I don't have the strength. I hate myself for my weakness. To be or not to be. That's not a question. Stupid Shakespeare.

I'm not drunk, if that's what you're thinking. I'm just tired. I'm so tired of trying to make sense of all this confusion. My point— and I do have one—is this.

You're the first thing that has made me feel alive in years.

My terror about what that means is huge. My therapist says my attraction to you triggers my guilt, like maybe I'm betraying the memory of my husband, but honestly, I think my therapist is full of shit. I've tried and tried to believe that nothing means anything at all, that life is just one big shit show of chaos, that belief in fate and God and a benevolent universe is for suckers, but wow. Meeting you sure changed all that.

There's also the distinct possibility that I'm crazy, so take the compliment with a grain of salt.

I'll make you a deal. You don't ask about my crazy, and I won't ask about yours. Don't ask, don't tell. It worked fine for the military for years, it should work for two nut jobs like us.

I saw a sticker on the back of a stop sign today that read, "Sometimes following your heart means losing your mind." It made me smile, right before it made me cry.

Come back, Theo. If I'm the reason you left, come back. A wise man recently told me that the thing that breaks you is the only thing that can put you back together. If we're each other's hammers, maybe we're also each other's glue.

Megan

After I hit Send, I feel a strange and overwhelming sense of relief. I fall asleep as soon as my head touches the pillow, and I don't dream.

I wake with a jolt sometime in the still black hours before dawn, my skin prickling with the recognition that I'm no longer alone.

I sit up in bed, listening hard into the darkness. My body floods with adrenaline. My heart starts pounding, and my hands begin to shake. I hear nothing but the gentle patter of raindrops against the windows and the restless sigh of the surf.

And then...

That familiar crackle of electricity skitters over my skin.

He's here.

I can't see him, but I know straight down to the marrow of my bones that Theo is somewhere nearby.

I'm struck with a wild elation that makes me feel as light as a feather, as if I might at any moment shirk the bounds of gravity and float up to the ceiling like a balloon.

Some part of me was expecting this. I summoned him, after all. I cast a spell with my letter, one I knew would work its magic and bring him to me in the night, my midnight valentine who stalks the darkness outside my house and inside my heart.

With shaking hands, I push aside the covers and slip out of bed. I walk barefoot from the room and down the twist of stairs, my nerves screaming, a roar like thunder inside my head. At the foot of the stairs, I pause with one hand on the banister. I close my eyes and open my mind, waiting until I feel it again.

I open my eyes and look at the front door.

And it strikes me, the sight of that closed door. For all our cryptic back and forth about the damn things, there was one thing Theo and I both missed.

Some doors have to be opened from the inside.

I cross the foyer, open the lock, turn the handle, and pull—

And there he is.

Soaking wet and shivering, standing with his head bowed and his arms braced on either side of the frame, rain dripping from the tip of his nose. His wet hair is plastered against his skull. A puddle of water shimmers around his feet.

He raises his head and looks into my eyes. His face is wet from more than just the rain.

He's crying.

Without a word, I take hold of his jacket and pull him into my arms.

He collapses against me with a groan, shuddering violently. He hugs me so tight, I'm breathless. His clothing is freezing cold, but his skin is hot. His face pressed to my neck feels feverish.

"It's okay," I whisper, holding him. "Everything's going to be okay."

I'm not sure which of us I'm reassuring.

"Come inside. Come in out of the rain, Theo. You're wet. Let me help you. Let me help you."

He reluctantly allows me to coax him through the door, though he refuses to release me. He's like a terrified animal, starving and afraid to be caged, but desperate for the food inside. I kick the door shut, and we stand in the shadowed foyer, clutching each other, shivering and breathing erratically, the rain growing louder until it sounds like a hail of bullets on the roof.

His hands are in my hair. He takes big fistfuls of it, buries his face in it, breathes it in. When he makes an inarticulate sound of anguish, I gently shush him again.

Calm descends over me, a serenity so powerful, it disorients me for a moment, but then I realize it's the same thing I felt upstairs in bed. That feeling like my soul is filling with air and I'm rising.

That feeling of finally being able to breathe after spending so long suffocating on hopelessness.

"We need to get you dry. Okay? Can you stay here for a minute?"

He drags in a breath and nods, though his hands stay in my hair and he makes no move to step away. I have to gently peel myself out of his arms. I leave him standing there like a statue, staring at the floor, and hurry upstairs to find some thick bath towels. When I come back down, he hasn't moved from the spot I left him.

I ease off his soaked jacket and let it fall to the floor. Then I drape one of the towels around his shoulders. When I put another over his head and start to gently rub his hair, he closes his eyes and sighs.

The weight of the world is in that sigh. I can tell by how his shoulders sag after he releases it that he's feeling what I'm feeling too. That strange unburdening of spirit. The aching bliss of finally letting go.

We're quiet as I blot the water from his face and hair, my hands as reverent and tender with him as if he were a baby. His fragility is so unexpected, his vulnerability so raw, I'm moved almost to tears. He could crush me with those big hands of his, all those powerful muscles, but instead stands emotionally naked and allows me to care for him.

His trust is devastating.

"You have a fever," I whisper, my brow crinkled with worry as I touch his forehead. "Theo, you're burning up."

He tilts his head into my palm and presses his hand against it. It's such a sweet gesture, and so intimate. I can't stop myself: I rise up on tiptoe and softly press a kiss to his lips.

He takes my face in his hands. Cupping my jaw, he touches his forehead to mine. He's trembling all over, his hands as feverish as the rest of him.

I kiss him again. I have to. There is no choice. His mouth is the oxygen I need to survive, and I no longer care about anything else but this:

His soft, trembling lips.

His low, sweet groan.

His heat and his taste and the astonishing intensity of how much I like all that, how quickly addicted I become to the feel of his mouth against mine.

Everything disappears. The rain, the night, and every ounce of my hesitation, every fear for the future or what might happen next. There is only now. Right now. Here, us, *this*.

I pull my T-shirt over my head and drop it to the floor.

Theo sucks in a startled breath. Wide-eyed, he stares down at me, his gaze raking over my naked breasts. He's frozen, unwilling or unable to move, so I take matters into my own hands and grip the hem of his wet shirt. I pull it up and over his head, pulling it past his chin, yanking harder when his hands get caught in the sleeves. The shirt and towel tumble to the floor.

Then he's standing bare-chested in front of me, his eyes incandescent like some nocturnal animal's, silvery bright in the dark.

I place my hands on his chest. With my fingertips, I trace his scars, the snarls and puckers of flesh, his roadmap of ancient trauma. Suzanne guessed right: he was burned, and badly. The left side of his body from shoulder to hip is a testament to the accident that stole his speech.

But to me, his scars are beautiful. So eloquent, these monuments to his pain. It's perverse, but I wish I had scars like these. I wish I could look at my body in a mirror and think, *Yes. There is the physical evidence of my suffering. It can't be all in my head, because there it is, carved on my skin like etchings on glass.*

I have nothing so concrete. All my wounds are on the inside, hidden in places they can never heal.

I press a kiss to his chest, right above his throbbing heart. Then I tilt my head back and look up into his blazing eyes. "I don't care if we're crazy. You make me believe that all the things I stopped believing in might actually exist. You give me faith, Theo. Until I lost it, I had no idea how impossible it is to live without."

His lids drift shut. He slowly exhales. Then he opens his eyes, picks me up in his arms, and heads toward the staircase.

Effortlessly, he takes the stairs two at a time. I cling to his strong shoulders, watching his profile, my mind clear, the nagging voice inside it mercifully silent. When we get to the bedroom, he strides straight over to the bed. Then he lays me down on the mattress, kneels beside the bed, slides one arm underneath me and the other around my hips, and rests his head on my stomach.

Then he simply breathes.

I touch his damp hair, running my fingers through the

strands. Rain slides down the patio windows in long, silvery trails, like tears.

He turns his head so his lips are on my stomach. They're moving swiftly and silently, as if he's saying a prayer.

It isn't until I feel water slide over my temples that I realize I'm crying.

Theo lifts his head and looks at me. His eyes burn as hotly as his skin.

I whisper, "Please," but I don't know what I'm asking for.

Still on his knees, he takes my face in his hands and gently kisses me. It's a reverent kiss, soft and chaste, at least at first. He's hesitant, his lips barely grazing mine, until I thread my hands around the back of his neck and pull him closer.

I curl my body toward his and take his tongue into my mouth. Desire flashes over me like a detonation.

He makes a sound of pleasure deep in his throat. His fingers twist in my hair.

Outside, a rolling boom of thunder rattles the windows. Waves pummel the shore with a wild, powerful sound that matches the crashing beat of my heart.

Then his lips are gone, but I get them again somewhere else —the tender flesh of my inner thigh. The heat of his open mouth on my flesh is shocking. He sucks, and the sharp scrape of his teeth makes me gasp.

"Theo. Theo."

His name is a plea, a soft, broken noise beneath the drum of the rain. He slips his fingers into the waistband of my shorts, then slowly eases my shorts and panties past my hips and down my legs. Then his big, rough hands are all over my body. Everywhere they roam, they're followed by his lips.

Breasts, stomach, thighs, neck—his shaking hands and greedy mouth map the contours of my body. I quake as he devours me, my eyes closed and my lips parted, dragging air into my lungs. When I feel his mouth between my legs, I release a low, guttural moan that makes him dig his fingers into my bottom.

Like grief, pleasure comes in waves. It builds and recedes and builds again until it crashes over you. Then you either swim, or drown. I've ridden hundred-foot-tall waves of grief—cresting the top so I can see the endless line of waves waiting to roll in before tumbling to the bottom and starting the ride up all over again—so I know how to survive without going under.

What I didn't expect was pleasure that could surpass the height and power of those waves of sorrow. I didn't expect I would so gladly stop treading water so I could drown.

With my nails digging into his shoulders and a cry of surrender raw in my throat, I convulse around that bright, burning spot of pleasure between my legs. I sink so deep into that pleasure, it's like a kind of death—there's nothing else. I'm obliterated.

Then he's lowering his naked body on top of mine. Somehow, he's undressed. It must've happened while I was busy dying.

He's hot, heavy, and shaking like a leaf, and I love it all. I love it that this is as momentous for him as it is for me, that he feels the burn and power of this lightning strike just as deeply as I do.

I open my thighs around his hips. He presses his face to my neck. Then it's as natural and effortless as breathing. A tilt and a flex and his hardness slides inside me, and both of us are groaning.

As with his kiss, it starts gently but quickly turns passionate. We're both frantic, greedy and grasping, wild with need. I meet every thrust of his hips with one of my own, grabbing his ass to take him deeper. Starting to buck, he rears up onto his hands and throws his head back. I draw my knees up around his waist and gaze in wonder at his beautiful body, all his muscles bunched and straining, the strong column of his throat painted pale from a sliver of moonlight filtering through the clouds.

He moans, faltering.

"What's wrong?"

Lowering himself to his elbows, he rests atop me and nuzzles my neck. With one hand, he reaches between our bodies and flattens his hand over my belly. Then he lifts his head and looks at me with a question in his eyes.

"You don't have to worry," I whisper, understanding. "I can't... we're safe."

We both know we're not talking about diseases.

He cradles my head and kisses me, and in his kiss, I feel his sorrow.

That brings on the tears again. I'm sorry too, sorry for what I've lost and can no longer have, sorry that if Theo pictured his life including fatherhood, by default that means his life won't include me.

He kisses my wet cheeks so tenderly, I feel like I might shatter. Then he stares down into my eyes as he starts to move again with small, perfect thrusts that soon have me panting.

Everything narrows to the space between our faces. The room vanishes, as does the storm outside, as does any final shred of my resistance.

I go over the edge before he does. My eyes closed and my head thrown back onto the pillow, my body arched against his. As if from a great distance, I hear myself cry out his name. He swells and throbs inside me, grunting faster and faster until the sounds merge to become one long, wavering moan as his entire body stiffens.

He spills himself inside me in a hot, pulsing surge as lightning tears a jagged white scar across the midnight sky and my soul sings a song of resurrection.

—————

22

*W*hen I open my eyes in the morning, the sky is clear.

Theo is gone.

Gathered in a water glass on the nightstand are a bunch of purple sweet peas.

Unmoving in bed, I stare at them for a long time. I listen to the waves break, listen to the seagulls cry, feel my pulse and the soreness in my body. For the first time in a long time, my mind is clear and still.

I sit up and bring the glass to my nose, inhaling the flowers' honey-sweet perfume. It's October. Sweet peas aren't in season, but somehow, they're in my bedroom.

I won't ask how.

Don't ask, don't tell. That was the deal.

As if in a dream, I rise, shower, and dress. In the kitchen, a fresh pot of coffee awaits me. Another gift from Theo. Smiling, I pour myself a mug and stare down into the inky liquid, remembering his hands on my skin.

When the phone rings, I float over to it, pillowed on clouds. "Hello?"

"Hi, is this Ms. Dunn?"

"*Mrs.* Dunn," I correct dreamily. "Who's this?"

"I'm calling from Seaside Pharmacy. We've got your prescription ready."

I take a sip of coffee before answering, savoring its nutty goodness. It's black and strong, exactly the way I like it. "Right. My crazy pills. Hold on to those for me for a few days, would you? I'd like to see how far down the nutso river I'll get before I really need them. This morning, I'm paddling way upstream."

I hang up before the young woman on the other end can respond.

At 11:00 a.m. on the nose, someone knocks on my front door. I've been standing at the patio windows, staring out at the ocean, my mind as blank as a clean sheet of paper. When I open the door, I find Coop and his team grouped on my porch. They're all wearing tool belts and carrying lunch boxes. Work trucks line the curb on either side of the street.

"Mornin', Megan," says Coop. A small smile hovers at the corners of his lips.

"Hey, Coop. Hey, guys."

The men solemnly nod. I stare at them, waiting, but no one says anything.

"You boys lost? Out for a morning drive and took a wrong turn?"

Coop's smile grows wider. "No wrong turns."

My face grows warm, and my heart beats faster. I whisper, "Theo?"

Coop's eyes are so blue. As blue as the sky above. He nods, grinning now. "The one and only. Sent word that we were to start work on the Buttercup as soon as I could get everyone together. So, I got us together. Here we are. We're gonna start on the master bedroom first. Theo said make sure that gets done before anything else."

The men look at me. My cheeks go from warm to burning.

Coop says, "You ready for us?"

I swallow, quickly nodding. "Yes. Please, come in." I swing the door open, and the men file inside.

Coop is last to walk over the threshold. He stops and gazes down at me. He keeps his voice low so only I can hear his words. "I take it you and Theo hashed out your problems."

My laugh is a little shaky. "I guess that's one way to put it. Is he...is he coming?"

Coop slowly shakes his head. "But he seems better. What I could tell anyway, from his emails. I'm sure I have you to thank for that."

"Well, you know what they say, Coop. The thing that breaks you is the only thing that can put you back together."

"Yeah, I think Einstein said that, right?"

I rise up on my toes and kiss him on the cheek, making him blush. "Yes. It was Einstein, for sure."

Coop chuckles, giving my arm a friendly squeeze. "You talk to Suzanne since you ran outta church like you were bein' chased by the Holy Ghost?"

"No." I think for a moment. "That must've been an interesting spectacle I made."

"Hate to tell you, Megan, but it was all anyone could talk about after. New girl in town starts laughin' like a hyena at the start of the sermon, then bolts for the doors at a hundred miles per hour—the general consensus is that you're either on drugs or an atheist. Drugs bein' the better option, by the way. Folks around here are pretty nonjudgmental, but nobody likes an atheist. You can't trust a person who doesn't believe in God."

I smile at that. "I can honestly tell you, Coop, that I'm not an atheist this morning."

"So it's drugs, then," he teases. "Guess I should make you pay

up front for the job in case you're incarcerated for possession.
That way we can still work on the place while you're dryin' out in
the poke."

I laugh, pressing a hand to my forehead because it feels like
my brain is cracking underneath my skull.

Coop shakes his head and sighs. "Okay, dopehead, outta my
way. I gotta get to work." He tweaks my nose and ambles past, his
boots thumping hollowly against the wood floor.

That night, I wait, but Theo doesn't come. He doesn't come the
next either, or the next. By Friday, I'm climbing the walls in frustration, my need to see him gnawing my guts like an infestation
of termites.

So much for paddling upstream.

Meanwhile, the men of Hillrise Construction are hard at work
turning my vision of the Buttercup Inn into reality.

One team works on the master bedroom—starting by ripping
out the bathroom sink, bathtub, and shower—while another
team goes to work on the roof. A construction Dumpster rental
company delivers two huge trash bins on flatbed trucks and parks
them along the curb. Every day, more workmen and equipment
show up until the place is crawling with both. Coop keeps me
abreast of all the plans and the progress, but I pay attention to his
briefings with only half my mind.

The other half is in Theotown, searching desperately for its
namesake.

A dozen times, I sit down at the computer to compose an
email to him, but I always end up deleting it. I pick up the phone
to call him but quickly hang up, my skin going clammy with a
cold sweat. A voice inside my head keeps screaming hysterical
warnings about looking a gift horse in the mouth.

I made a pact when I said in my email that we wouldn't talk

about each other's crazy. I have to keep my word, even if it makes me grow even crazier.

Finally, on Friday night, he returns.

In the darkest heart of the evening, I'm lying in bed staring at the ceiling when I hear footsteps downstairs. My pulse soaring, I jerk upright and stare at my closed bedroom door. For several long minutes, I listen to him rove around in the dark, going from one room to the next, pausing briefly before moving on.

I know it's him, and I know what he's doing. He's checking on the work that's been completed in his absence.

When heavy boots begin to ascend the stairs, my heart pounds so hard, it's painful.

Outside the door, the footsteps pause. Electricity sizzles over my skin. Then my bedroom door handle turns.

It takes a lifetime for the door to crack open. When it slips a few inches wider, Theo silently eases into the room. We stare at each other through the shadows for a long, breathless moment, and everything I am or ever thought I was dissolves when I see the look of ardor in his eyes.

I launch myself from the bed and fly into his open arms.

My sudden assault doesn't budge him a single inch. He simply stands with his legs apart, holding me up like he's holding up air. My legs are wrapped around his waist, my arms are wrapped around his shoulders, my face is buried in his neck. Shuddering, I suck in a breath, taking his woodsy scent into my nose. "You're here."

He nods. His pulse throbs against my lips. Against my chest, his heart drums as madly as mine does.

I whisper, "I've been waiting. It feels like I've been waiting forever."

He presses the softest kiss to my temple, his lips a featherlight brush against my skin. Then he carries me slowly over to the bed.

He lays me down, peels me out of my shorts and T-shirt, and throws them away with a low growl. He tears off his own shirt and jacket and discards them just as quickly. He opens the top button of his jeans, his hands fumbling, but my impatience is too great. I sit up, bat his hands out of the way, and rip open his fly.

His erection is a big, straining bulge beneath a pair of white boxer briefs. I press my cheek against it, nuzzling the pulsing vein that runs the length underneath. Theo sinks his trembling hands into my hair.

I pull down the waistband of his boxer briefs, and his gorgeous cock springs free. I grip it and lick it from base to crown, swirling my tongue around the engorged head. Theo sucks in a hard breath through his teeth.

When I take the length of it down my throat, he groans. He fists my hair and flexes his hips, forcing me to take him deeper.

I want more of his groans. I want him unleashed, as raw and starving as I am.

I scoop the velvet heft of his balls out of his underwear and caress them with one hand while I stroke his pulsing shaft with the other, still sucking the crown. I immediately get that groan I wanted, a deep, guttural one, paired with an involuntary shudder. I look up and find him gazing down at me with his hair falling into his face, his eyes filled with hazy wonder.

And a dark, dangerous lust. The intensity of it makes my heart skip a beat.

He pulls away and pushes me onto my back. He lifts my legs and hooks both of my ankles over his shoulders. Then he slides his hands down my shins to my thighs. Staring down at me with burning eyes, he runs a thumb back and forth over my wetness until I'm panting and rocking my hips in time with his strokes.

"Theo. Please. Your mouth."

Without hesitation, he sinks to his knees and gives me what I need.

Gasping, I arch against the mattress. He swirls his tongue around and around, sliding a big finger deep inside me, then another. My trembling hands find his hair. Moaning softly and starting to sweat, I grip it as I flex my hips against the strokes of his tongue. The room is cool, but I'm almost unbearably hot. My skin is so tight. My heart pounds so hard it might burst.

"Not yet—with you inside me."

My words are fractured and strained. I'm holding back, barely in control. He must hear the desperation in my voice, because he stops licking, grabs my hips, and drags me to the edge of the mattress. He shucks off his boots, tears off his jeans and briefs, positions himself at my entrance, then plunges deep inside me, so deep, I throw my head back to scream.

Nothing comes out. Pleasure has stolen my voice. I can't make a sound as he starts to fuck me, hard and fast, pulling my hair and sucking on one rigid nipple, scraping it with his teeth.

He fucks me like he owns me, body and soul.

And he does. But I own him too. Every look and touch is evidence of his total surrender. Every kiss is one more link added to the chain.

He breaks away from my breast and takes my mouth in a hard, possessive kiss. He makes an animal sound deep in his chest that's incredibly erotic. He's close to his climax, and he's falling apart.

I fall apart first.

With the initial hard contraction deep inside me, he groans. On the second contraction, I start to thrash, losing control of my body. I find my voice and moan, loud and long, the hard, rhythmic clenching and unclenching of muscles and the aching throb of pleasure breath-stealingly intense.

He comes in a hot swell, jerking and gasping as I writhe beneath him. His fingers twist in my hair. His unshaven jaw is a welcome rough scrape against my skin as he moves against me.

When it's over and we're both wrung out, sweating and panting against each other, racked with tremors and utterly spent, I burst into tears.

I curl against Theo's chest and sob like a baby.

He strokes my back and hair, gently kisses my cheek and neck. He holds me tight, his arms like a vise, and throws one heavy leg over me so I feel cocooned, safe and snug in the small slice of heaven we've created in the moonlit shadows of my room.

When the worst of it is over and I'm quietly hiccupping in his arms, I whisper, "Do you still think we can never be friends?"

He cups my face in his hand and tilts it up so we're gazing into each others' eyes. Then he kisses me with such depth of feeling, it brings fresh tears to my eyes. I break away first because I can barely stand how much it hurts, and hide my face in his chest.

We stay like that, locked in each other's arms, until I fall asleep to the sound of his deep, even breathing.

In the morning, he's gone again. Once again, fresh sweet peas sit in a glass of water beside my bed. But this time, there's something else. A haiku, handwritten and left on my pillow.

Isn't it simple?
Whatever we are, or not,
There is only you.

I read it over and over, my eyes filling with water. Then I tuck the poem carefully in my wedding album and pick up the phone to call Suzanne.

It's time I find out where Theo lives.

23

"*W*ell, well, if it isn't Usain Bolt," says Suzanne drily when she hears my voice.

"Hi, Suzanne."

"That was a world-class sprint you made out of church, girlfriend. You training for the Olympics?"

"Yeah, my bad. I'm sorry. But in my defense, I told you I wasn't a big fan."

She snorts. "Had I known not being a fan meant you'd start cackling like a psychopath and burn rubber the second the poor pastor started talking, I'd never have brought you!"

I knew I'd have to eat some crow, so I apologize again, hoping to unruffle some of Suzanne's highly ruffled feathers. "You're right, I was completely out of line. It was disrespectful and uncalled for. I'm really sorry."

"What you should be sorry for is all the gossip you started. Now everyone thinks you're a nutcase!"

"Everyone is right."

Suzanne doesn't even pause to draw a breath before she answers, her voice dismissive.

"Oh, please, honey, you're not crazy. Besides, if you were, you wouldn't think so. The truly insane think they're completely normal and *we're* all off our rockers. Trust me, my uncle Roy was locked up in the loony bin because he was such a nutter. Screaming bloody murder about government surveillance and spiders coming out of his skin. Compared to him, you're a shining example of sanity."

I start to laugh. "That makes me feel so much better. As long as I'm not as nuts as Uncle Roy, I've still got a chance."

"Exactly. Everything's relative, babe." Her voice sours. "Now here's the part where you apologize for not calling me back for almost an entire week after I left you a bazillion messages."

I adopt a solemn tone and try to sound as contrite as possible. "I'm sorry about that too. I'm very, truly, sincerely, utterly, and completely sorry—"

"Oh, for God's sake, stop talking," she interrupts crossly. "I accept your terrible apologies." She sighs and changes the subject. "Have you eaten yet? I was thinking of doing brunch at Booger's."

"Actually, I was planning on running some errands. And, um…I wanted to ask you where someone lives."

"*Someone?*" she repeats, laughing. "Gee, I wonder who it could be?"

"Please don't bust my balls."

"Sorry, that's what ballbusters do. Have you heard from Theo since we last talked?"

When I don't respond fast enough, Suzanne shrieks. "Wait —*have you slept with him?*"

It's my turn to sound cross. "Why does your brain go right there? Seriously, you're like a fifteen-year-old boy."

"You *did*," she says, a thrill in her voice. "Sweet baby Jesus in heaven, tell me *everything!*"

"No," I say emphatically. "I will not."

"Killjoy," she mutters. Then, brightly, "Okay, how about this *one* thing—"

"I won't tell you anything to do with his prowess in bed or the size of his penis."

"What kind of a girlfriend are you? And who says 'penis'? You sound like a doctor."

"Can we please get back on topic?"

"Oh, you mean the topic of Theo's home address?" she drawls. "That you don't have but I do? That you would like me to give you? Without any reciprocity whatsoever?"

I huff out a breath. "Fine. I'll tell you *one* thing." When she squeals happily, I shake my head in disbelief. "Okay, let me think." I close my eyes, trying to recall something that isn't too revealing but will satisfy Suzanne's horny streak. Instantly, I'm lost in memories of Theo's eloquent eyes, his strong, possessive hands, his incredible intensity.

I murmur, "He's so beautiful, it breaks my heart."

At the top of her lungs, Suzanne shouts, "ARE YOU KIDDING ME RIGHT NOW?"

I start to laugh, which only angers her more.

"You have GOT to give me SOMETHING here, Megan!" she hollers. "I haven't gotten laid in about A HUNDRED YEARS, and I'm in no mood to listen to you chirping 'penis' this and 'beautiful' that like you're a damn VIRGIN on her HONEYMOON! How big is the man's DICK?"

I have to answer through my laughter. "It's enormous. It's big, brawny, and works like a champ. Satisfied?"

She starts muttering under her breath about shitty friends and the unfairness of life and various other things until I interrupt her tirade.

"Just give me the address, Suzanne. Please."

"How are you sleeping together and you don't know where he lives?"

I think about how to answer that. "We, um, actually...it never came up."

She grouses, "Right. Because you were too busy having

incredible, mind-blowing sex that you selfishly won't share details of with your girlfriend."

"Suzanne. The address. *Please.*"

"Wait a minute, I have more questions!"

I mutter, "Of course you do."

"The last I heard, Theo had left town—because of you, I might add—but then within the space of a week, he's back and in your pants? How did this happen? What am I missing here?"

"Honestly, your guess is as good as mine."

I can almost hear her eye roll through the phone. "I know Coop gave you a letter or a note that Theo left for you. I pestered him after church to tell me what he wanted to talk to you about. So what was in the note?"

"A quote from the Bible."

That shuts her up for a good fifteen seconds. Then she asks hopefully, "Was it a sexy quote?"

"Are there such things in the Bible?"

"I don't know, I haven't *read* the damn thing!"

"But you sit in a church every week and listen to someone who has."

Her voice drips sarcasm. "I'll ask the pastor if she's been skipping all the juicy parts."

"It was a quote about doors, if you must know, that related to something we'd been discussing earlier." *It also related to a tattoo my dead husband had on his back, but I'm trying hard not to be crazy, so we're not going there.*

Hearing my explanation, Suzanne is dubious. "So he leaves you a note about doors, then he splits for destinations unknown, then he's back in a jiffy, tickling your lady parts? I'm not the brightest bulb, honey, but there are holes in this story bigger than my boobs."

"In between the splitting and the tickling, I wrote him an email."

She ponders that for a while. "Must've been some email."

"Yeah, it was. So...skipping over the details—"

"Bad friend!"

"—what I *can* tell you is that I've seen him twice since he supposedly left town, but he's not coming every day with the rest of the crew to work on the Buttercup—"

"Whoa, whoa, rewind! Hillrise is working on the Buttercup?"

"Oh. Yes. Did I leave that out?"

She groans in exasperation. "Do you even know *how* to do the girlfriend thing, girlfriend?"

"I'd apologize again, but I think my apologies just irritate you."

"So does your god-awful storytelling! I've got a five-year-old niece who tells more coherent stories about her imaginary pet bunny, Mr. Nibbles!"

"Okay. Starting over. You were caught up to where I had a public meltdown in church. And you know Coop gave me Theo's note, and now you know what was in it. Then, when I got home, I wrote Theo an email that basically explained how I was feeling about everything. Then later that night, he showed up and...uh...we..."

Suzanne scoffs. "Don't pop a vessel trying to find a delicate way to say 'We screwed our brains out,' princess."

I say softly, "We didn't, though, Suzanne. We made love. Sweet, intimate, passionate love."

She mutters, "Dear God in heaven, what did I do to deserve this shit?"

"I'll assume that's a rhetorical question and continue. Both times after we made love, he disappeared. When I woke up in the mornings, he was gone."

She gasps in outrage. "He *didn't*!"

She sounds so horrified, I feel defensive on Theo's behalf. "But he left me flowers and a poem." When she doesn't respond, I sigh. "You're right. It sounds bad when I say it out loud."

She says sarcastically, "You think?"

"Are you deliberately trying to make me feel worse? Because it's working."

"So your plan is to do what? Go over to his house and confront him about why he's acting like a dickhead and abandoning you after your 'sweet, intimate' lovemaking?"

She has a point. I don't have a plan, I just want to see him. But what if he doesn't want me at his house? What if he wants me to leave him alone?

Oh God—what if I'm not the only woman on the receiving end of his nocturnal visits? Maybe he has a trail of haikus he's left on pillows all over town!

Suzanne intrudes on my dark musings with an annoyed "Hello? Anybody there?"

"Still here," I answer, though my mind is taking a trip into Paranoiaville.

"Listen, I'll give you his address, but why don't you send him another one of your magical emails first?"

"I was trying to give him space."

"Space?" she repeats, incredulous. "No, he doesn't get to have space, *he's been inside you!* You can crowd him all you want!"

"You make a good point."

"Oh, I'm full of 'em. Here's another one: showing up unannounced at a man's home doesn't exactly count as giving him space. Not that he's allowed to have space, because he's already dipped his willy in your honey pot, I'm just saying."

"You're ragging on me for saying penis while you throw out ridiculous euphemisms for genitals like willy and honey pot?"

She ignores me, switching into concerned-friend mode. "Tell me the truth now, honey. Are you okay? I've been worried about you."

I stand from where I've been sitting on the edge of my bed and walk to the patio windows. Looking out at the restless ocean, I say, "Define okay."

"That really doesn't help my peace of mind."

"I'm just confused, I guess. I don't know how to handle this. I haven't been with anyone since my husband died." My laugh is small and uncomfortable. "I wasn't with anyone before him either."

A blistering curse comes over the line, then Suzanne says hotly, "And Theo has the *nerve* to ghost you after sex!"

Ghost. That word strikes a jarring chord in my ears. I back away from it as if it's a hissing snake. "You said it yourself, Suzanne—he isn't in his right mind. I'm sure this is as difficult and unexpected for him as it as for me."

"It better be," she says with vehemence. "Or I'll rip off his balls myself."

Despite how unsettled I am, I have to smile. "Not so long ago, you were defending him when I called him an asshole. Look at you now."

"Yeah, take note. This is how you girlfriend, girlfriend. It's us against them. Hoes before bros and all that. Now get a pen so I can give you your lover's address—and call me the *second* you hear from him! I'm not letting you deal with this alone."

After Suzanne gives me the address and we disconnect, I spend half an hour engaged in my new favorite form of exercise: pacing. Back and forth I march over my bedroom floor, chewing my thumbnail and working myself into a frenzy.

Why didn't I ask him where he's been when he was here? Why didn't I ask him when I'd see him again? Is this what it's like to date nowadays? Is this what I should expect, intense, soul-searing sex followed by a disappearing act that would make Houdini proud along with flowers, a fresh pot of coffee, and a cryptic poem on my pillow?

Okay, the flowers and the poem are nice touches. I'm calling the flowers a "nice touch" so I don't have to call them what they really are: prime magical-thinking material. But the more I think about the disappearing, the more it bothers me.

I really hope he didn't leave because of how loudly I snore.

On the other hand, compared to whatever else it could be, that's not such a bad reason.

"Oh, for God's sake, Megan, Suzanne is right," I scold myself. "You and Theo slept together. If he didn't want you feeling weird, he shouldn't have run out in the middle of the night. Just contact him!"

That decision made, I feel better. I get my laptop and compose a short email to Theo saying I can't wait to see him again. Then I spend five minutes afterward hating myself for every word, because on a re-read, it sounds desperate.

I forget all about my desperation when I receive an automatic response from Theo's email server that says he's out of the office and not responding to email.

A strange feeling forms in the pit of my stomach. I decide to try Theo's phone. When it goes straight to voicemail, the strange feeling intensifies into anxiety.

I don't know what it is, but something's off.

When I hear the low rumble of engine noise coming from the street outside, I head downstairs. It's Saturday, but Hillrise is working through the weekends to get the project as far as possible before the rainy season starts in full force. When I swing open the front door, Coop's already walking up the steps of the porch, wearing his trademark smile.

"Mornin', Megan!"

"Morning, Coop. Question for you: why hasn't my deposit check to Hillrise cleared my account yet?"

Wearing his usual outfit of flannel shirt and jeans, he leans against the doorframe and grins down at me. "'Cause I haven't deposited it."

I inspect his face. "I sense there's a reason other than that you just haven't had time to get to the bank."

His smile widens. When he doesn't answer, an alarm bell goes off in my head.

"No. Oh, no, Coop, that's *not* happening!"

"What're you talkin' about?" He blinks, the picture of innocence.

"You're going to deposit that check *first thing* Monday morning. These guys need to get paid. You need to get paid. There's too much material and labor costs on this project to do it for free!"

"Aw, that's real sweet. But don't you worry about me and the boys. We're gettin' paid. And the bills for the material and equipment are gettin' paid. Hillrise's got plenty of dough."

I throw my hands in the air. "If you're not taking my money, I'm firing you!"

He bursts out laughing. "Now there's some female logic if I ever heard it! If somebody told me I'd get my house renovated at no cost, I'd be doin' somersaults on the front lawn!"

"I'm serious, Coop, this is bullshit!"

He shrugs, as if there's nothing he can do about the situation. "Sorry, ma'am, I don't make these decisions. You'll have to take it up with the owner."

Fuming, I blow out a hard breath. "I would, but the owner isn't available by email or cell phone. You have any idea how I can get a hold of him?"

He gazes at me for a while, his eyes thoughtful. "Carrier pigeon?"

I send him a withering scowl. "Oh, you're funny. Ha. Friggin'. *Ha.*"

He presses his lips together to try to stop from laughing, which only pisses me off even more.

"Coop, what the hell is going on? *Where's Theo?*"

Workers start to file up the pathway to the front door, talking and joking with each other. Coop pulls me aside into a quiet corner, then keeps his voice low. "He's gettin' help, okay?"

"Help? What does that mean?"

Coop drags a hand over his blond head and sighs. Then he props his hands on his hips and looks me dead in the eyes. "It means he checked himself into a facility in Melville."

Facility. I swallow, fighting the same anxiety I felt upstairs. "What kind of facility?"

He says gently, "You know what kind."

Horrified, I whisper, "A mental hospital?"

"They got a good program over at Acadia. Great success rate. And it's not full-time, he can leave at night and over weekends if he wants to." He looks uncomfortable when I keep staring at him in disbelief. "It's not court mandated or anything. He volunteered."

I stumble over to the stairs, cursing the lack of chairs in the house. I sit heavily on the second step and grip the banister, trying to stop the room from spinning.

Theo checked himself into a mental hospital. According to what Coop told me at church, he was stable before I moved here —but now he's taking a vacation at a funny farm.

Images come back to haunt me with sickening clarity: the anguish in Theo's eyes almost every time he's looked at me; him so wrecked, standing wet and crying outside my front door; the email that brought him to me in the middle of the night, all the things I wrote about losing your mind to follow your heart, and not asking about each other's crazy, and being each other's hammers and glue.

"Oh God," I say, shaking and sick. "Did I do this?"

Coop sits beside me and takes my hand. "Listen to me now. After his accident, Theo changed. It was like he became a different person. He never got the help he needed, because he was just too goddamn stubborn."

Dr. Singer would say Theo and I have a lot in common. I laugh, and it sounds deranged.

"This is a good thing, Megan. He's finally doing something to help himself. He wouldn't admit it to me when he first left, but I got it out of him. And I hope you don't take this the wrong way, but...yeah. It's because of you. You've inspired him to try to get better. He wants to get rid of his demons once and for all."

Demons.

Theo wants to get rid of his *demons*.

My blood runs Arctic cold.

A theory blooms to life inside the cracked and shadowed corridors of my brain and quickly spirals out of control. It's a theory that explains everything, start to finish, from the first moment I laid eyes on Theo and he reacted so strangely to my presence, all the way to his voluntary stay in a sanitarium.

It's a theory that would have Dr. Singer in fits.

It's Magical Thinking with capital letters, in blinking neon lights.

It's a theory that goes like this:

Maybe I'm not the only one who thinks my dead husband has returned to me in the body of another man.

24

"*Megan?* Your face is all funny. You need some water or somethin'?"

Coop is concerned. He should be, because I'm about two seconds away from a full-blown meltdown. The words Theo wrote me appear in my mind like vapor, as if breathed there by a ghost.

What I'd have to say if we talked about the problem wouldn't be romantic, or funny. It would be scary as hell.

And let's not forget this award-winning mind fuck: *How can you remember someone you've never met?*

My mental illness supplies a smug answer: *Because you knew them in another life.*

"I have to go now." I rise unsteadily to my feet.

Coop stands too, still holding on to my hand. "Go? Where you goin'?"

"I have to...pick up...the pharmacy."

If Coop was hoping for a more coherent explanation, he won't get one. My mind is a jumble of fractured thoughts and memories, each more disturbing than the last. I'm tumbling down a rabbit hole, one I'm afraid I'll never climb out of. I'm Alice, only this isn't Wonderland.

This is Crazyville, and I've just elected myself mayor.

I grab my purse and keys and head to my car, stumbling over my feet in my rush. As soon as I get my prescription from the pharmacy, I'll call Dr. Anders to make an emergency appointment.

My brain can no longer be trusted at the wheel. It's driving erratically on a narrow mountain road, taking corners too fast, swerving dangerously close to the edge.

I tear through town like a bat out of hell, screeching to a stop in front of the pharmacy and running inside in a panic. The register is all the way in the back of the store, so I have to hazard aisle after aisle of greeting cards and pain relievers, vitamins and suppositories, little old ladies squinting at dusty bottles on shelves. When I find the prescription pickup window, I throw myself at it like a *Titanic* passenger going for the last life raft.

"Megan Dunn hello I'm Megan Dunn you should have a prescription ready for me?" I blurt it out in one long, breathless rush, impatiently drumming my fingers on the counter.

The pharmacist is a thin bald man about a hundred years old who moves at the speed of cold molasses. He looks at me, blinks slowly, then pulls his glasses down the bridge of his nose. "You'll have to get in line, ma'am."

This is when I realize there's a row of people standing behind me, staring at me with varying degrees of annoyance.

"Oh. I'm so sorry." Avoiding eye contact, I slink to the back of the line.

"Megan?"

When I glance up, I'm looking at a pretty brunette with piercing blue eyes.

"Hi. Colleen Elliott. We met at Sunday Anderson's party, do you remember?"

Dear God. It's Theo's ex-fiancée.

I stammer, "Oh—uh—h-hi! How are you! N-nice to see you again!"

My voice is too loud. Colleen quirks an eyebrow, and her smile falters. The woman in line in front of her turns and gives me a snooty once-over, sniffing in disapproval.

I wonder if she saw my performance at church.

Colleen says, "It's nice to see you too. I didn't really get a chance to talk to you at the party. I think you left pretty quick after you came, right?"

The woman in front of Colleen leans in. "She does that."

Yep, definitely a churchgoer. Goddamn small towns. I snap, "Mind your business, Nosey Parker!"

She turns around with another sniff, shaking her head.

Colleen now looks as if she's sorry she said hello, but she's trapped in line and can't get away. Her smile goes brittle. "So how are you settling in? I hear Hillrise is working on the Buttercup?"

Boy, are they. I laugh. "Yep, oh yeah, Hillrise is working on the Buttercup, and man are those guys *good!*" I thunder it, unable to control my volume. I'm smiling so hard, my face might crack.

Eyes widening, Colleen takes a step back. "Yes," she says faintly, hand at her throat. "Theo always does a wonderful job."

A crystal-clear mental image of Theo, thrusting and groaning on top of me, forms in my mind. I produce another unstable laugh, because of course I would.

Nosey Parker shoots me a disapproving glare over her shoulder. I need to deflect the conversation away from me before I completely crack. "Anyway, how are *you?*"

Colleen's face takes on a dreamy, secret expression. She looks down at the basket in her arms and smiles. "I'm good, thanks."

I glance into her basket, see the pregnancy test kit, and want to vomit.

Colleen laughs softly, her cheeks going pink. "This is the fourth one I've bought. I have an appointment at the doctor in a few days to confirm what these things are telling me, but I just can't seem to stop taking them." She glances at me under her lashes, her blue eyes sparkling. "I've always wanted to be a mother."

Me too. "Congratulations." My voice has lost all its animation and now sounds dead.

Nosey Parker leans in again. "In *my* day, if a woman got pregnant without being married, it *wasn't* a cause for congratulations."

Colleen and I both whirl on her and shout, "Mind your business!"

When the woman turns around with her nose in the air, Colleen lets out an exasperated huff that tells me she expects this won't be the first time she'll be on the receiving end of narrow-minded judgment from the womenfolk of Seaside. It makes me feel kinder toward her, and a little protective.

I clear my throat and try to sound like anything other than a woman standing out on a narrow ledge. "How bad is your morning sickness?"

"Pretty bad," she admits, making a face.

"That's good."

She blinks at me, surprised. "It is?"

"Yeah. It's a sign your hormone levels are high. I had it really bad too." Shocked by my admission, I bite my tongue.

Colleen draws her dark brows together into a quizzical frown. "Oh, I didn't know you have children."

I clear my throat again, wanting to die. "I don't."

We stare at each other. I see it the instant she makes the connection. She says softly, "I'm so sorry."

The sympathy in her eyes is excruciating. "Ancient history," I say, my voice cracking.

"Well, you're still young. I mean, it's not too late..."

She trails off, unsure, probably because I look so miserable. I draw a breath and square my shoulders. "Are you having any food cravings yet?"

"Ugh. No. I can barely keep anything down at this point."

The pharmacist calls the first person in line to the counter, and the rest of us shuffle forward. "Have saltines and seltzer water. Fresh ginger brewed into tea also. And make sure you take prenatal vitamins. That's really important."

"Thanks," says Colleen gently.

Jesus. She looks like she wants to give me a hug.

But the line moves forward again, sparing me. Colleen and I stand in awkward silence for a few moments until she makes an unexpected confession.

"Honestly, it's not so much the morning sickness I'm worried about. It's telling my boyfriend."

Boyfriend? Suzanne said Colleen was still pining after Theo. "I take it this is an unexpected development in your relationship?"

She sighs, twirling a lock of dark hair between her fingers. "Yeah. And it's a brand-new relationship too, so..."

So we've got some major baby-mama drama. "Do you think he'll be okay with it?"

The twist of her lips is less than confident. "I don't know. I wouldn't describe him as a family man. He's obsessed with his work. This is the first time he's ever really been in a relationship. Honestly, he's not what I would have thought of as my type." Her laugh is quiet. "I guess I'm just attracted to contractors."

A thunderbolt blasts through the roof and strikes me with a million volts of supercharged electricity. "Contractors?"

Blushing, she smiles dreamily at me. "Yeah. He owns Capstone Construction out in Portland. His name's Craig."

I'm so stunned, I can't speak. I stare at Colleen in dismay, which she must take as interest because she keeps talking, her voice dropping to a just-between-us-girls tone.

"He took me to a really lovely hotel last Friday. It was the first time he told me he loved me."

Last Friday was the night he took me to dinner and propositioned me. Since then, he's tried calling me every day, though I've avoided answering.

I'd like to keep my balls, he said when I threatened him with my butter knife. *If things go the way I hope they will, we're going to need them.*

I should've neutered that strutting rooster when I had the chance.

Anger hardens my voice. "You know, Colleen, I wouldn't worry about telling him. In fact, I wouldn't worry about him at all. Concentrate on yourself, on whatever makes you feel good, on whatever's good for the baby. He should be worried about losing you, not the other way around. And if he acts like a dick when you tell him about the baby"—*which he definitely will*— "drop him like a hot potato and get on with your life. You're too good to put up with any bullshit."

Colleen looks startled by my vehement little speech.

Without turning around, Nosey Parker says loudly, "Amen."

I dig a piece of paper and a pen from my handbag, scribble my number on it, and give it to Colleen. "If you ever need to talk, call me. I'm a really good listener."

"That's so sweet. Thank you, Megan."

She looks surprised, like she can't believe the girl the whole town is gabbing about could be so nice. The line moves forward again, and soon it's Colleen's turn. Before she steps up to the register, she gives me the quick, awkward hug I was dreading, her basket poking into my chest.

"And if *you* ever need to talk, you can call me too," she says softly. "Suzanne has my number. I mean it, anytime."

Then she's chatting up the pharmacist, and I'm left wondering how long it'll take before she finds out through the grapevine that Craig and I had dinner. More importantly, how many curse words and threats of bodily dismemberment I can work into the phone call I'm going to make to that worthless, egotistical, polka-loving peacock.

Distracted for the moment from my pending mental break-down, I get my prescription and get back on the road. It isn't until I find myself driving past the turnoff to the Buttercup that I realize where I'm headed.

I don't know the way, so I pull over to the side of the road and punch Theo's home address into my GPS.

I'm not sure what I was expecting, but it wasn't a modern masterpiece of glass and steel jutting from a steep rocky cliff, overlooking the ocean and surrounded on the other three sides by dense forest. Masculine, austere, and starkly beautiful, it's straight out of *Architectural Digest*.

I swing shut the driver's-side door, then slowly walk up the driveway toward the house, gravel crunching underfoot. The sea breeze is brisk, snapping my hair around my face. The sun shines glaringly bright. Set back about a hundred yards from the house is an old barn, out of place with its old-fashioned style and state of disrepair. It looks as if it's been standing neglected in the same spot at the forest's edge for a hundred years. If it wasn't for the padlock and chain wound around the handles of the sliding doors—both as shiny as newly minted quarters—I'd think no one had been inside it in decades.

I walk up a white marble pathway flanked on both sides by a water feature built to resemble a burbling brook. It flows away from the front door, disappearing into an almost invisible dip in the marble at the driveway's edge. The door itself is a massive slab of steel at least ten feet tall, with a slim steel handle of the same height. Windows on either side of the door give a view of the inside, which is decorated all in white and just as modern as the outside. The furniture is sparse but fits the airy, contempo-rary space perfectly. The interior walls are devoid of artwork or pictures. Windows are the dominating feature.

The entire west-facing wall is made of glass, giving the viewer the impression the house is floating in midair above the ocean.

Feeling strangely scared, I ring the doorbell.

After several minutes go by and it's evident no one is home, I decide to go around the side of the house. Skirting plantings of bamboo, horsetail, and Zen-like stone gardens, I make my way around the house until I come to a high glass wall. There's no door. Beyond the wall is a rectangular infinity pool with a view of the sea.

The lack of furniture on the sleek cement deck makes me suspect that this pool never gets used. It's only for show.

It looks as lonely as I feel.

I retrace my steps absentmindedly. I don't know what I was hoping to find here. A clue, perhaps, into the mystery of Theo Valentine. But this home gives no hint as to the nature or character of its occupant. It's unnervingly sterile, as if it were built so the owner could live inside a blank canvas.

Or wanted to *be* a blank canvas.

Perhaps its austerity is a clue, after all. Perhaps this is the kind of home you buy or build when what you most need is a clean slate. A place to pretend the past doesn't exist.

A place to be reborn.

"Stop it," I chastise myself, the harsh sound of my voice jarring in the silence. No other noise can be heard up here except the whisper of the wind through the trees and the murmur of the waves breaking on the rocky coast far down below.

And the dark, familiar voice of my insanity, wondering why Theo would keep a padlock and chain on a decrepit barn door. Who could he be trying to keep out?

Or what might he be trying to keep hidden within?

I stand staring at the barn for a long time, wondering if it's my imagination or if I really *can* smell that hint of sweet peas perfuming the cool morning air.

25

One of the side effects of the drug that Dr. Singer prescribed me is nausea. Severe nausea, the rolling, violent kind like seasickness, only worse because it never goes away. Paired with ringing in my ears and a disturbing sensation of dizziness, the medication renders me useless.

After six days of puking my guts out and stumbling around in a fog, I flush the rest of the pills down the toilet. I call Dr. Singer to get a different prescription and am told by his secretary that he's gone on vacation and won't be back for two weeks.

So much for him being available for me to talk to anytime.

Dr. Anders doesn't have a spot open for another few days, so in the interim, my leaking mental dinghy is adrift in shark-infested waters.

I know I'm unwell. I'm dangerously obsessed with Theo, and his continued absence only makes it worse. I drive by his house at all hours, hoping he'll be there, but he never is. I take a trip out to Melville and find the facility he checked himself into, then sit in the car and stare at the building until a security guard approaches warily, wanting to know what I'm doing.

I tell him I don't know, because I honestly don't.

I write email after email to Theo, none of them sent. I save them in the drafts folder, unwilling to delete them, as if somehow that might make things worse.

All the while, Coop and his workers are busy transforming the Buttercup from ugly duckling into beautiful swan, using Theo's plans as their guide.

The master bedroom—a spectacular suite that makes me swoon, it's so gorgeous—is finished in record-setting time. The roof and plaster repair work are coming along at a remarkable clip. Every day, I'm amazed by the progress, and if I hear a familiar footstep downstairs in the middle of the night, I know it's only my mind playing tricks on me, because Theo never appears.

Then, on Halloween, he finally does.

"It's a Halloween party, Megan. That means you're supposed to wear a costume, not the clothes you wear every other day of the week!"

Suzanne has her hands propped on her hips. She's looking me up and down with an expression of disgust. It's Tuesday night, I've just arrived at her house, and we're supposed to be on our way to Booger's for their annual Spooktacular event, but I'm not sure Suzanne is going to let me out of her house without donning some ridiculous getup like the one she's wearing.

"I refuse to be seen in public looking like a roll of toilet paper, Suzanne."

Aghast, she looks down at herself. "I'm a *mystical mummy!*"

"Mystical? That explains all the glitter in your cleavage."

"Seriously, I can't let you out like that." She waves a hand at my jeans and Bowie T-shirt, grimacing like *I'm* the one with the tragic fashion sense.

"Let's tell people I'm a roadie. If you have a portable amp handy, I could carry that as a prop."

Her eye roll is exaggerated. "Oh, right. Let me go grab my portable amp, I'm sure it's around here somewhere."

"It could be underneath that wig."

The blonde bouffant wig perched on her head is as big as a ten-gallon cowboy hat and decorated with shredded bits of the same white gauze she's wrapped around her body. The gauze is supposed to resemble the linen bandages used to dress mummies, but the overall effect is that Suzanne recently suffered an unfortunate accident at a toilet paper factory.

"Don't you diss my wig. This thing cost a fortune!" She pats the towering wall of synthetic fiber, making it jiggle. Then her eyes go round, and she shouts, "Oh!"

With that, she runs down the hallway toward her bedroom, trailing bits of gauze in her wake.

I look at De Niro, Pacino, and Stallone, lounging on the sofa and regarding me with catlike disdain. "Don't worry, boys. Mommy's the *normal* one here."

In moments, Suzanne reappears from her bedroom holding a wig so purple, it glows. She tosses it at me, forcing me to catch it. "Put that on."

I curl my lip. "This color doesn't occur in nature."

"I'll tell you what else doesn't occur in nature—these shoes!" She sticks out a leg, clad in a six-inch spike-heel sandal with leather straps that crisscross the length of her calf from ankle to knee. The shoes are meant to look Egyptian, but they bear a striking resemblance to dominatrix wear. Mistress Charmin the mystical mummy.

"So wear flats," I suggest, making her retch.

"Flats! Ha! The day I wear flats is the day I've given up all hope of attracting a man!"

"Speaking of men," I say, aiming for a casual tone, "do you think Coop will be at Booger's tonight?"

Suzanne is busily digging through her handbag. She produces a lipstick and compact, then proceeds to paint her lips a very unmummy shade of scarlet red. "Coop? I dunno. Maybe."

"I mean...wouldn't you like to see him there?"

She looks away from her compact and narrows her eyes at me. "What's that supposed to mean?"

Considering how peeved I was when she tried to set me up with Doug, the height-challenged building inspector, I have to tread carefully or risk being labeled a hypocrite. "Nothing. Only..."

Suzanne drops the compact and lipstick back into her bag, then turns to me with her arms folded. "Only what?"

She's suspicious already. I might as well spit it out. "Only I'm sure he'd love to see *you* there."

It takes a minute for her to process that, then she rears back like I've slapped her across the face. "Don't be ridiculous!"

"Why is that ridiculous?"

"Preston Cooper is the last man on earth who'd be interested in a girl like me, that's why! He likes *sweet* girls"—she simpers, batting her lashes—"homebodies who are duller than dirt who no one ever gossips about because they never do anything interesting! Girls like his wife!"

"Ex-wife."

"Put on the damn wig."

She's annoyed by the turn in the conversation, so I let it go. "Who else will be at this shindig?"

"If you're worried about the church ladies who've been talking about you, yes, most of them will be there. So will pretty much everyone else in this town. Booger's annual Spooktacular is second only to the Christmas boat parade in popularity. Which is why you need a costume!"

I jam the wig on my head, make a few adjustments so all the purple strands are out of my eyes, and deadpan, "Ta-da. Costume."

"You're the worst." She slings her handbag over her gauzy

shoulder and heads for the door. "Let's get outta here before the cats decide I'm a scratching post and shred me."

Once in the car, Suzanne spends so much time staring at my profile, I start to get weirded out. "What're you looking at?"

"I haven't seen you since church. You've lost weight."

"Maybe I should've gone as the mummy," I mutter, taking a corner too fast.

"Have you been sick?"

"Jesus, do I look that bad?"

"No, you actually look great—bitch—just thinner. And sort of...haunted."

I drag in a breath and grip the steering wheel harder. "I went on Lexapro for a few days, but it made me so sick, I stopped taking it. I couldn't keep anything down."

"Megan, I *told* you you're *not* crazy." Her tone is the same one my mother used right before I got a spanking as a kid.

"My shrink might disagree."

"Fuck him!"

"He's not my type."

"Quit being sarcastic, this is serious! Just because you're going through a rough patch doesn't mean you need to take drugs!"

"Those drugs can save people's lives, Suzanne."

"They can also end them!" she shoots back hotly. "You ever see the list of horrible side effects for those antidepressants? Uncontrollable thoughts of suicide is right at the top!"

I assume this is her experience with her institutionalized Uncle Roy talking, but I'm too irritated to get into it. People who've never had depression don't have a clue what it's like. I can't count how many times I've been told to "just get over it" or "focus on the positive" by well-meaning friends.

But then she says something that stops my irritation dead in its tracks.

"I mean, hell, if my boyfriend locked himself away in a psych ward, I'd be upset too, but you wouldn't see me medicating my damn...self..." She trails off into silence, staring at me with wide eyes.

"How do you know Theo locked himself away in a psych ward?"

"Um..."

Realization punches me in the solar plexus. "Oh my God. *Everyone* in Seaside knows where Theo is, don't they?"

She looks apologetic, scrunching up her shoulders. "Maybe?"

I shout, "How?"

"Well, honey—now don't get upset—Leanne's cousin's hairdresser, Maxine, has a stepbrother who's up at Acadia right now, having a little rest after his brain got knocked askew from spending one too many years balls-deep in cocaine. Maxine went to visit the stepbrother last week and saw Theo wandering around the grounds. Said he looked really out of it. So she told all her clients at the salon, one of whom was Leanne's cousin, and the cousin told Leanne, and Leanne—who's a major flaptrap, by the way, don't *ever* trust that woman with a secret—told her book club and her knitting circle, and—"

"I got it!" I holler, red-faced. I don't know who any of those people are, but I know how the gossip line works, and how fast a juicy bit of news burns through it.

"Sorry. I know it sucks. If it's any consolation, nobody knows about you two."

I groan. "I'm not worried about me—I'm worried about him! What will this do to his business? Will people treat him differently? How's he going to feel, knowing everyone's judging him and talking behind his back?"

"Probably the same way he's felt for the last few years while they've been doing it."

I groan again, miserable at the thought of Theo being subjected to stares and whispers.

Suzanne pats my arm. "Believe it or not, everyone's pulling for him. Maybe this will turn out to be a good thing. He's needed to get help for a long time."

I stew in silence for several minutes, until Suzanne asks tentatively, "So, um, did you ever go to his house?"

I exhale in a gust. "God, I feel like such a jerk for doing that. I hope he doesn't have security cameras. The last thing the poor man needs is the woman he's having random booty calls with creeping around his property like a total lunatic."

I fail to mention all the drive-bys, but Suzanne makes me feel bad enough for the one visit I admit to by saying, "Yeah. Let's hope he's never seen the movie *Fatal Attraction*."

I say sourly, "Thanks."

"About those booty calls—"

"No."

"No, you're not talking about them, or no, there haven't been any more than the two you weren't talking about in the first place?"

"Both."

She sighs. "Bummer."

"Tell me about it."

"Any idea when you'll see him again?"

"No."

"What does he say about it when you ask him?"

"I *don't* ask him. He isn't responding to emails, and his phone is turned off. Plus, I sort of set up this don't ask, don't tell situation regarding our relationship." When she stares at me cockeyed, it's my turn to sigh. "These things always sound better inside my head than they do out loud."

Suzanne is beginning to look disturbed. "So...what? You just have to wait for him to show up?"

"Basically."

"Oh, for fuck's sake, we can't have that! You're not some ditzy Disney princess, wasting all your pretty years pining for your knight in shining denim!" She thinks for a moment. "What if you sent him a letter at Acadia?"

"Is that what you'd do?"

She scoffs. "Oh hell, no, honey, I'd already have broken into the damn place and chewed through his underwear."

"Of course you would." I pull into the parking lot at Booger's, stop in front of a valet stand, and we head inside.

Booger's is packed. It's wall-to-wall zombies and witches, ghosts and pirates, fairies and vampires. A few Star Wars and Marvel comics characters round out the mix. Everyone is laughing and mingling, crowding the dance floor, guzzling drinks. Suzanne drags me through the crush to a table on the far side of the room, near the temporary bar that's been erected in one corner to handle the overflow of guests. It's manned by a guy dressed as the Joker in a bright purple suit. I want to give him my wig.

I also want to leave.

It's too packed, too loud, and my social anxiety is kicking in with a vengeance. Why the hell did I agree to this? I *hate* parties.

"Oh no," says Suzanne, examining my expression. "You're not going anywhere, girlfriend. Sit your ass down in that chair and pretend to enjoy yourself. I'm gonna get a drink—what do you want?"

"Ginger ale."

She pushes me into a chair and heads off to the Joker, trailing wisps of gauze like snow. The instant she leaves, a man lowers himself into the chair opposite mine.

It's Craig.

He's the only other person in the place in normal clothes, in his case, tan slacks and a black cashmere sweater. His hair is perfect. His smile is perfect. His eyes are as hungry as a crocodile's.

I grit my teeth in disbelief at how much the universe loves to fuck with me. "What're you doing here?"

"You've been avoiding my calls."

"So true. Funny how I wouldn't want to talk to a lying, philandering dick."

If he's surprised by my hostility, he doesn't show it. "How am I a liar?"

"Go away."

"Or a philanderer?"

"Are you hearing impaired? I said *go away*."

A muscle flexes in his jaw. "At least give me the courtesy of an explanation. When I dropped you at your place after we had dinner, I thought everything was great. I thought we had a real connection."

There's a sneer in my laugh that makes his eyes darken. "You're good, I'll give you that. All your talk of 'I don't play games' and 'You'll always know where you stand with me.' Women must eat that shit up. I mean, *I* thought it sounded genuine."

I pause, staring at him with what I hope is pure disgust on my face. "I'm sure Colleen thinks so too. Tell me, how long did it take you to call her after you dropped me at my front door? Ten seconds? Twenty?"

After a beat, he leans back in his chair, crosses his legs, folds his hands in his lap, and smiles. "You're adorable when you're jealous."

He thinks I'm jealous? The ego on this idiot. He's lucky there isn't any cutlery on the table, because he'd have a fork embedded in his forehead right about now.

I say with freezing calm, "Time to fuck off, Craig. And if you don't want me telling your *girlfriend* Colleen what a giant piece of shit you are, make it quick."

"She isn't my girlfriend."

"If you don't get out of my face within five seconds, I'll find something to stab you with."

His smile grows indulgent, like he's dealing with a cute, fussing baby. "Don't be silly. You'll do no such thing."

I lean in on my elbows, rest my chin on my hands, and smile back at him with all my teeth showing. "Haven't you heard, Craig? I'm. Fucking. *Nuts*."

When he blinks, I know I've finally broken through.

"Oh, Craig! Hi! Fancy seeing *you* here!" Suzanne stands at the side of the table, holding two drinks and gazing at Craig with all the warmth of an iceberg.

I haven't told her about my talk with Colleen at the pharmacy, so her reaction is all about his brush-off when the three of us had dinner. I've always liked a woman who can hold a grudge.

"Hello, Suzanne," he says smoothly, rising. "How nice to see you again. You look beautiful." He ogles her cleavage, not bothering to be the tiniest bit discreet about it.

Jesus Christ. The man is single-handedly eroding my faith in humankind.

"I know," says Suzanne flatly, and pushes past him to sit down.

Then the universe decides it hasn't had nearly enough fun for the evening and produces Colleen.

She's wearing a tight black Catwoman costume and looks fantastic. Nary a baby bump in sight. "Hi, ladies," she says, smiling. She glances at Craig, standing there with his plastic grin fixed on his face. "Have you met Craig?"

Suzanne and I both say, "Yep!" and glare at him.

As Colleen's face registers confusion at all the odd tension in the air, the music changes. What was an upbeat pop number fades into the slow, sultry voice of Etta James, singing her signature blues love song, "At Last."

Closing my eyes, I soak in the song's passionate vocals and sweeping violins. I pull the stupid purple wig off and drop my head into my hands, wishing I were any place else on earth so I could burst into tears.

"Sweetie," says Suzanne, touching my hand. "What's wrong?"

"This song," I say, my voice breaking.

"What about it?"

I start to chuckle in small, agonized gasps that are closer to sobs than laughter. "It was *our* song. Mine and Cass's, from the time it was playing on the radio when he gave me a promise ring when we were fifteen, to our first dance at our wedding reception. Every time it came on, he'd tell me he loved me."

I love you, sweet pea. I'll love you till the end of time.

I hear his voice exactly as if he's standing right beside me. Tears, hot and burning, quickly form behind my eyes. *Shit*—I'm going to cry. I've got to get out of this room before I have a meltdown.

But instead of running away when I open my eyes, I freeze, the impulse to flee retracting in one hard, reflexive movement, like a hand clenching to a fist.

Across the dance floor, half-hidden in the shadows of a doorway, stands Theo.

He's staring right at me.

He's smiling.

26

*T*he room fades to black. Everything and everyone else disappears, and all that remains is him, standing there motionless, gazing at me with his smile so warm and his heart shining so brightly in his eyes.

He's freshly shaven. It makes the hard angle of his jaw gleam like the edge of a blade. He's wearing his usual outfit of boots, black leather jacket, and jeans, but his hair has been combed and trimmed. He looks scrubbed. Refreshed.

Knock-out, breath-stealing, uterus-scorching beautiful.

Someone says, "Is that Theo?" Then his name is all over the place, whispered in every corner of the room, an astonished repetition of *Theo Theo Theo* in dozens of hushed voices, none meant to carry but collectively as loud as a bell.

He moves out from the shadows of the doorway and gracefully crosses the dance floor, his gaze locked on mine. People scurry out of his way as he approaches the table, jostling each other in their hurry to give him room. He stops beside my chair. Without breaking eye contact, he holds out his hand.

When our fingers meet, that familiar zing of static electricity sparks between our skin. He clasps my hand, and I float breath-lessly to my feet.

Theo leads me to the middle of the dance floor and takes me in his arms, then we stand there unmoving, staring into each other's eyes as the music swells to a crescendo and Etta's voice becomes the soaring soundtrack to the beating of my heart.

I say, "Hi."

In response, he bends his head to my neck and deeply inhales.

I tighten my arms around his shoulders and hide my face against his chest, not caring that we've got hundreds of gaping witnesses. My heart pounds so hard, I can feel it in my fingertips. "You sure know how to make an entrance, Sunshine."

A low rumble passes through his chest. A chuckle?

He shifts his weight, then we're gently swaying. Our bodies pressed together, we move slowly in time to the music, as effort-less as a sigh.

"I've missed you."

He puts a finger under my chin and tilts my head up so I'm looking at him, then taps himself on the chest and holds up two fingers. *Me too.*

"You seem...better."

He slowly nods. His pupils are dilated. He blinks, and it's as lazy as his nod.

He's high.

Like ice water, a cold flush of horror slices through my veins. When I stiffen in his arms, he cocks his head, looking at me with half-lidded eyes.

"Theo, are you stoned right now?"

His face registers faint surprise, then he shakes his head. He mouths something, and it takes me a moment to recognize what he's trying to say:

Meds.

He's on medication. Why that should be such a surprise, I

don't know, because generally, when a person checks himself into a facility for hard-core psychiatric care, medication is involved.

I whisper, "Are you...are you okay?"

Smiling dreamily, he nods again. He taps his temple and makes a *poof* motion with his hand. If he were anyone else, I wouldn't know what that meant, but this is the man who once told me he hears voices and sees ghosts. He's saying they're gone. The meds have banished them.

Must be some strong fucking meds.

Strong enough to kill demons.

Fear sinks cold fingers into my heart. The song ends, the music changes, and suddenly, everything that was so magical is jarring and strange. "I want to leave, Theo. Will you come home with me?"

When he takes my face in his hands and gently kisses me, I take it as a yes. I order him to stay right where he is, run back to the table, and tell Suzanne I'm leaving.

She sips her drink and grins. "Honey, I'm surprised you're still here."

"How are you gonna get home?"

She waves a hand. "Taxi. Or maybe the Joker—he's kinda cute." She raises her glass and toasts the bartender, sending him a wink.

I don't bother to see if he winks back. I give her a kiss and run back to Theo, ignoring all the eyes following my every move. I grab his hand and lead him off the dance floor, snarling at anyone too slow to get out of my way.

I don't give a shit about being polite right now. I have to be alone with this man, or I'm liable to commit murder.

The drive home takes half the time it normally would because I break every traffic law in existence. The entire time, Theo simply looks at me, stroking my hair and smiling, undisturbed even when we tear so fast around corners, the tires squeal.

I don't like his unnatural calm. I don't like the glassiness in his eyes, that strange new haze that has taken the place of everything that was once so sharp. I don't like the way his right hand trembles at regular intervals, or the way his shoulders occasionally twitch, or the way he keeps swallowing, as if his mouth is dry.

There's always a price to be paid for sanity, but in this case, I think it might be too high.

"Theo, what medication are you on?"

He reaches into his coat pocket, removes two small orange vials, and hands them to me. I flick on the overhead light and squint at the labels. One is valium—that's probably causing the glassy eyes, but it should be out of his system by morning. The other one bears an ominously long name I've never seen before. It must be the demon killer causing all the twitching.

I hold that bottle up. "Is this something you'll need to be on permanently?"

He nods.

Fuck.

I hit the light and drop the bottles into the cup holder. When I huff out a worried breath, he leans over and rests his head in my lap, nuzzling my thighs and stroking my knee, sighing in contentment. By the time we arrive at the Buttercup, he's fast asleep.

I pull into the driveway, shut off the car, and sit in the darkness, listening to the engine tick and Theo's deep, even breathing.

How the hell did he get to Booger's? There's no way he could've managed to drive. Coop said Theo could leave Acadia at night and for weekends if he wanted to, but the staff must monitor the patients' conditions. I can't believe they'd let him float out the door like this, high as a kite!

Abruptly, I'm angry. Angry at the employees at Acadia, angry at the universe, angry at his stupid medication and its stupid side effects.

Most of all, angry at myself.

If I'd never moved to Seaside, Theo would've been all right. Maybe not stable, maybe not exactly sane, but all right. Surviving.

Which is all any of us can reasonably expect in this shitty, fucked-up world. But now here he is, passed out in my lap, a lion reduced to a woozy lamb.

I fish around in his coat, not exactly sure what I'm looking for. Then I feel something in an inside pocket and pull it out. It's a small white card on which Theo has written the words *If found, please return home.*

Underneath that, he's written my name, address, and phone number.

My face crumples. Hot tears slide silently down my cheeks. I slip the card back into his pocket, then sit in the car for a long time, thinking, my mind a dark snarl that goes over and over every possible scenario for what needs to happen next. Ultimately, I decide that no matter what the truth is—whether I'm dealing with a miracle or just two people suffering from mental illness—Theo is now my home too. And there's nothing in this world that could make me leave his side.

Crazy or not, we're in this shit together.

That decision made, I get Theo inside, get him upstairs, and put him to bed.

Then I fire up my computer and google a contact number for Acadia.

I didn't expect Theo's doctor to be available. I didn't expect anyone to be available except maybe a night receptionist, but when I tell the woman who answers the phone that I'm Theo Valentine's wife, there's a long pause, then she says, "Hold the line, please."

The wait stretches so long, I have time to pour myself a whiskey, drink it, and refill my glass. Then a man with a brusque Boston accent and an attitude to match picks up the phone.

"This is Dr. Garner. Who's this?"

"Megan Du—Valentine. Theo Valentine's wife."

It's a ridiculous gamble. I have no reason to believe Theo might have listed me as a contact on his medical papers, and even less reason to think he might've listed me as his spouse. But the same magical thinking that had me stringing coincidences together like Christmas lights has me thinking there's a chance that he did.

Sure enough, I'm right.

"Hello, Mrs. Valentine," says Dr. Garner. "How can I help you?"

I'm so relieved, my legs give out. I slide down to the floor and sit there shaking, the phone clutched in one hand and my whiskey in the other. The only thing holding me up is the kitchen counter against my back. I clear my throat, then try to sound like a rational person and not the barking fruitcake I really am. "I want to talk to you about Theo's treatment plan."

"I'm not at liberty to discuss that."

"That's very interesting, Dr. Garner, because the HIPAA Privacy Rule specifically allows a doctor to discuss a patient's health status with his family."

If he's impressed by my knowledge of federal health privacy laws, he doesn't let on. In a voice as dry as dust, he replies, "Yes. It *allows* for discussion. It doesn't require it; disclosure is at the doctor's discretion."

Fuck. This guy is a brick wall. "I'd think you'd want to do anything you could to help Theo's recovery."

There's a pause, then Dr. Garner says, "Forgive me for being blunt, Mrs. Valentine, but I could say the same thing about you."

Like a hissing cat's, my hackles go up. "What's that supposed to mean?"

"Are you aware of the nature of your husband's hallucinations?"

I gulp, my defensiveness vanishing as quickly as it appeared. "He...he mentioned ghosts. Voices."

"Schizophrenia is characterized by delusions—"

"*Schizophrenia?*"

My horrified shout cuts Dr. Garner short, then he continues in a sharper tone. "I don't know how familiar you are with severe mental illnesses, Mrs. Valentine, but Theo needs care for the rest of his life to manage the symptoms of his disease. That means medication, therapy, and—most importantly—support from family and friends."

The doctor's voice gains an even harder edge. "He's made it clear he can't talk to you about his condition, so frankly, I'm not inclined to talk to you about it either."

I drain the rest of the whiskey in my glass. It burns a fiery path down my throat, mirroring the blaze of insanity scorching its way through my brain.

Maybe the reason Theo can't talk to me about his hallucinations is because I play a starring role in them. Maybe what he thinks are hallucinations are something else entirely.

For instance, memories.

In a shaking voice, I say, "Dr. Garner, do you believe in reincarnation?"

"No," he says flatly, "and I don't believe in Santa Claus or the Tooth Fairy either. If you want to help your husband, convince him to continue his stay at Acadia."

"Continue? You mean..."

"He's completed the treatment period he signed up for. I don't believe he's a threat to himself or anyone else, so there's nothing I can do to keep him here, but I *strongly* believe a stable, therapeutic environment like the one we offer here is in his best interests."

I stand, balance myself on the kitchen counter for support, straighten my shoulders, and take a grounding breath. When I blow it out, I'm filled with new resolve.

"I'll tell you what's in his best interests. Being home with me."

I hang up, go upstairs, and crawl under the covers next to

Theo, who's sleeping as still and silent as death on Cass's side of the bed.

I wake in the quiet gray hours before dawn, burning hot and disoriented. I spend a moment in that hazy space between dreams and reality, my limbs and eyelids heavy, my heart thudding a slow and steady pace.

A hand, strong and rough, slides up my thigh.

Here's the source of all that heat: Theo's wrapped around me like a blanket. His legs are drawn up behind mine, his chest is pressed against my back, one muscular arm pillows my head. His lips brush the nape of my neck.

His erection is a different heat, rock hard and throbbing against my bottom.

He slides his hand over my hip and rib cage and cups my breast, lazily thumbing my nipple until it stiffens. His mouth, hot and wet, opens over my shoulder.

I whisper, "Good morning."

In response, he presses his teeth gently into my skin.

"Did you sleep well?"

He sucks where his teeth have just been, sliding his hand down my belly and between my legs. I inhale a quiet breath when he touches that most sensitive part of me. With slow, stroking circles, his fingers work their magic. Within moments, I'm softly moaning, turning my head for his kiss.

He takes my mouth. The kiss is deep and erotic, as unhurried as his hands. Soon I'm making a mewling sound in my throat, needing more.

He gives it to me.

Spreading my legs with his knee, he slides his erection between my thighs and uses his hand to guide it between my wetness. But he doesn't push inside—he strokes back and forth, his shaft sliding through my folds as he continues to work me with his fingers.

I make a small sound of pleasure, rocking my hips in time to his soft, even strokes.

He goes on like that, maddeningly slow, until I start to breathe raggedly and push harder against him. A noise rumbles through his chest, deep and dark, the sound of his desire. He grasps my inner thigh, lifts my leg higher, and cants his hips until he gets the right angle. With one sure thrust, he slides inside.

I arch, moan, shudder. He flattens his hand over my stomach and holds me against his body as he starts to pump into me, shallowly at first, until the greedy movement of my hips forces him deeper.

Then he rolls me onto my belly, fists a hand in my hair, and fucks me until I'm gasping.

I come hard, my fingers digging into the mattress, animal noises of pleasure raw in my throat. He grunts his approval, his breath ragged, his body heavy and hard against my back. I think he's going to come too, but he slows, withdraws, then flips me over. Then he lowers himself between my thighs and kisses me deeply as he pushes inside.

It's so good. So natural. He feels like heaven.

He feels like mine.

I hook my ankles around his back and twist my fingers into his hair, pulling hard because I can't get him deep enough, close enough. I want more of him. More of everything.

He starts to lose himself. I feel it in the way his arms shake, hear it in the deep rasps of his breath, see it in his face as his brows draw together in the kind of pleasure so acute, it's almost pain. With every thrust of his pelvis, my nipples drag against his chest. He bends his head and takes one into his mouth, then sucks hard as he starts to buck uncontrollably, pumping deep and groaning around my flesh.

"Ah—Theo!"

His entire body jerks. He makes a sound like he's dying. His hands twitch against my head as his orgasm rips another sound from his lips. A new sound, one I've never heard him make before.

It's a name.

My name.

"*Megan!*"

All the lingering doubts about my sanity and the impossible puzzle my brain has pieced together are destroyed by finally hearing Theo speak.

Because now I know why he stopped talking.

His voice isn't his own.

It belongs to a man with sky-blue eyes and a smile like sunshine, whom I first met when I was six years old.

27

I erupt into sobs so hysterical, Theo freezes in shock. Clinging to him with every ounce of strength in my arms, I bury my face in his neck and pour out my euphoria in wave after uncontrollable wave of tears.

"I knew it!" I wail, my voice muffled against his skin. "I knew you'd come back to me!"

Theo's frozen muscles relax. He exhales, pressing a kiss to my neck. With an edge like a purr, a low laugh rumbles through his chest.

"Sweetheart," he whispers, his lips near my ear. "I was only gone for a few weeks." His tone turns gently teasing. "Are you always gonna get this emotional after sex?"

The words are Theo's, but the voice is one I know well, its timbre a shade more husky, but otherwise unchanged. The echo of that voice has lived in my mind for five long years. I'd recognize it anywhere.

"No—you know what I mean!" I lift my head and stare into his eyes. "Cass, Cass, I love you! I never stopped, not even for a second! I always knew you'd come back!"

Theo stops breathing. He falls still, as still as a corpse. Into his eyes comes a look of pure horror. "What?"

I'm crying so hard, I almost can't see. Insane with joy, I press frantic kisses all over his neck. "Why did you try to stay away from me? Why didn't you tell me sooner? Why didn't you come find me in Phoenix?"

He abruptly pushes away from me, withdrawing his body and warmth in a whip-crack move so fast, it's blinding. He leaps up and stands nude at the foot of the bed, gazing down at me with wide, wild eyes, his hands trembling.

He whispers, "What the hell are you talking about?"

Time stops.

All the clocks in the world stop ticking.

Gravity releases its hold on me and blasts me off into black, frozen space.

I sit up in bed and draw the covers over my naked breasts, and we stare at each other across the silence of the room until I find the courage to speak. "You don't have to pretend. I won't...I won't tell anyone." My laugh is small, choked with fear. "Who would believe us anyway?"

After a pause in which I hear every beat of my banging heart, Theo says through gritted teeth, "Who would believe us about *what*?"

My blood crystallizes to ice.

No.

No, this can't be happening.

Tears are still sliding down my cheeks, but I can no longer feel them. I no longer know how to blink, or move, or even breathe.

"Cass—"

"I'm not your dead fucking husband!" Theo roars in my dead husband's voice.

The acid bite of bile forces its way up my throat. I swallow it down, shivering uncontrollably. The air has gone so cold, we could be in a crypt. I say hoarsely, "Why are you lying?"

All the light leaves Theo's eyes. They go dead. It's like watching storm shades being slammed over windows. "This is why you want me? Because you think I'm him?"

Listening to those words in that voice causes a fissure in my brain. I feel it—a quick, hard *snap*—like ice cracking underfoot.

I jolt to my feet, right there on the mattress. Clutching the sheet to my chest, I draw a breath so ragged, it sounds like a death rattle. My voice is even worse, as hollow and eerie as if I'm speaking from beyond the grave.

"I don't think you're him—you *are* him. *And* you're you. You're both, and you're perfect."

"Stop it," he says flatly.

"No. Why did you stop talking after your accident, Theo? Why haven't you spoken a word to anyone in five years?"

He answers without hesitation. "My vocal cords were damaged from smoke inhalation in the accident. My voice changed, and I hated how strange it sounded."

A hysterical laugh tears from my throat. "Smoke damage? Is that how they explained it to you at Acadia? Because I think we both know it's something else."

"Megan, *stop*—"

"Did you ever see me before I moved here, Theo?"

All the blood drains from his face. He's as white as the sheet I'm clutching in my fist. He whispers, "I...I had a brain injury, Megan. My hallucinations...they're not real."

"Then why did you ask Coop how you could remember someone you'd never met?"

Theo swallows, briefly closing his eyes. In a rasp, he says, "My doctor said I couldn't get well unless I started talking again, unless I *forced* myself to. I didn't want to do it for the first time in front of everyone last night at the party—"

"How did you know me, Theo?"

With a strangled cry, Theo runs over to his clothes, left in a pile on the floor on his side of the bed. He yanks on his jeans, shirt, and jacket while I sink farther and farther into the black delirium rising like floodwaters inside my mind.

They drugged him. Those sons of bitches at Acadia, that soulless bastard Dr. Garner—they fed him drugs, told him he's schizophrenic, and brainwashed him into believing a miracle was mental illness.

I'm not having it. I'm not having any of it. This is my soul mate, and I won't let anyone take him away from me.

Not again.

I shout, "You're afraid of yellow balloons!"

Theo flinches as if I've punched him in the gut. Backing away slowly toward the bedroom door, he stares at me as I give witness to the truth of who he is at the absolute top of my lungs.

"Your mother's name was Mary! Your father was Dan! When you were ten years old, you got a beagle and named him Snoopy!"

Theo slaps his hands over his ears. Shaking his head and still moving backward, his face crumples, and he starts to cry.

"You loved hot dogs and bear claws and Mad Max movies! You photographed lightning strikes and painted landscapes in oils! You proposed to me in the same place we first made love when we were sixteen, under the blooming acacia at our favorite spot in the bend in the Salt River! You had a tattoo of Matthew verse seven across your back, because you were a seeker who believed that the only way to get at the truth was to knock on every door until you found it!"

His sob tears a hole in my heart, but I have to keep going. I can't stop, no matter how much he might want me to. I have to break through this wall of denial once and for all.

I step down from the mattress and stalk toward him, one step forward for each stumbling step he takes away, my body racked with tremors, my voice rising to a scream.

"And whether you choose to accept it or not, the truth is that you died at 12:02 in the morning on the seventeenth of May five years ago—your name was Cassidy Michael Dunn, and *you were the love of my life!*"

Crying openly now, Theo turns and sprints from the room.

As his footsteps pound hollowly down the stairs, I lose the strength in my legs. I sink to my knees, the room spinning. In a few moments, the front door slams with a boom that rattles the windows. The roar of a car engine breaks the still of the morning outside, followed by the angry squeal of tires spinning against pavement, then another roar as the car takes off at top speed down the street. I don't have to look to know the car is mine. Theo obviously took my keys from my purse.

I kneel in the same spot for a long time, blank and drained. My mind doesn't sharpen until I hear the wail of sirens far in the distance.

Then the blankness is replaced by a terror so powerful, I'm still frozen in place when the phone begins to ring.

I run.

I run so hard and with such focus, I don't see Coop's red truck blast past me down the boulevard leading into town. I can't see anything, I can't hear anything except the solemn voice of the young man calling from the hospital. The words play on a dark, terrible repeat inside my head.

"We found your number in his clothing. There's been an accident."

Accident.

Three simple syllables with the power to ruin lives.

I pump my arms and legs as hard as they can go, my chest heaving, hot tears streaming down my cheeks. I'm barefoot, but I don't feel the cold asphalt of the road under my feet. I don't feel the misty morning air on my face, or hear my harsh, labored gasps, or smell the sea breeze. I'm half-dead already.

If Theo's gone by the time I get to the hospital, the rest of me will follow.

"Megan!"

My name sounds as if it's been shouted at me from underwater. It's muffled, distorted, a long way away. I keep running.

"Megan!"

A red truck pulls next to me in the street. The window is down. Coop is shouting my name. I remember I called him to come get me because I didn't have a car, and sob in relief.

I slow just enough to yank open the door and throw myself inside. Without waiting for the door to close, Coop slams his foot against the gas pedal, and we rocket down the street.

"How bad is it?"

My teeth chatter so hard, I can barely manage to answer Coop's question. "I don't know. They didn't say. They just said come quick."

"Fuck."

No more words are spoken. In a few short minutes, we screech to a stop outside the emergency room doors of the only hospital in Seaside. I'm out of the truck before Coop has time to shut off the engine.

I burst through the doors and look wildly around, panting in panic. I throw myself at the admission desk, startling the plump brunette sitting behind it when I start shouting.

"Theo Valentine! I'm here for Theo Valentine! Where is he? Where is he? I have to see him!"

"Ma'am, please, calm down!" She rises, hands held up, eyes wide.

I know I look like a madwoman, but I don't care. Furious, I pound my fists on the desk and scream, "*Take me to him now!*"

Coop grabs my shoulders and peels me off the desk.

"Mornin', Angela," he says to the brunette, firmly wedging me under his arm. "Sorry 'bout that. We're all upset—got a call they brought Theo in."

I lean against Coop and weep into his flannel shirt, so scared, I'm delirious.

"Yes, not long ago," says the brunette, sounding rattled. "I'll see if I can get someone to come out and talk to you. Why don't you have a seat in the waiting room?"

"Thanks."

Coop drags me away from the desk and down a short hallway, catching me every time I stumble, his arm the only thing holding me up. When we round the corner and enter a sterile, brightly lit room filled with rows of chairs and one sickly plant dying in a corner, I pull up short, shocked to see Colleen sitting there in her Catwoman costume, crying.

She looks up, catches sight of me and Coop standing in the doorway, and cries harder.

She wails, "I can't go through this again, Coop!"

I don't know what's happening. My mind is broken. Nothing makes sense.

Coop gently sets me in a chair opposite her, makes sure I'm steady, then kneels in front of her and takes her hands. "What happened, Colleen?"

Through her sobs, she tells the story. "W-we were at the Halloween party at Booger's. Craig and I... We got into a fight. He was flirting with every girl there, just being obnoxious about it. And I know it was bad timing, but I was so mad, I told him about the baby—"

"Baby?" Coop says, startled.

Colleen nods, her shoulders shaking. "We haven't been dating very long. He wasn't h-happy"—she hiccups, wiping the back of her hand across her face—"and said it probably wasn't even his."

His voice hard, Coop says, "Do I know this idiot?"

"Craig Kennedy. From Capstone Construction," she whispers.

Coop curses under his breath. "Okay. Go on."

"We left the party late and went back to my house. We kept fighting. H-he was drinking. He was drinking a lot."

Fighting nausea, I close my eyes. *Not again. Please God, not again.*

"When he was leaving, I tried to stop him. I grabbed his keys, but he pushed me down and left. I was terrified he was going to hurt someone, so I followed him in my car and I...I called 9-1-1."

"That's good," murmurs Coop. "You did the right thing."

Colleen looks up at him. Mascara tracks long black streaks down her cheeks. Her face is red and wet, and her eyes are haunted. "It didn't matter, though," she whispers hoarsely. "He ran through that red light anyway. He hit that little car with his big sedan without even tapping his brakes. I saw the whole thing. Thought I'd die from shock. I ran up the curb on Broadway before I could get control of my car."

Her face crumples, she squeezes her eyes shut, and she winds her arms protectively around herself and starts rocking. "When I went over to the sedan, Craig was bleeding on his face, but his airbag had deployed. I think he was just disoriented, not badly hurt. Then I went to the other car...and...I saw Theo inside. Craig T-boned his car in the middle of an intersection, just like what happened to Theo last time."

She folds over into herself, dissolving into loud, body-racking sobs. "Why would God do this to me again, Coop? How could he make me go through this *again*?"

Because God is a monster, I want to tell her. *A monster who hates us both.*

Before Coop can give her the hug he's about to give her, I stumble over to Colleen and grab her, throwing my arms around her and squeezing her hard. She clings to me, sobbing.

I'm not sure who I feel worse for. Which of us has God fucked over the most?

I whisper, "You don't have to go through it alone this time, Colleen. We'll go through it together."

"I know you and Theo are dating," she sobs. "I saw you together at the party, then Suzanne told me you'd been seeing him, and I'm so sorry…I'm just so fucking sorry—"

She breaks off into choked gasps and can't go on.

"Okay, take it easy now, girls," murmurs Coop. "We don't know anything yet. Theo could be just fine."

"Excuse me."

A man's voice from the doorway makes us all jump. It's a doctor, tall, silver-haired, grim-faced. He looks over the three of us with a weary eye. "Which of you are with Mr. Kennedy?"

Colleen stands shakily. "That's me."

"Will you take a step outside, ma'am? The police are here. They'd like to talk to you."

Colleen goes pale. "How is he?"

Sighing, the doctor smooths a hand over his hair. "Physically, he's fine. He suffered only a few minor cuts on his face. But if he has an attorney, you should call him."

"He's being charged with drunk driving?" says Coop.

The doctor looks at Coop for a moment, his gaze steady. "For the time being."

I know exactly what he means. I hear a low, agonized moan, but don't realize until Coop hugs my shoulders that the person making it is me.

"What about Theo Valentine? What's his condition?" Coop's voice is as harsh as fingernails scraping down a chalkboard. When the doctor hesitates, Coop snaps, "Just fuckin' tell us, man, we're family!"

"I'm afraid it doesn't look good."

Colleen bursts into a fresh round of sobs, Coop curses, and I make that sound again, the one like an animal dying.

The doctor says, "His internal injuries are too severe for him to be moved safely at the moment, but as soon as he's stabilized, we'll have to fly him to our sister hospital in Portland."

"Why?" barks Coop, the only other person in the room capable of speech.

"They have a neurosurgical unit there. We have to relieve the pressure of the subdural hematoma—"

"I don't speak doctor!" Coop roars.

After a beat, the doctor says quietly, "His brain is bleeding. His spleen is ruptured. He has half a dozen broken bones, including a shattered rib that punctured and collapsed a lung. Blood is filling his pleural cavity, which could collapse the other lung. Most importantly, his brain wave activity is minimal. His situation is very grave. I'm sorry to have to ask you this, but does he have a DNR?"

Though Coop has reined in his temper, he's staring at the doctor with a dangerous look in his eyes. "What's a DNR?"

At the same time, Colleen and I whisper, "Do not resuscitate."

28

*T*here was no room on the helicopter for anyone but the pilot, an EMT, and Theo, so when he'd finally been stabilized, Coop, Colleen, and I watched the copter take off from the roof of the hospital and head east until it disappeared into the horizon.

They wouldn't let us see him. I took that as a terrible sign.

We did see Craig, however.

After the police gave him blood and urine tests for alcohol and interviewed Colleen, they led Craig out of the emergency room in handcuffs, shuffling and disheveled. Coop had to physically restrain me from attacking him.

Poor Angela, the woman behind the desk. She was so frightened by my banshee shriek and wild flailings as I lunged at Craig, she fled down the hallway and never looked back. A tall, burly orderly replaced her, giving me a hard stare when he sat down.

My reputation in Seaside must be growing legendary.

Colleen insisted she wanted to make the drive to Portland with me and Coop, but I ordered her to go home and rest. "You've got to take care of yourself," I whispered. "For the baby, okay? I'll call you as soon as we know anything."

We embraced for a long time in the parking lot, crying in each other's arms.

There was a chance Theo would pull through, but knowing God like I did, I wasn't holding my breath for any more miracles. He was a bully who'd give you candy only so he could laugh at your tears when he stole it away.

Coop and I made the long drive together to the hospital in Portland in silence broken only by the radio playing a blues station.

When "At Last" came on, I had to switch it off.

There's only so much pain a person can take.

The surgery took twelve hours, some of the longest and darkest of my life—which is saying a lot. When the doctor came out afterward and found Coop and me in the waiting room, it was almost midnight.

"We've done what we could," he said, at which point my knees gave out and Coop had to carry me to a chair. I listened to the rest crying quietly on my back on a row of plastic hospital seats, all welded together and hard as winter ground.

"He's in a medically induced coma. That was necessary because of the swelling in his brain. We'll know more in a few hours, but I have to be honest with you...be prepared for the worst."

He said something else, but I was no longer listening. I couldn't hear anything over the sound of my sobs.

At ten o'clock the next morning, a pretty blonde nurse came and told us we could see him.

By then, I felt like death, and Coop was looking pretty hellish too. Neither of us had eaten or slept. Neither cared. We went into Theo's room together, holding our breath and holding hands, quaking in fear at what we'd find.

I took one look at him and fell against Coop with a strangled cry of horror.

No one should look that bad and still be alive.

He was black, blue, and purple, and various shades of green. Both eyes were swollen shut. Lacerations slashed ugly red lines across his face and arms. His lips were bruised and disfigured by swelling. His head had been shaved on one side, and a tube stuck out of his skull, leaking yellow fluid. He was hooked up to a ventilator and various plastic tubes and beeping machines, and if it wasn't for the slow and steady rise and fall of his chest, I'd be certain he was dead.

After he caught his breath, Coop said in a tight voice, "Well, he's looked better."

I burst into tears and buried my face in his chest.

"C'mon, now," he whispered, hugging me. "Dry your tears and go say hello."

Heart pounding, I crept over to the bed. When I touched Theo's hand, it was cold. I leaned over and kiss his forehead, and that was cold too.

Shaking, I whispered, "Don't you dare leave me. Hold on. I need you. I love you. Come back to me."

Theo made no response. Not a flicker of life crossed his face. His body was still there, but I had doubts about the rest of him.

Then the hardest part began.

Waiting.

29

"Just go home, Coop. There's nothing more you can do here. You heard the doctor—they're not going to bring him out of the coma for at least another few days, at the earliest. Go home to your kids, get back to your life. Make sure your crew doesn't build a bar in my living room. I'll call you the minute I have any news."

Coop sighs, scrubs a hand over his face, and nods. It's been three days since Theo had surgery. His vital signs are stable, but he's still in critical condition. The doctors look at him like they can't believe he's still alive, and though that makes me want to punch them all in the face, it gives me a grim kind of hope. If he's made it this far, maybe he'll make it all the way.

"You gonna be okay here?" asks Coop, his face creased with worry.

"Okay or not, I'm not going anywhere."

He looks at me for a long time. "You know, his parents both passed. He's an only child, no real family to speak of."

I whisper, "I know. You said."

"My point is that he's lucky to have you."

My laugh sounds hollow. "No, Coop. *I'm* the lucky one. You have no idea."

He looks like he wants to say something more, but then he shakes his head and exhales heavily, giving my shoulder a squeeze. "I'll check on the Buttercup on my way home, see how everything's goin'. I'll call you later tonight."

He pulls me from the chair I'm sitting in beside Theo's bed and gives me a bear hug. Then he clasps Theo's hand in farewell. "See you soon, buddy," he says, his voice choked.

He turns and lumbers out, tears shining in his eyes.

Suzanne has already been out to bring me a change of clothes and have a breakdown at the sight of Theo. I had to take her into the hallway and prop her up in a chair so she could catch her breath.

Colleen and I have been talking on the phone every day. I have a feeling we're going to become very good friends, no matter what the future holds.

Craig was charged with DWI and spent two days in jail. Depending on the outcome with Theo, other charges might be pending.

As for me, I've been sleeping in chairs and drinking too much coffee, and spending a lot of time on my knees in the hospital's quiet little chapel, bargaining with God. Which is about as useful as trying to bargain with the earth to spin in the opposite direction, but it gives me something to pass the time.

Three days turn into four, four into seven. I check into a hotel near the hospital and rent a car. I receive daily updates from the doctors, but learn nothing new. I exist in a strange twilight zone of fluorescent lights and cafeteria food, endless terror and crushing guilt.

I crucify myself over all the things I should've told Theo while I had the time.

We always think we have enough of that precious commodity, until fate steps in and proves us wrong.

Then, on the tenth day after Theo's accident, I get an early phone call from Coop.

"How's it goin'? You been over to the hospital yet?"

"I was just on my way over. I've already talked to his doctor, though. Still no change."

"Well, uh...I think you should, uh..." He clears his throat. "There's somethin' I want you to take a look at. Come on out to Seaside today."

I'm combing my hair, still wet from my shower, but fall still when I hear the strange note in Coop's voice. "What is it?"

Coop draws a breath. "It's not somethin' I could explain. You need to see this, Megan. I wouldn't make you leave him if it wasn't really important."

"Is it the Buttercup? Is everything okay?"

"It's not the Buttercup. We're makin' good progress on the house. This is...a lot more important."

"Coop," I say flatly. "I hate mysteries. And my nerves can't take any more drama. What the fuck is so important that I have to come back to Seaside to see?"

Coop says quietly, "What I found in Theo's barn."

Goose bumps erupt all over my body. I think of that big, shiny chain threaded through the door handles of the ramshackle barn, and shiver.

"Theo uses his house as Hillrise's headquarters—it's like a showroom up there, just a beautiful example of his work—and I had to get some paperwork from the office for a client. Copy of an old invoice for their taxes. Anyway, I couldn't find it in the computer, so I thought maybe we'd have it in storage in the barn."

"And?" I prompt impatiently when he stops talking.

His answer is so soft, I have to strain to hear it. "And now I guess I know why Theo never let me go out there."

"Coop," I shout, "give me a slight fucking break, would you? What's in the goddamn barn?"

He says simply, "You."

His voice is so strange, it's starting to scare me. "I don't understand."

"Me neither. I'll meet you there at noon. I'll text you the address."

He hangs up before I can say I already have it.

I make the ninety-minute drive to Seaside in an hour and ten. When I tear into the driveway at Theo's house, Coop is already there. He leans against his truck with his arms folded over his chest, gazing down at his boots. When he looks up and our eyes meet through the windshield, my heart stops.

Because my big, burly, confident Coop looks scared as shit.

I shut off the car and get out, the keys shaking in my hands. He speaks as soon as I'm within earshot.

"Did you ever meet Theo before you moved here?"

Suddenly, I'm breathless. My heart starts to hammer. "Why do you ask?"

He works his jaw, looking off into the distance for a moment. Then he pushes away from the car and pulls a set of keys from his pocket. "Let's go in."

I follow in rising panic as Coop ambles toward the barn, gravel crunching under his boots. It's a bright, beautiful day, the air clear and cold. Coop unlocks the shiny padlock on the chain around the barn doors and drags the unwieldy wooden doors apart. They groan on rusty hinges, cantankerous as old men. With a jerk of his chin indicating I should follow, he disappears inside.

It takes a moment for my eyes to adjust to the dimness. Hazy rays of light filter through cracks in the wood roof, lending the interior an otherworldly air.

Empty horse stalls line one side of the long room. On the other side, a tall, rickety wooden ladder leads up to a loft.

Discarded pieces of lumber litter the dirt floor, and several of the wide beams supporting the roof show signs of water damage. A whisper of animal musk—dried dung from long-dead horses—hangs in the air.

So does the sharper, newer tang of oil paint and acetone, scents I'd recognize blindfolded.

"Doesn't seem like a good place to store documents," I tell Coop, trying to keep my voice steady though my pulse is racing and I'm starting to sweat.

"Guess Theo moved 'em out when he took up his secret hobby."

He's standing next to the ladder, looking at me with that odd, unnerved expression. I don't bother asking which hobby he's referring to, because I already know.

I look up at the loft, then back at Coop. He says quietly, "I hope you don't spook real easy, 'cause this near scared the livin' daylights outta me."

He starts to climb.

I watch until he reaches the top and steps off the ladder, then I follow. When I get to the top, Coop grasps my hand to help me off, then steps back without a word, watching me closely to see my reaction.

But he's already disappeared. I'm alone, all alone in what can only be described as a shrine.

Hundreds, perhaps thousands, of oil paintings in different sizes are stacked upright, leaning against the barn walls. More crowd every inch of the walls, hung haphazardly from nails. More are scattered carelessly on long rustic wood tables and all over the floor, piles and piles of them, an unending sea of canvas.

Some are unfinished. All are unframed. And every one of them depicts the same subject in various clothing, poses, and stages of undress:

Me.

Me walking in a vineyard with a glass of wine. Me in a bubble bath, laughing. Me riding a horse, washing the dishes, reading a book.

Me walking down the aisle in my wedding dress, holding a bouquet of purple sweet peas, the light of true love aglow in my eyes.

He even got the details of the scalloped neckline and the seed pearls on the bodice right. I press a hand over my thundering heart as tears threaten to crest my lower lids.

Coop's quiet voice barely penetrates my cocoon of shock and memory. "They're dated. I didn't check them all, but enough to gimme the willies."

I find enough presence of mind to turn my head and look at him.

Keeping his gaze steady on mine, he says, "Theo painted these *before* you moved to Seaside, Megan. The oldest one I found, near the back of that stack in the corner, is dated one month after his accident five years ago. How's that possible?"

I drift over to the nearest table and run my fingertips over a half-finished painting of me sleeping, my hair spread over the pillow, a small smile on my lips. There's a frenzied quality to the style, lots of quick, short strokes, as if he raced through it, abandoning it halfway in dissatisfaction.

You make all my broken parts bleed.

How awful it must have been for him, how terrifying, to finally see in flesh the person who'd been haunting all his waking hours like a ghost. No wonder he looked at me with such fury that first night at Cal's Diner. He probably thought he was losing his mind.

I murmur, "Maybe he painted them since we met and dated them wrong. He's been ill, you know that."

Coop snorts. Spreading his arms wide, he says. "He painted *all these* since September? I don't think so. And I found other weird shit in his office in the house too."

"Like what?"

"Like two hundred fuckin' recipes for key lime pie. Like an entire folder of clippings from magazines of pictures of Denver fuckin' omelets. Like almost five years' worth of invoices from some hydroponic flower growers in Holland and Japan—he'd been having flowers delivered here every week from halfway round the world! Like what the fuck is wrong with all the flowers in Oregon?"

Sweet peas aren't always in season here.

I turn my face to a ray of light slicing through a crack in the roof and close my eyes.

"And he has all this fancy French wine in a closet—cases of the stuff—and he doesn't even drink wine! He hates it!"

I form a mental picture of the elegant label of the Château Corton Grancey that Cass and I always drank on our anniversary. The wine we first enjoyed on our honeymoon, served to us by the old man we picked up on the side of a country road who turned out to be the head of one of the oldest and finest wineries in France. I whisper, "Burgundy's always a good investment. Especially a grand cru."

There's a short pause, then Coop says, "I never said it was from Burgundy."

I look at him.

His eyes intense, he adds more quietly, "Or a grand cru."

"He told me he'd been collecting," I hear myself lie, knowing the truth is impossible.

After a long time wherein we simply gaze at each other, Coop looks down at his feet. "You're right. He's been sick. This is all just...evidence of that. And him askin' me how he could remember someone he'd never met, and his obsession with the Buttercup, and him never speakin' another word after his accident...that's all part of his sickness too."

He glances at my wedding band, then once again meets my eyes. "Right?"

There's a moment, one brief moment where I consider telling

him and letting the chips fall where they may. But the moment passes when I decide this thing is so unbelievable, the weight of trying to understand it has almost broken Theo and me—it would be wrong to burden Coop with the knowledge of it too.

Some mysteries are meant to live in the dark, quiet places of our hearts, kept safe and sacred.

"You're a good friend, Coop. And a good man. And now I have to go, because I need to be there when he wakes up."

I hug him hard, then scramble down the ladder and run to my car, my spirit soaring and my heart on fire, adrenaline pumping through my veins. I tear out of the driveway so fast, a spray of gravel spits out from the tires.

I have to get to that hospital as soon as I can.

I need to be there when my midnight valentine comes back to me.

*O*nly Theo doesn't come back.

Not that day, not that week, not the next. The doctors take him out of the induced coma, but he doesn't wake up. They remove the ventilator, and he starts to breathe on his own, but he doesn't wake up. By the time Thanksgiving arrives, he's developed bed sores from lying in one position so long, and I've developed a hatred for myself so burning, I can't even look at my reflection in the mirror.

I did this.

I pushed him so hard, his only choice was to run away. I could've let him come to it in his own time, or gone along with his treatment plan if it made him feel better to pretend schizophrenia was the root of all his problems. I didn't have to shove the truth down his throat, but I did.

I punish myself in a variety of imaginative ways, but my favorite is denying myself food.

Which makes all the vomiting I'm doing more than a little strange.

"You're sick again, honey?"

The head nurse on Theo's floor at the hospital is a motherly

Latina named Ana with big, brown eyes and a tendency to dispense random hugs. She's gazing at me in concern outside the hallway restroom where I've just been puking my guts out.

I lean against the doorframe, wiping the beads of sweat off my brow with the back of my hand. "You heard, huh?"

She makes an apologetic face. "I think the whole floor heard. It sounded like an exorcism was happening in here."

"Must've been that egg salad sandwich I had for breakfast." I attempt a feeble laugh, avoiding her eyes. "Damn cafeteria food."

She snorts, propping her hands on her hips. "I think you actually have to *eat* some food before it can make you sick, *chica*."

I mutter churlishly, "I eat."

"Ai!" She pinches my arm, startling me into looking at her. She shakes her finger in my face. "Don't you lie to me! I have six kids—I've got a black belt in lie detection!"

I'm too tired to argue with her, so I sigh instead. "Okay, fine. I probably picked up a bug from hanging around this place so much. Didn't I read somewhere that hospitals make people sick more than anything else?"

Her eyes round. "*Dios mío.* Do you have a fever?"

"No."

"Body aches?"

"No more than usual."

"A strange rash? Enlarged lymph glands? Extreme weakness or chills?"

I wrinkle my nose in disgust. "Why, is the plague going around here or something?"

Her eyes go from round to narrow. She pinches her lips and looks me up and down. "Well, I can tell you what—no matter what else might be wrong with you, you're anemic for sure." Clucking like a hen, she lightly slaps my cheek. "Look at this, pale as a ghost."

"Thanks for that vote of support," I say drily.

She grabs my arm and steers me down the hallway toward the

elevators. "I'm sending you down to Tommy in the lab to get some blood drawn."

"No! I'm okay, Ana, really—"

Glaring at me, she says something in sharp Spanish that shuts me up.

"Fine. But if Tommy doesn't hit the vein the first time, I'm kicking him in his balls."

She clucks again, pressing the call button for the elevator. "Such a temper. I heard about your performance in the emergency room in Seaside Hospital, you know."

I look at the ceiling, shaking my head. "Unbelievable."

Tommy turns out to be a hipster with sleeves of pinup girls tattooed on his arms, silver rings decorating his thumbs, and a bald head capped by a gray fedora set at a jaunty angle. When he catches me eyeing it, he grins.

"It makes my head look less like an egg. Have a seat."

I sit, stick my arm into the squishy blue armrest on his small counter, and squirm in my chair when he pulls a lethal-looking needle from a plastic wrapper and jabs the opposite end into an empty vial.

"Make a fist." He ties a length of urine-colored rubber around my biceps, and taps the little blue bulge on my inner arm. "Nice veins," he says, impressed.

"Thanks. I'm an ass girl, myself."

He laughs, displaying a set of dimples. "We all have our weaknesses, I suppose."

To distract myself from the pointy spike of steel about to be jabbed into my body, I ask, "So, how'd you get into the vein business, Tommy?"

"After my brother overdosed from heroin when I was fifteen, I decided I wanted to be a doctor."

He discloses that bit of personal information so nonchalantly, I'm stunned. "Oh. God, I'm so sorry."

He slides the needle home expertly. I hardly feel a pinch.

"Yeah. It sucked. I was the one who found him, slumped over the toilet with his arm still tied off. Shit like that really changes your perspective on things."

I say faintly, "It sure does."

He fills up one vial, exchanges it for another, casual and competent, talking as he works. "I enrolled in the premed program at Portland State but dropped out after a year. College wasn't really my thing. I'm crap at taking tests. But I still wanted to do something in the medical field. I knew a guy who worked here, said the pay was decent, and they had on-the-job training, so I got my certification and that was that."

He's filled all four of his little vials by now and removes the heinous needle. I get a cotton ball topped by a purple Band-Aid to cover the tiny hole in my arm, then we're done.

"Well, I can honestly say you're the best phlebotomist I've ever known, Tommy. Good job."

"Thanks." He looks at me for a moment. "You doin' okay?"

I'm taken aback by the question and run a hand over my hair in embarrassment. "I look that bad, huh?"

"I see a lotta people come through those doors. You get a feel for 'em."

My laugh is uncomfortable. "Oh yeah? And what's my vibe telling you? Woman on the verge of a nervous breakdown?"

The corners of his lips lift into a small, mysterious smile. "Woman on the verge of something. You take care now. Happy Thanksgiving."

He leaves me sitting in the chair, wondering what the hell that was all about.

I decide people who draw blood for a living are weird.

When I get back to Theo's room, I pull up short, shocked to see Coop and Suzanne setting up a makeshift Thanksgiving dinner table on the empty bed next to Theo's.

"You guys," I whisper, my voice cracking. "What're you doing here?"

"Are you kidding?" says Suzanne, hustling over to give me a hug and a kiss. She pulls away and beams at me, holding me by the shoulders. "Where else are you supposed to be on Thanksgiving other than with family?"

"But, Coop..." I look at him, taking up most of the space in the room with his blond bulk and his grin. "Your kids."

"They're with their mother today. I'm gettin' 'em for Christmas. Which works out great, seein' as how I can't stand my mother-in-law."

"*Ex* mother-in-law," says Suzanne over her shoulder.

Coop grins at her. "Right. Ex."

When Suzanne looks back at me, her cheeks are red, which tells me everything I need to know about what these two have been up to since I've been staying in Portland.

"That nice nurse lady Ana said she wasn't supposed to let us in here with all this food, but most of those stuffy-ass doctors are gone for the holiday, so she snuck us in. *And...*"

Her signature skyscraper heels clicking on the floor, she trots over to a paper bag on the desk under the TV and pulls out a dish wrapped in aluminum foil. She holds it up like a trophy. "I made key lime pie!"

When my lower lip starts to quiver and my eyes fill with tears, she looks horrified.

"Oh, shit, don't tell me you're on a diet! Is that why you look like a stray cat?"

"I love you, Suzanne," I say, and burst into tears.

"Sweetie, it's okay." She must have handed the pie to Coop, because her arms come around me in a gentle hug. Then she pats my hair as I fall apart, sobbing into her boobs. She murmurs into my ear, "I love you too. Even if you are ruining my new silk blouse with your snot." She sighs. "Why are the prettiest girls the ugliest criers?"

By the time I manage to get myself together and Suzanne and I break apart, Coop has finished putting out the food. Everything is there: turkey breast, stuffing, corn, sweet potatoes. They've even brought cranberry sauce. It makes me want to burst into tears all over again, but I've got something more important to focus on now.

The smell of the food is turning my stomach.

"You're lookin' a little green over there," says Coop, glancing at me sideways as he pulls paper plates from a bag.

"I'm just tired. This looks amazing, you guys. Thank you so much."

We each fill a plate with food, then drag chairs around Theo's bed and eat in silence interrupted only by the steady beeping of Theo's heart monitor.

After a while, Coop says quietly, "He's thin."

"You would be too if all your meals were liquid."

Coop glances at the lump under the blankets where the feeding tube is inserted into Theo's abdomen. His eyes register pain, and he quickly looks back at his plate. "Anything new?"

I pick at the stuffing on my plate with my fork, moving it around so I look busy. They went to all this trouble. I don't want to insult them by not eating. Or, worse, eating and throwing everything right back up. "Nothing. His vitals are all stable."

"What about the EEG?"

I whisper, "No change. His brain waves look like the surface of a lake."

Suzanne says casually, "My grandma Rhoda was in a coma for two years before she came out of it. Just woke up one day and demanded chocolate pudding. She didn't have any brain waves either. Didn't mean a thing in the end. If God wants you to wake up, you're waking up. If she doesn't, you don't."

Sounding exhausted, Coop says, "Why does God always get blamed for everything? Maybe God's just letting life do what it will, and watches us to see how we handle it."

"God as watchmaker as opposed to chess player," I say. "That's what my dad thought."

Suzanne says, "I have no idea what that means, but I do know that everything happens for a reason. Even the bad things. It's all part of a bigger plan we can't understand. God is the greatest force of love in the universe."

I mutter, "I think God's a kid who likes to sprinkle salt on snails."

The conversation moves to other topics. Coop updates me on the progress Hillrise is making on the Buttercup, which is impressive. If the weather cooperates, they're on schedule to have all the work done in late January. Just in time for me to open the B&B for Valentine's Day.

The fucking irony.

I try my best to make a dent in the pile of food on my plate, but only manage to get a few bites down. They stay for another hour, then we pack up the leftovers and throw out the trash. When Suzanne goes to the restroom, Coop unexpectedly pulls me into a hug.

In a low voice, he says, "What're you gonna do?"

I know what he means without having to ask. "Wait," I say, my voice breaking. "No matter how long it takes."

He pulls away and gazes at me with so much pain in his eyes, it's awful. "And what if this is as good as it gets?" He gestures to Theo lying unmoving and unresponsive on the bed. "What, then?"

"I'm not giving up hope," I say with quiet vehemence. "Not now, not ever. If I have to grow old in this fucking hospital room, that's what I'll do. If he wakes up and has the IQ of a cup of coffee and needs to be dressed and bathed and hand-fed for the rest of his life, that's what I'll do. I love him, Coop. No matter what. I'll love this man and take care of him until the day I die."

My throat closes, so my next words are strangled. "And even then, I'll keep loving him. I'll love him till the end of time."

Coop hugs me hard, his breath hitching, then walks out abruptly so I don't see him cry.

Suzanne comes back from the bathroom and we say our goodbyes, then I'm so tired, I settle into the chair beside Theo's bed and close my eyes, intending to nap for only a few minutes. But when I open my eyes again, it's dark outside and Ana is standing over me, whispering my name.

"Megan. *Mija*, wake up."

I blink up at her and scrub a hand over my face. My back is stiff and my left leg has fallen asleep. The pins and needles are painful. "What time is it?"

"Just after midnight."

"Is everything okay?"

When she hesitates, my heart takes off like a rocket. I jump to my feet and knock her out of my way in my hurry to grab Theo's hand. I search his face in panic for any signs of distress, but he seems to be in the exact same condition he was in when I fell asleep.

"Honey, he's fine," she says, touching my shoulder. "It's, ah... it's you, actually."

I turn and stare at her. "Me? What do you mean?"

She glances at Theo. Then, her usually expressive brown eyes revealing nothing, she jerks her chin toward the door. "Let's go talk over there."

Oh my God. There's something terribly wrong with me. It's cancer. It's a rare, infectious disease. It's the Zika virus. It's Ebola. It's the fucking plague!

When I continue to stare at her with my mouth open, terror tightening my stomach to a fist, Ana gently takes my arm and steers me toward the door. She stops in the doorway and keeps her voice barely above a whisper.

Which must be why I can't understand what she says.

"You're pregnant."

I blink, then squint at her. "Excuse me? What did you say?"

"I said you're pregnant, honey. Congratulations."

I wait for the punch line. When one isn't forthcoming and Ana simply stares at me with a small, soft smile, I realize she's not joking.

"Ana, that's not possible. I can't get pregnant."

She lifts her shoulders. "According to your blood test, you can."

That hipster idiot, Tommy. He switched my test results with someone else's! Some poor pregnant woman is going to be told her morning sickness is only anemia!

I say flatly, "No, Ana, I can't. I'm telling you—it's impossible. It would be a miracle."

Her entire face lights up with a smile. "Well, God is in the miracle business, honey, so maybe you should thank him."

There's a noise in my head like a thousand wolves howling at a full moon. I can hardly hear myself think over it. Incredulous, I whisper, "I'm...I'm pregnant? *How?*"

She lifts her brows, an expression of humor on her face. "Oh, did you miss that day at school? See, there's this thing called a sperm—"

I grab her arms and shout into her face, "I'M PREGNANT? WITH A BABY?"

Dissolving into laughter, she says, "No, with a piñata. Of *course* with a baby!"

A loud, frantic beeping emits from one of the machines hooked up to Theo.

We both freeze, then Ana reacts first. She hustles over to his bed, peers at a black box with some green flashing numbers, then turns around and runs past me, shouting for a doctor.

"Ana!" I scream after her, panicked. "What's happening!"

She's headed for the nurses' station down the hall, yelling over her shoulder as she goes. "His heartbeat is skyrocketing!" She disappears around a corner.

I whirl around and run to Theo's bedside, so frantic, I catch my foot on the leg of a chair and almost fall. I grab his hand and collapse onto the bed, panting, terrified at all the flashing I see on the machines. It's not only the heartbeat monitor that's going mad—several other devices screech with alarms.

This is it. He's dying.

I start to sob uncontrollably. "Don't you dare leave me, Theo! Don't you dare! I love you! I need you! I'll never forgive you if you leave me alone!"

Pressure on my hand, so faint I almost can't feel it, cuts off my hysterical screams as if someone pulled a plug. I freeze, looking down at Theo's hand clasped in mine...his hand that's weakly squeezing.

Time slows to a crawl. Every beat of my heart is a boom of thunder in my ears. I look up at his face and watch in utter astonishment and joy as the second miracle of the night occurs.

Theo slowly opens his eyes and looks at me.

His gaze is hazy at first but gains focus after several moments. Then we stare at each other for an endless span of silence as I wait without breathing to see if he recognizes me.

Is he even in there at all?

Squeezing his hand hard, I lean over his chest and plead, "Theo? Theo, can you hear me? Can you speak?" When he doesn't respond, tears begin to flow down my cheeks again. I feel my face crumbling, and the last of my hope unravels at the blankness I see in his dark, dark eyes.

Sobbing, I beg, "Please, if you can hear me, please say something!"

Finally, after what feels like forever, the corners of his lips curve to a ghost of a smile.

In a weak, scratchy voice, the words halting and almost unintelligible, he whispers, "It wasn't enough."

"What? What do you mean?" I can barely speak, I'm crying so hard. My entire body is racked with sobs. When his lips move but no words come out, I lean closer, putting my ear near his mouth and begging him to say it again.

On the faintest of exhalations, he does.

"One lifetime wasn't enough to love you."

I fall to my knees as a team of doctors and nurses bursts into the room.

EPILOGUE
THEO

Two months later

*F*ucking yellow balloons.

It's the dumbest thing to be scared of, right? Right. So imagine my surprise when I woke up in the hospital after my accident—my first accident, that is—saw a kid carrying a yellow balloon down the hallway, and got so scared, it felt like I was having a heart attack.

That was the first clue something strange was going on.

At first, I assumed it was the brain injury. Getting your head rammed by a steel rocket doing eighty miles per hour isn't good for the old noggin, we can all agree on that. But then the voices started. Faint little whispers at my ear. One female, one male. The male was a pain in my ass, to be honest. Always going on about lightning strikes and football stats and B&Bs. Made no sense whatsoever.

The female voice, though. Hearing her was like hearing an angel.

She had this amazing laugh, as silky smooth as flowing water. That laugh was sexy as fuck. It rang in my ears like music.

Yeah, I had a thing for the imaginary voice in my head. Don't judge me.

And don't get me started about how my own voice had changed and now sounded exactly like the other whispering voice in my head—the irritating male.

If things weren't looking fucked enough, I had all these memories that didn't fit. Things I hadn't done, places I'd never been, people I'd never met before.

Then the dreams started.

Nightmares, technically, because they were so scary. It wasn't so much the dreams themselves that were scary, but how vivid they were. It was like I was *there*, in them.

Like I was living someone else's life at night.

Then there were all these new habits and desires I suddenly had. Bear claws for breakfast every day? Sure, why not. French wine that costs two hundred bucks a bottle? Yeah, gotta have me some of that.

Oil painting, though I'd never picked up a brush before and couldn't draw a straight line to save my life?

Bring it on.

If all that wasn't bad enough, I developed an obsession with this old, empty Victorian house on the coast. More than an obsession—a *compulsion*. I had to be near it. I couldn't stay away from it for more than a day, at most. It was like the thing was a giant fucking magnet, a powerful black hole drawing me helplessly in. I spent hours wandering its rooms, wondering what the hell was happening to me.

The only logical conclusion was that I was going insane.

Oh—I forgot to mention the precognition.

I knew she'd be there, that night at Cal's Diner. I knew it in my goddamn bones. By that time, I'd spent five years with her voice in my head and her face taking shape over and over on my canvases. Part of me hoped that by painting her, I'd get rid of her, like there was a finite amount of her that would eventually deplete, but the supply was apparently endless.

I loved her long before we met.

If that sounds ridiculous—it is. But it's also true.

I ached for her the way the desert aches for rain. Longing was something I'd never felt before, but it inhabited me so completely, I almost couldn't function. Then, one rainy night, she appeared. Boom—she's at the counter at Cal's ordering a Denver omelet with extra bacon and key lime pie.

Exactly like I knew she would.

The fear I felt in that moment put the sighting of the yellow balloon to shame.

Because it wasn't possible. Any of it—*all* of it.

And what was I supposed to do anyway? Walk up to her and say, "Hi! You don't know me, but I've painted you naked and had sex with you in my dreams and I'm pretty sure we were married before—it's great to finally meet you!"

I don't think it would've gone over.

So I got mad. I got mad and I tried my damndest to stay away. The more I tried, the more I fell apart, until I was hanging on by a thread so thin, you could see right through it. When Dr. Garner told me I was schizophrenic, it was such a relief.

I mean, I didn't believe it, but it was a hell of a lot better than the alternative. It was something solid I could hang on to. It made *sense*. Taking the drugs to set my brain straight made sense. Everything made sense again until Megan brought up that goddamn yellow balloon and I couldn't pretend anymore.

Cue the sound of squealing tires.

That fight-or-flight response is such a bitch. I chose flight, and ended up in an accident—*again*.

And Jesus, am I looking rough.

"Honey, stop."

Her soft voice comes from behind me. I look away from the

bathroom mirror as she winds her arms around my waist and rests her chin on my arm.

"Why couldn't they at least have fixed my nose? I feel kinda bad for it, having to hang out on my face like that, all crooked and sad."

Megan tightens her arms around me and tries to hide a smile. "Your nose is perfect."

"My nose is tragic."

"It's beautiful."

"Yeah. Except it's not." I grab her and pull her around to face me so I can kiss her. I can't get enough of that mouth.

She melts against me with one of those little sighs that makes my dick instantly hard, but pulls away with a playful laugh when I squeeze her ass.

"They're waiting."

"Let them wait," I murmur, then take her mouth again. Kissing her deeply, I wrap my arms around her so she can't get away.

She's so sweet. So fucking sweet. I don't think she has any idea how much I love her. How I can't breathe when she's not within eyesight. How I'd gladly die for her, kill for her, do anything big or small that she asked.

All the other bullshit aside, I fell for her the normal way too. Because of who she is. Because of her courage, her strength, her intelligence. Because of her kindness and that gooey soft center she hides underneath her tough outer shell. The fact that she's a knockout didn't hurt, I'll be honest, but she would've been my dream woman even if she wasn't *literally* my dream woman.

We had a long conversation about it where she told me the same thing. I'm not just a placeholder for her past. It's hard to explain, but I know that when she looks at me, she sees *me*.

And when I look at her, I see my entire world.

"Theo," Megan says breathlessly, looking up at me with those gorgeous eyes. They're the color of the ocean, blue and green combined, shifting hue with the light. "Theo, if we don't go down now, it'll be an hour, and I'll never hear the end of it from Suzanne."

"Pfft. You'll never hear the end of it no matter what. She lives for drama."

"C'mon, she's worked really hard helping me put this party together!"

I caress her cheek, then bend and inhale against her neck. God, I love the smell of her skin. Warm vanilla and something sweet, like a cookie fresh from the oven. I wanna sink my teeth into her every time I get a whiff.

When I slide my hand up from her waist and gently squeeze one full breast, she warns, "Honey."

I whisper, "I'll be quick," and use my hips to bump her back until she's trapped between my crotch and the bathroom sink.

Her laugh is throaty. It sends a thrill of lust up my spine.

"*No*, honey." She flaps her hands at me, trying to push me away.

Grinning, I grasp her wrists and wind her arms around her back. "Now what're you gonna do?"

"Well, your balls are in the direct line of fire for a nasty jab from my knee," she says sweetly, smiling. "I think that would do the trick."

I pretend to glower. "Unfair." Then I tickle her, because I love the way it makes her shriek.

"Stop! No! You asshole!" She squirms and wriggles in my arms, desperate to get away, but I'm too strong. I don't relent until she's helplessly laughing and has called me every curse word in the book.

Then I drop to my knees in front of her and rest my cheek on her belly. "Hey, little bean," I whisper, framing the small swell of her stomach in my hands. "How you doing in there?"

Megan's soft hands come to rest on my head. She combs her

fingers through my hair, and I can feel how they tremble. "She's doing great. She says she loves her daddy."

I look up at her. Her eyes are soft and glimmer with tears, and are so full of love, it fucking kills me.

I say hoarsely, "I love her too. And her mommy." My voice breaks. "So much."

She presses her lips together and blinks really fast in that way she does when she's trying hard not to cry.

From somewhere downstairs comes the sound of Suzanne's aggravated holler. "Jesus Christ on a crutch, people, are you coming or what?"

I stand, give Megan a kiss against her laughing mouth, then grab her hand and lead her out of the bedroom. When we get downstairs, Suzanne, Coop, and all the guys from Hillrise are in the main parlor, milling around with drinks in their hands. There's a bar set up in the corner, and two uniformed servers stand off to one side, holding silver platters filled with those tiny bites of food they serve at parties that you have to eat about a hundred of before you get full.

Everyone turns when we come in.

"There you are! Come over here and say a few words before the guests start to arrive."

Suzanne has on a red dress cut so low, it might be illegal in some states. Coop—staring down at her with a huge grin and his arm wound around her shoulders—is too busy appreciating the view to look up at us.

Megan and I walk near the fireplace. Through the parlor windows, I see the valet stand set up at the curb on the street outside. More than three hundred guests RSVP'd for the grand reopening of the Buttercup Inn, but we'll probably get more. People love free drinks.

Megan squeezes my hand, looking at me expectantly, but I shake my head. I still don't like to talk around other people. Old habits die hard, I guess.

She turns to all our friends with a smile. "Okay, so we just want to thank you guys, so much, for everything you've done to make the Buttercup so amazingly beautiful. Honestly, it's better than I dreamed." She pauses to press a hand over her heart. I sling an arm around her shoulders and draw her closer, knowing she's gonna struggle today.

The word bittersweet was invented for times like this.

She takes a breath and continues. "Coop, Suzanne...you're our best friends. We wouldn't have made it through all this without you. We love you."

Suzanne swipes at her eyes. Coop nods his big head, his grin growing wider. "Love you too, marshmallow." His eyes meet mine. More quietly, he says, "And you, brother."

My chest gets tight.

Maybe one day, I'll talk to Coop about what happened. One day when we're old and gray and all our grandkids are running around our rocking chairs out on the back porch. But for now, we both leave it alone. He can tell I'm still processing. I'm damn lucky to have such a good friend.

Megan says, "To all the guys at Hillrise, tonight is a celebration of your hard work and talent. I know you're as proud of the Buttercup as I am, because she's perfect. Thank you from the bottom of our hearts. I'd toast you with champagne, but I'm not allowed."

She rests a hand on her belly, smiling, and everyone laughs.

My heart swells. I have to swallow a few times and take some deep breaths before I'm under control again.

Then I catch sight of the first car pulling up outside and squeeze Megan's shoulder. She follows my gaze and claps in excitement.

"Oh! People are starting to arrive!"

"Already?" shouts Suzanne, instantly panicking. "Oh, fuck, let me make sure the caterer is ready!" She breaks from Coop and runs from the room, hands flailing, heels clacking against the floor.

"Wait for me!" shouts Megan, already following.

I pull her back by her arm and give her one final, firm kiss.

She looks up at me, breathless, happiness shining in her eyes. "I love you," she whispers.

I bend my head to her ear. "I love you too."

She's gone with a laugh, spinning out of my reach. I watch as she runs from the room, hair flying, long legs flashing, ass like an apple in a pair of tight blue jeans. And I know with the same sixth sense that told me she'd be there at Cal's Diner that night that I'll love this woman forever. Whatever happens, she's the true north my soul will always point to.

I'll love her in every one of my lives.

ACKNOWLEDGMENTS

My plan for this book, from the time I conceived the idea right up until I wrote the final chapter, was that Theo died at the end. He died in the hospital after the accident, his organs were donated, then many months later, Megan met the man who'd received Theo's heart. But when it came time for Theo's heart to stop beating, I couldn't do it. My fingers just started writing the happy ending he and Megan deserved, and here we are.

I've always been fascinated with the topic of reincarnation. During the research for this book, I read some incredible stories about people convinced they'd led other lives. Stories of people who were drawn to certain places, had vivid, recurring dreams about things they'd never done or people they'd never known, developed unexplainable fears and odd habits after near-death experiences, or simply knew from the time they were born that they once were someone else. Many, if not most, of the world's religions hold a belief in an afterlife at their core.

Fact or fiction, it sure makes for interesting reading. In one case, a three-year-old remembered being murdered in her past life, identified her murderer, and led police to the location of her former body.

The poor kid.

And now for the other stuff:

The quote about death Coop referred to in chapter 12 is paraphrased from the book *Tuesdays with Morrie*, by Mitch Albom.

Thank you to my editor, Linda Ingmanson, for catching all my mistakes. Thank you to Teri Clark Linden for doing such a fabulous job bringing Megan, Theo, and friends to life. Thanks to Jay for helping me through the rough spots in the manuscript, and for not laughing (too hard) when I cried over my imaginary friends. Thanks to Letitia Hasser for her beautiful cover design. Thank you to all the bloggers and reviewers who have been so supportive of my work.

And thank you to all my readers, for whom I'm incredibly grateful.

If we never meet in this life, perhaps we'll meet in the next.

ABOUT THE AUTHOR

J.T. Geissinger is a #1 international and Amazon Charts bestselling author of emotionally charged romance and women's fiction. Ranging from funny, feisty romcoms to intense, edgy suspense, her books have sold over ten million copies and been translated into more than twenty languages.

She is the recipient of the Prism Award for Best First Book, the Golden Quill Award for Best Paranormal/Urban Fantasy, the HOLT Medallion for Best Erotic Romance, and is a three-time finalist for the RITA® Award from the Romance Writers of America®.

Please subscribe to her monthly newsletter to get updates on new releases.

www.jtgeissinger.com

ALSO BY J.T. GEISSINGER

For a complete current book list, please visit www.jtgeissinger.com

Standalone Novels

Pen Pal

Perfect Strangers

Rules of Engagement

Midnight Valentine

Queens & Monsters Series

Ruthless Creatures

Carnal Urges

Savage Hearts

Brutal Vows

Beautifully Cruel Duet

Beautifully Cruel

Cruel Paradise

Dangerous Beauty Series

Dangerous Beauty

Dangerous Desires

Dangerous Games

Slow Burn Series

Burn For You

Printed in the USA
CPSIA information can be obtained
at www.ICGtesting.com
LVHW040729010924
789836LV00035B/877